The Year of the Comet

Books by John Christopher

The Little People
The Possessors
The Twenty-Second Century
A Wrinkle in the Skin
The Year of the Comet

John Christopher

Cosmos Books, an imprint of **Wildside Press**
New Jersey . New York . California . Ohio

The Year of the Comet

Published by:

Cosmos Books, an imprint of Wildside Press
P.O. Box 45, Gillette, NJ 07933-0045
www.wildsidepress.com

For more information, contact Wildside Press.

ISBN: 1-58715-395-5

1

AFTER he had put the remains of the meal down the chute and snapped the table back into the wall, Charles Grayner slumped automatically in his fireside chair and his eyes, as automatically, went to the flickering telescreen. It was silent, the figures prancing without accompaniment. At one time he had followed the usual practice of leaving sound switched on as well as vision, for company, but in the last year or so he had found himself growing into the habit of silence. Growing old, he reflected. Anyway, it had become a new habit to cut the sound off as soon as he came into the house in the evening.

He cut the whole thing off when he left in the morning, but the daily help put it on again. He knew her viewing habits by now; she alternated between three channels—Red League, Honey, and Cosy Bright. He derived some amusement from guessing which one had been left on, without turning the sound up and without looking at the controls. Tonight it was too easy. He recognized the singer: Loulou del Keith. She was a Cosy Bright exclusive.

He pressed the sound button on his chair arm, and the voice, rising on an even throatier wave of sound from the electric violins, caressed him lovingly. She leaned forward and the camera closed in purposefully for a second before breaking upwards for a fade close-up. Dewy-eyed and yet lascivious. As the camera broke away, preparatory to another run-in on her corsage, his hand dropped to the control panel. He checked himself for a moment and then pressed the ninth button decisively.

Sight and sound went, and were replaced. The music now was Mozart, a string quartet that he knew. K—— what was it? He didn't know that much. On the screen was the El Greco 'Cleansing of the Temple.' Dinkuhl had used that juxtaposition before—twice at least. He felt a mild irritation; he had been one of those who had protested against this business of deliberately associating musical works and paintings.

The quartet ended, on a flat note. Dinkuhl's face came through, characteristically smiling, half mocking, half enraged.

'This,' Dinkuhl said, 'is Channel KF.' His voice was soft but flexible; it could resonate into anger. 'I propose to save a lot of people a lot of money. Well, when I say a *lot* of people——' He shrugged. 'I've hired a boy to go through my stenoflips for me. He has instructions to destroy any one that tells me I have to stop linking Mozart and El Greco, or Haydn and Rubens, or Beethoven and Rembrandt. So save yourself a couple of quarters.'

Dinkuhl smiled. 'And this means you. You precisely. You one or two hundred malcontents, saboteurs, out of that great concourse of one or two thousand enthusiasts who hear and attend to Channel KF. So you don't deserve an explanation, but you're going to get one anyway.

'Had we the money, friends, we would hire for your delight musicians of unparalleled comeliness. And if we couldn't find such, we would hire a group of the lovelies from Red League or Superlux, and patiently would we instruct them in the art of holding fiddles and a viola and a

6

'cello in just about the right operating positions. Well, that may be beautiful, but it's still a dream. So we give you paintings instead, and I pick them, that being the way things are.'

He paused. 'Do you object that you would prefer to see the musicians, in all their ugliness, in all their squalor? In that case I recommend that you go right out and see them— in the flesh, my friends, in the disillusioning flesh. Few of you will have to travel more than five hundred miles to find a concert hall. But this is TV, and there is only one Channel KF, and I shall continue to kill two birds with one stone. Some of you, at least, must be tone deaf.'

Dinkuhl backed away from the camera, turned his back on it, and began rooting around in one corner of the studio. The confusion appeared to get worse every day; there must at times be a clear-out but Charles had never seen the place showing the effects of one. He was fairly sure that the mice, which the camera occasionally picked up rioting in the background, were a deliberate importation.

Dinkuhl came back to face the camera. 'Now I remember,' he said. 'I fixed it all up before. Ladies and gentlemen, the KF newsreel!'

The music was a neat parody of the signature tune for the Red League newsreel, in a minor key, mocking. The screen showed the night sky, caught the Moon, and dissolved into a familiar moonscape—the view from the Tycho observatory.

'Here,' said Dinkuhl, 'on the frozen, challenging surface of the Moon, men serve their mistress, Science. Here, in the great observatory, the secrets of the universe are unriddled one by one, or hundred by hundred, or thousand by thousand, or whatever the score now is. Puny man reaches out into the vastness of intergalactic space, seeking, seeking, admitting no obstacle, no defeat. We're pretty good, aren't we? Inch by inch, light year by light year, the cosmos yields up its mysteries, like a woman, as someone with inspiration has possibly said already.'

The scene shifted to the interior of the dome, and to the main room, housing the giant reflector. A figure stayed hunched over an eyepiece.

'And out there,' Dinkuhl said, 'along with mystery, there is beauty. Let us look, with these stalwart watchers of the skies, not at a new planet but at the—*the*—new comet.'

The screen was patterned with brilliant stars; the bright smudge of the comet was central, beneath Jupiter.

'There it is, below the giant Jupiter. More than two thousand years ago, as astronomers have calculated, this great comet last swept in its parabola round the sun. Think of it, my friends. More than two thousand years. While eighty generations of men have come and gone, while kingdoms have waxed and waned, while the human race has climbed so painfully to its present eminence, that majestic luminary, that celestial gas-bag, has been plodding round a course trillions of miles away in the outer dark.'

His voice became more brisk. 'And now for several months it will increase in brightness as it approaches the sun, swings round it, and prepares to leave us for another two millennia. During that time, the TV newsreels will keep you informed of the details and chart the path of the comet among the twinkling stars. To you, in your fireside chair, the comet, from outer space. What an encounter!'

The camera came back to Dinkuhl's own face. He lowered his head so that light gleamed from the bald patch at the crown, and smiled up from under bushy eyebrows.

'You know what I suggest?' Dinkuhl asked. He leaned forward to the camera, his mouth pursed almost as though to kiss. 'I suggest you get up out of that goddam chair, and go outside and have a look for yourself. You can find it with field-glasses or, in the rare event of your possessing what used to be called normal vision, with the naked eye. Right under Jupiter. If you can find Jupiter, that is. Anyway, Channel KF proposes to help you on your way in the simplest and most effective manner by closing down for half an hour. That is the end of the newsreel. We are going out on the roof to have a look at the comet ourself. Goodbye.'

The screen went blank. Charles got up. He hesitated for a moment, and then went over to his sports locker. The glasses were hanging on the inside of the door. He remembered, as he passed through the hall, to flip down the switch on the call amplifier. It was a long time since there had been a call while he was out in the garden or, for that matter, even while he was in the house; the action was a routine one. The door slid to behind him and he was aware of the night air, damp and a little frosty.

He put on the small lights that edged the garden path, and then put them off again for even they took something from the night's royal darkness. He made his way, blindly at first, down the path, to the point, beyond the arbour, where his view of the sky would be uninterrupted. There was some cloud in the east, but otherwise bright starlight; no moon. Jupiter was in Taurus, on the edge of the Milky Way. He raised his glasses and found the comet. He looked at it until his arm began to ache and his hand shook the glasses. Nothing much—a smear of whiteness, with one of the planet's moons set in it like a pearl. He reflected: once a portent, dethroner of kings, justifier of prophets. And now, the wide world over, just something for the newsreel lyricists, for Dinkuhl to parody in turn.

He was preparing to go back to the house when he heard the loud ring of the call amplifier; automatically he quickened his step and then, deliberately, slowed again. His eyes were sufficiently used to the starlight by now for him to see his

9

way clearly. He pressed the door open, and cut the amplifier out. The din dropped to the usual persistent buzz.

In the lounge, he pressed the button for the information panel on the callscreen. The letters sprang into being at the left-hand side, ran across, and jerked back again, in a never-ending series:

GRAYNER FROM LEDBETTER—UC DIV HQ DETROIT—
URGENT URGENT—PERSONAL—GRAYNER FROM LED-
BETTER——

Ledbetter. He wasted no time in putting the callscreen on reply circuit. While his Accept call was going out he pulled a chair over and sat down. He tried to be at ease, reminding himself that at thirty-eight he was past the stage of being upset by unexpected calls from HQ. At least, he should be.

It was not Ledbetter, of course, who took the call. A young man, with a sleek look and the little rubylite badges on his lapels, spelling out United Chemicals, which in current fashion were replacing the old anodized aluminium UC signets. He smiled, clearly well practised in the art of making older men at ease in their inferiorities.

'Grayner?' he said. 'We haven't met, have we? I'm Official Paulton.'

'Glad to know you,' Charles said evenly.

'Manager Ledbetter wants to see you; he asked me to fix an appointment. Can you get up here in the morning?'

Charles looked at him. Paulton made him nervous; there was not only the impression of a personality screen set up to dazzle, but also the feeling that if you stretched your neck a little in the right direction you would be able to see right round it. He said slowly:

'It's rather short notice. I like to be able to arrange things at the lab whenever I have to be away.'

10

Paulton looked to one side, openly checking a dossier.

'Let me see, your establishment is——'

Charles cut in. 'One junior assistant and two lab boys. All the same, I like to have things mapped out.'

Paulton smiled. 'It won't kill the economy even if they loaf for a day. Can you make it by ten hundred?'

He thought of saying his gyro was out of action, but rejected the idea. Since they were apparently anxious to get him in Detroit they would certainly arrange for him to be picked up.

'All right.'

'Ten hundred. Look me up first. My room is F 73. You know your way around the place, I take it?'

'I've been there before.'

'See you then.'

Paulton let his smile fade into a look of sober concentration, and then switched off. The callscreen blanked. Charles sat where he was for several minutes. The first thing he told himself was that there was no point at all in trying to work out possible reasons for the call to see Ledbetter. From that stage, nevertheless, he went on to do precisely that.

His niche in the Saginaw laboratories was a small but apparently secure one. At times he had resented the smallness; more recently he had felt himself valuing the security. There had been, since Ledbetter took over the year before, a shaking up that had brought down quite a few in the Saginaw hierarchy. He had congratulated himself on being too unimportant, and in what was clearly enough a blind alley, to be counted worth the shotgun. Now he was forced to wonder about that.

But if this were a demotion—a removal back, perhaps, to the general lab—it was difficult to see why he should be called urgently in to Detroit to be informed of it. That was a routine matter and would be dealt with through routine channels.

It would not need an interview with Ledbetter to confirm it.

Unfortunately the same argument applied to the suggestion, which he could not help entertaining for a moment, that there might, after all this time, be a promotion for him. Promotion procedures followed iron-clad rules; protocol had it that everything went through the local Manager, and there was no reason why there should be any urgency. For that matter, he had to admit to himself that there could be no justification for a promotion, anyway. Sixteen years' research in the radio-active properties of diamonds had not, he knew, fitted him for the control of any larger project. One assistant and two lab boys. After sixteen years you could do that, and that was all you could do.

That left him up in the air. No demotion, no promotion—then why the call to Detroit? He grinned to himself. Could one of his reports have given someone the idea that he was on to a synthesis? But that didn't fit either. Recent reports had covered no new ground, and Ledbetter was anything but the kind of fool to read fantasies into them.

To hell with it, he thought, but knew it would not be dismissed so easily. He went over and switched on the telescreen. It glowed softly, but nothing came through. Channel KF still taking a break. Impatiently he buttoned Red League.

It was Superquiz. Ramon Astell was doing his usual clowning with the quiz-members. Charles watched it for a time superciliously; then, unable to resist the carefully designed idiocy, he began to laugh.

For a moment Paulton looked puzzled when he saw his face. Charles was standing in the corridor outside room 73 on F floor and the small inset callscreen transmitted his features to the panel on the wall facing Paulton's desk. Then Paulton's face cleared.

12

'Grayner, of course! Come on in.'

The door beside him slid open, and closed after him as he went through. Paulton had genuine interest and recollection on his face when they met in the flesh. His control, Charles reflected, was admirable; many would have overdone the forgetfulness. He shook hands with a warm grip.

'I'd like to plead pressure of work,' Paulton said, 'but——' He smiled and a gesture took in the bare desk and the tele-screen alive on the wall—he had ostentatiously knocked the sound off while Charles was entering. 'I guess I don't im-prove with idleness.'

Charles smiled and said nothing. If Paulton wanted, for some obscure reason of his own, to put over the popular impression of Admin life as being the true one, he saw no reason why he should rise to it. Paulton was watching him astutely enough behind that self-deprecating smile.

'Anyway,' Paulton went on, 'that's no good reason for wasting your time as well. I told George ten fifteen—to allow for your not being quite on time—but we'll breeze right in. He won't be doing anything.'

Ledbetter's rooms, of course, were on B. Paulton led him through to the room marked 'Manager G. D. Ledbetter,' and whistled at the door. It opened, and they went in. Ledbetter was talking into a dictaphone. He looked up grimly as they entered, but went on to finish the stenoflip he was engaged on. Then he said to Paulton:

'I propose to have the sound-key changed on that door. When I do I shall make a point of not letting you in on the new one. Who's this?'

'Grayner,' Paulton said. 'It won't make a lot of difference —about the door. Grayner. You told me to get him here to see you.'

Ledbetter said: 'Yes, of course. All right, you can go, Harry. Next time you come in, use the callscreen.'

Paulton, retreating, said: 'I'll try to remember.'

Charles had been studying Ledbetter. He had seen him on newsreels and in the UC telezine, but those had been formal occasions. Now he was entirely friendly and relaxed. He slid a cigarette box over, and Charles took one. Ledbetter took one himself. The small flame jet rose from the desk-lighter and they both bent forward to light up. Ledbetter settled back again in his desk, his cigarette between his fingers and his other hand pulling at his long chin in a reflective manner.

He had got his managership young and his present seniority had been reached in a vault over several more likely shoulders. He was probably a year or two younger than Charles himself; he was long-limbed and looked, in repose, as though he were midway between two series of violent actions.

He said to Charles: 'You'll be wondering why I've got you to come along here.'

Charles was determined to preserve his wariness, but he could not help responding to some extent to the intimate friendliness of Ledbetter's approach. He could see now why he had come up so fast; some of his recent seniors must still be rubbing their eyes.

Charles said: 'Well, naturally. And the notice was rather short.'

Ledbetter nodded. 'The reason I wanted to see you is that I am in the middle of the usual thing that new Area Managers go in for. I'm having a reorganization. It's expected of me, I gather. Once over, I can settle down and let things run themselves until my translation elsewhere or my decease.' He looked directly at Charles. 'You will have noticed some of the earlier changes in your own plant?'

Charles nodded. 'I'd hoped maybe I was in too small a niche to be noticed.'

14

Ledbetter examined him again; searchingly this time. 'You've been in that niche too long.'

From one of the drawers in his desk he produced a microfilm capsule and clipped it into the projector. The telescreen on the wall lit up and displayed what was immediately recognizable as one of Charles' own recent reports. 'The effect of zeta irradiation on the photoelectric properties of a type II diamond (Cape white).'

'You write a very fair report. But you're not ambitious?'

'You have my psychoplan.'

'That, too.' Ledbetter smiled. 'There has been some revision of the methods of evaluation. In fact, you might say that the only thing Psycho & Med don't revise is their charming air of infallibility. Frankly, an error was made in your case. You aren't really the dead-end type.'

'I always suspected it. But it's a little late to do anything about it now, I imagine.'

'Ye-es. In any major respect, anyway. I could let you have official condolences——-'

'Thanks, I'll take them as read. You didn't call me in simply to offer the condolences—official or otherwise?'

Ledbetter's hand reached out towards the controls of his aromofact. 'Any objections to a whiff of the bounding wave?' Charles shook his head and watched him finger one of the buttons. The tang of seaweed and salt-water was in the air; his report faded off the telescreen and was replaced by a rocky seascape. He had the impression that Ledbetter was showing off, but he did not resent it.

Ledbetter said: 'This is one of the few gadgets they've given me that I'm genuinely attached to. I get away to yachting whenever I can. No, of course I didn't bring you up here simply to tell you P & M snafued your psychoplan sixteen years ago. If there had been nothing that could be done about it, I should have seen to it that you weren't informed

15

at all. You can weave a damn sight more tangled a web undeceiving people than the other way round.

'Now, let's get it straight and lay it on the table. Alpha —I'm in a mood for change. Beta—you should never have been tossed into that lab in the first place. Gamma's the rub. Gamma—you've spent sixteen years messing around with radio-active diamonds. That restricts the possibilities of what we can do with you to a somewhat startling extent.'

Charles said: 'Very interesting. Delta——?'

'Coincidence,' said Ledbetter, 'rears its ungainly but attractive head. There's a little place going at a spot called San Miguel. South of San Diego. Wonderful climate and the wide Pacific. I wish I was there myself. Area HQ is at Los Angeles—a guy called Mettrill. You'll like him.'

Charles said: 'Establishment?'

Ledbetter leaned back. 'I thought you would ask that. L category.'

He kept his eyes fixed on Charles' face. Charles felt himself flushing slightly.

'It's a wonderful opportunity,' he remarked. 'From one assistant and two lab boys to one assistant and two lab boys. What do I do for the next sixteen years—electrify diamonds instead of irradiating them?'

Ledbetter grinned. 'Think of the climate! It's not quite as bad as it looks. Still diamond, of course—what else could we give you? But you will be picking up some interesting threads. This for instance.'

He removed the microfilm of Charles' report and replaced it with another. The monotonously rolling sea gave way to neat lines of text and a number of equations. Charles let his eyes skim across them. He glanced at Ledbetter, and the Manager set the film in slow rolling motion up the screen. The report unfolded itself before them. In the list of refer-

16

ences at the end there were half a dozen papers of his own. He looked at Ledbetter.

'Where was this published?'

Ledbetter let the seascape come back before he answered. 'It hasn't been published.'

'Because?'

'Because that is one of the advantages of your new post. Don't publish if you don't want to. Don't do a damn thing if you don't feel like it. Sit and wriggle your toes in the ocean all day if you have a mind. The lab's on its own—on the edge of an orange grove I understand. You might call yourself a scientific hobo, with endowment.'

Charles' mind had been engaged with the paper that had just been projected for him. Things began to click into place.

'Do I come under Contact Section?' he asked.

Ledbetter smiled and turned the sea scents higher.

'No.'

'You're certain of that?'

'People,' Ledbetter said, 'have some odd ideas about Contact Section. I can't vouch for the other managerials, but in UC their budget doesn't run to special laboratories. And what would Contact Section do with non-insulating diamonds? Non-insulating callscreens are about their line of country.'

Charles said patiently: 'Then it will be all right for me to publish whatever I want?'

'I didn't say that. All right—abandoning the smoke-screen —you weren't supposed to have asked so many awkward questions at this early stage—yes, you're guessing in the right direction. The new job is restricted. You are under San Diego for admin but any reports you make go direct to Graz.'

'To Tapron?'

'To Nikko-Tsi, for Preston.'

17

'And what do they want me to turn out?'

'I'm not in the secret. This report of Isaacssohn's you've just seen—it doesn't mean anything to me because it's not my line, but I suspect that there isn't anything vital in it anyway, or I wouldn't have been given it to show you.'

Charles said: 'It's fairly routine stuff, as a matter of fact. Bombardment conductivity; we've done a certain amount at Saginaw.' Ledbetter nodded his appreciation. 'There are one or two points in it, though——'

'They, I take it, were meant to whet your appetite. Do they?'

'Yes.' He hesitated before he shot the next question at the Manager. 'What became of my predecessor? Radiation poisoning or the managerial variety?'

'A good question. Isaacssohn, I understand, was by way of being an amateur sailor like myself—plenty of scope in a place like that as I've indicated. I don't know the details of what happened, except that his boat came back, keel upwards, and he didn't. It's a tricky coast, I understand.' Charles thought for a moment that he looked at him oddly, but there wasn't enough in it to get hold of a meaning. 'A very tricky coast. I should stay away from it when the flow tide's getting near the turn.'

'I doubt if I shall do any sailing at all.'

Ledbetter shook his head. 'What a waste! I take it you are accepting, then?'

'Do I have any choice?'

'On a job like this you have the full rights in practice that you normally have in theory. Look at it from their point of view.'

Charles nodded. 'When do you want me to start?'

Ledbetter glanced at the note-pad inset on the desk under his right hand. 'You will be turning your gyro in at Saginaw.

18

We'll pick you up with your things in the morning and you'll join the ten hundred stratoliner here.'

'Tomorrow morning? As soon as that?'

'You can make it?'

'Easily. But what's the hurry?'

'God knows. It probably helps to keep a file tidy in Graz. There are wheels within managerial wheels. By the way, in your new position you are up five hundred a month. You qualify for a Cat C gyro *and* limousine, too.'

'Wonderful.'

Ledbetter looked at him keenly. 'Had you come as far up from the bottom as I have you would think so. One other triviality—you don't object to ex-Israelis?'

Charles looked at him with some surprise. 'How many of them?'

'Only one. Isaacssohn was, and he picked one for his assistant. Natural enough, I suppose. If you have objections we can arrange for her to be shunted, I imagine, but you will probably need her to begin with at least. I have the impression that a lot of the valuable side of Isaacssohn's work may only be traceable through her.'

'I've never worked with any. I don't see any reason why I should want to get rid of her.'

'That's fine, then.' Ledbetter glanced at the chronometer on the wall. 'You'll have some packing to do, so I won't keep you any longer.'

Charles stood up: 'And what about what happens to my own lab? I shan't have time even to tidy things up.'

'I don't imagine it's necessary. I did want to consult you about that, of course, though. It very nearly slipped my mind. We propose letting Casey take over, since he's been with you for five years. He's a little young, but we believe he's all right? What are your views?'

19

'Yes, he'll do. What do P & M think? Does he fit the niche satisfactorily, by present reckoning?'

Ledbetter grinned. 'By present reckoning.'

He left the UC HQ building in the first place because he wanted to drop in, for the last time, on Stone's, the little gramophone record exchange at the corner of 27th and Main. He had very little packing to do—a couple of hours in the evening would clear it—and he had decided against going back to the lab. They might as well have it that way if they wanted it, and it was true enough that Casey would manage all right. He and Casey had got on well enough but there would be little grief on either side at the parting; for Casey, in fact, there would be the entirely understandable satisfaction of getting an establishment of his own a good few years before he could reasonably have expected it.

There was only old Stone himself in the shop when he reached it. The shop was, of course, no more than a hobby: it did not support Stone but Stone supported it, on his pension. He had been a Manager in Atomics and was now, at last, enjoying life. He was a sturdily built old man, but going to fat.

Charles told him of his own impending translation. He shook his head, but the ruefulness was not deep-rooted. He said: 'I'm not even sure if my customers still add up to double figures.' But essentially he was unconcerned.

Charles asked: 'Anyone in the business in San Diego?'

'There's only one shop in the west—Michael Kominski's in Los Angeles. I'll get you the address.'

He went rummaging among his untidy papers in the battered walnut desk at the end of the shop, and Charles meanwhile browsed through the shelves of assorted records near the door. He found a set of the Munich John Passion, with one record missing, and wondered whether it was worth while taking it in the hope of filling in the gap some time in the future. But it was priced too low; that represented Stone's own considered opinion that the odds against were very high. He put the records back as someone came into the shop.

He recognized Dinkuhl, of course. The odd thing was that Dinkuhl recognized him; they had been introduced once, some years before, in circumstances that were now vague.

The proprietor of Channel KF said: 'Charlie Grayner! Nice to find you again. Having a last look round before you light out for the land of sunshine?'

They shook hands. Charles said:

'You astonish me.'

Dinkuhl grinned. 'You don't show it.'

'You do, though. I suppose it would be rude to ask you where you got your information from?'

'It must be six or seven years since I saw you.' Dinkuhl shook his head, clearly delighted with his own powers of recollection. 'At the Sullivan place, before they got a transfer to Melbourne. It is you who are going to California, isn't it? I thought it must be. Source of information? That, Charlie, is one thing you never ask a TV man.'

'You make it sound important,' Charles said.

'Everything,' Dinkuhl said expansively, 'is important. Similarly everything is trivial. What the hell happens to you, *qua* you, is trivial. But if I were in your shoes I should regard getting away from this putrid section of the stinking cheese to one slightly less high as very important indeed. I'll never forgive Gillray for refusing to let us transfer to Frisco.'

Stone came back with the address written on a slip of paper. Charles took it and thanked him, and slipped it in his wallet. Dinkuhl appeared to have abandoned him in order to look through the shelves which Charles had recently left. He remembered now that at their previous meeting Dinkuhl had been alternately intimate with and then apparently forgetful of the people around him. His telescreen personality was not, it seemed, at all different from his natural one.

Charles said to Stone: 'The John Passion? What are the chances of filling it?'

Stone began: 'Well, Kominski's got a lot of stuff he's never properly looked through——'

Dinkuhl turned round. He had the set in his hands; he thrust them at Charles.

'He's an old fraud. Don't believe him. You won't get that missing record on this continent, and incidentally I've been through Kominski's stuff myself. On the other hand it's worth having incomplete. You take them.'

Charles smiled. 'Since you recommend them.'

Dinkuhl did not return to looking through the records. He waited while Stone made out his laborious accounts and constructed his usual clumsy parcel. Then he put his hand on Charles' arm.

'You've got time enough. Come back with me and have a glass of something.'

It was flattering; and it was true that he had time to spare. Charles nodded. 'Thanks.'

Dinkuhl had an old runabout automobile into which he had contrived to fit a petrol engine he had rescued from somewhere. Their progress was a conspicuous and stinking one. He drove not to the studio but to his house, about a mile away, overlooking Lake Erie. It was twentieth-century Scandinavian in architecture, but had apparently been more soundly constructed than the average. It was still in good condition and as hideously ugly as on the day it was completed. Dinkuhl drew Charles' attention to this while he put the car away in the built-in garage.

'If I must live in Detroit, I've got no intention of risking an æsthetic breakdown by inhabiting a house of decent appearance and proportions. The hell of it is that, over the years, it has begun to grow on me.'

He led Charles upstairs to a large room on the first floor, with a view on to the lake. The place was untidy and had not been dusted for some time. There was something definitely unusual about the room, too, and it took Charles a few minutes to find out what it was. The wall lacked a telescreen.

Dinkuhl brought Charles a drink in a very fine-looking wide-bowled glass. Both bowl and stem were delicately engraved—diamond engraving, Charles reflected with professional interest. The liquor in the glass was a pale amber colour.

Dinkuhl held his own glass up. 'Cheers,' he said.

They drank. The taste was odd. Charles held the glass up in inquiry.

'What is it, Manager?'

'Call me Hiram,' Dinkuhl said. 'You like it? It's a little something I knocked up myself. Turnip-and-tomato wine. Not bad, though? Not at all bad.'

Answering his own question, he simultaneously topped up both their glasses. He fished out of one pocket the old-fashioned spectacles he sometimes wore in the studio and put them on to study Charles more closely.

'Well, then,' he said. 'What are you going to do for culture in the Far West? You're one of the customers—you wrote me a letter about a month back.'

'I can give up TV,' Charles said. He smiled. 'Even KF. I might take up reading.'

'It is an unhappy fact,' Dinkuhl said, 'that the only people who can give up TV are precisely those who commonly patronize KF. Well, I guess it may last out my time.'

'I never did understand why Telecom let you keep running.'

'For only one reason, but a good one. Our charter got

incorporated, in some strange way, in their constitution. I give the credit to my then predecessor, a guy called Bert White. The proprietorship of KF is a self-perpetuating office for which the chief qualification is low cunning, but White was exceptional. Short of rewriting their own constitution, a desperate step that might stir up a regular horde of hibernating skeletons, they've got to go on giving us rights of telecasting. They just have to get what satisfaction they can from watching us slowly fade away; but it is slow.'

Charles said: 'I never knew your charter was pre-managerial.'

Dinkuhl stared at him. 'You could not seriously have thought that Telecom spawned us of their own free will? I was under the impression our pedigree was better known. We represent one of the few remaining strands of capitalism in the modern world. You know what KF stood for, in the first place?'

Charles shook his head.

'Koola Frutes—a fruitjuice combine. The big shot who ran it got culture in his old age and it went to his head. He put his fortune into the establishment of an independent, self-perpetuating TV network. KF has been lucky in its directors—up to me it has, at any rate. We tried to accommodate ourselves to managerialism, and we made a good play at that. The sands may be running out, but it's been a long long time.'

'But if Telecom can't touch you?'

'There's something else that can. Money. Comes the Roman Empire, feudalism, capitalism, managerialism—one little problem is constant: how to balance a budget. It will not have escaped your notice that we have had inflation with us the last couple of hundred years? We're the fixed income boys. We've retrenched and cut down and done everything bar live on immoral earnings. And the result? With one

24

station, beaming a small circle round this environ of Hades, the end is still in sight. And Gillray, and all the rest of Telecom, will laugh their silly heads off when it comes.'

Charles said: 'I'm sorry to hear that. Very sorry.'

'What do you think our scrounging appeals have been aimed at—buying me a spaceyacht?' Dinkuhl regarded him cynically. 'How much have you come through with?'

'Ten dollars, once. I would have managed more if I had known as much as this about the set-up.'

'At ten dollars you're well above average. If it had been a spaceyacht I wouldn't have had the spittoons to date. Why should people contribute to TV? It's a free service, isn't it? I know one thing: KF can't run another twenty years under managerialism.'

'And they won't let you move west for the passing?'

'That,' Dinkuhl said, 'is what has irked me. Really irked me. They have control over extensions in areas under their jurisdiction. We had a station in Frisco once, but they choose to regard reopening as an extension and it's their say. If they'd let me have that, I'd have taken it. I was even looking forward to the closing ceremony. But in Detroit . . . not if I can prevent it.'

'Can you?' Charles asked with interest.

'Have some more wine.' Charles watched Dinkuhl refill his glass without demur; the taste remained strange but the residual warm glow was very pleasant. 'Had I the talent for manœuvre, for politics, for downright chicanery, of my illustrious predecessors, I would be fairly confident. As it is, I doubt it, I doubt it.'

'The methods you're going to adopt are secret, I suppose?' Charles inquired tentatively.

Dinkuhl smiled sourly. 'As secret as your transfer to San Miguel. There's only one line I can try. Under managerialism,

25

we're sunk. So I shall try switching us to the one tiny oasis where managerialism doesn't send its camels—to Israel.'

'Well, good luck.' Charles thought about it for a moment. 'Not very hopeful, is it?'

Dinkuhl said: 'I like you, Charlie. You put things well. I can always join Red League again—you know I started with that outfit?'

'No. I didn't know.'

'The day I tossed my Telecom membership card in the lake was the happiest day of my life. I'm not even sure which lake it was now. I suppose they would make me out a new one.'

Dinkuhl glanced at his watch; it was extraordinarily big and he wore it on his wrist instead of on his watch-finger.

'But pending Israel or Red League, the show must go on. I must get back to rehearse an Indian I found working for Hydroponics not far from Seattle. A real Indian—guaranteed walkee and talkee. I hope to coach him into a withering denunciation of contemporary society, but I've got my work cut out. The old coot's too damn happy by far. Come with me—I'll drop you by the UC building.'

After the wine, the smell of petrol was a little sickly. Charles was glad when Dinkuhl kicked the door open to let him out.

'On your way. One thing.' Charles looked at him. 'I hear the boating's tricky on that coast.'

Charles said: 'I've already been told that.'

'This,' said Dinkuhl, 'is official. The voice of the KF Newsreel.'

He grinned, pulled the car door to, and went off in a stinking, noisy cloud.

2

CHARLES still had the habit, on first acquaintance, of appraising young women for romantic possibilities, although for some years it had been a relatively academic one. Sarah Cohn did not make a good initial impression, even academically. She was attractive enough—dark and rather square-faced and giving an impression of neatness and grace in small things—but her personality was unattractive. She was nervous, and the nervousness manifested itself in brusqueness; she succeeded in communicating her lack of ease to Charles. It was not a good start to a working association that would necessarily be close. It was comforting to remember that Ledbetter had told him he need not keep her if he didn't want to.

The lab was on high ground, facing the sea and perhaps a hundred yards from it. There was a good view of San Miguel, which was about a mile away, and the back looked into an orange grove which appeared to stretch indefinitely. At intervals during the day one of the giant robot tree-tenders would rumble down the aisles separating the rows of trees, spraying some aerosol that effectively blanketed the tender smell of the ripening oranges. It wore off gradually, but by then the tree-tender was probably approaching on a new round. This was the winter crop and it could hardly be left

27

alone for half a day. In among the trees the radiant heaters squatted on their long poles, waiting for the nightfall which would activate them. You had to hand it to Agriculture, Charles felt, for efficiency, but it was a pity that it had to include de-scenting an orange grove.

The equipment in the lab was very good. The first thing he noticed was the five-thousand kV electrobombard he had asked for, and failed to get, when it was announced a year before. There were three cyclotrons. Money had been spent here, and he felt he knew UC policy well enough to be sure that that meant they had expected to get something out of it. The difficulty was finding precisely what.

Isaacssohn's notes were scrappy; scrappy enough to be just about useless and yet, tantalizingly, not quite scrappy enough to discard entirely. The reports were on file, of course, and he spent the first couple of days almost exclusively in familiarizing himself with them. The trouble was that the reports, on the face of it, did not add up to a picture that jelled. The work that had been done had covered a number of different subjects, though experiments on diamond, selenium and germanium predominated, but even for the latter three it was difficult to determine any consistency of approach. It was the kind of work, clearly enough, which would gain considerably in meaning with the application of the key—the key being the trifling matter of what Isaacssohn was driving at. A lot of things might make sense, that granted.

This need obliged him to fall back on Sarah. He found her in the north room, engaged in the graphitization of a specimen of carbon. He stood behind her without saying anything for a couple of minutes. She might have been so absorbed in her work as to be unaware of him, but he knew she was not. He said at last:

'And the next step?'

28

She turned round slowly, holding a pair of asbestos tongs. She looked at him steadily, and behind the steadiness she was obviously jumpy and hostile.

'Slow bombardment, drying out for twenty-four hours, and checking lattice changes by positron diffraction.'

'To establish?'

She hesitated; she still looked at him but her gaze was edgy. 'It's a continuation of a series of experiments Dr Isaacssohn put in hand.'

It was a warm day outside; the distant rumble of the tree-tender had a somnolent note. Charles said impulsively:

'I'd like to have a talk with you, Sarah. You can spare half an hour?'

She nodded her head towards her workbench. 'And leave it?'

'Luke can look after this stage of it, can't he? If he can't, he should be able to.'

In the corridor she moved in the direction of his little private office at the back. He checked her.

'Since it's so fine, I thought we might walk out towards the shore. The sea's not all that familiar a thing to me; I come from lake country.'

To whatever suspicion and distrust already existed was now added, he realized, the routine suspicion that a pass might be about to be made. It was flattering that he could be taken for a wolf still.

She said distantly: 'If you'd prefer that.'

They walked down to the shore in silence. There was a path down the slope and at some time in the past there had been an attempt at a garden here. But the ground could hardly be worse—barren rocky earth, quite apart from spray, if not flooding, in bad weather—and it had long tailed off into a few unpromising cacti. The path drifted into beach at a spot where half a dozen flat-topped rocks huddled

29

together with an air of imitating a cromlech. This was clearly enough a common resort of the people attached to the lab. A power line, which had taken its own more direct way down the slope, found its terminus at this point. For a portable telescreen, Charles reflected gloomily.

To the south there was something of an anchorage—a rough breakwater with a couple of concrete posts built on. The breakwater had probably served a small fishing community at one time. More recently the concrete posts had, he imagined, provided the tie-up for his predecessor's boat.

He nodded towards them. 'What became of the boat?'

She was still standing, as though awaiting orders. He said: 'We might as well sit down, I guess,' and she sat on a stone a few feet from the one he took.

She smoothed her skirt down and looked not at him but away out to sea. 'The boat? They took it away.'

'They?'

'Your friends.' She glanced at him. 'Contact Section.'

He had begun to be angry before he realized it; he repressed the feeling decisively. It had been a shock to her; probably she had got on well with Isaacssohn—there might even have been something more in it than that. And Contact Section . . . those members he had encountered had not impressed him by their qualities of tact and the handling of difficult situations. All the same, it was essential that she should not settle into an attitude of surliness towards him. Either that must change or she must go: there could be no other alternative.

It was a pity that, as he very well knew, he did not himself have any great talent for handling awkward personal relations. He said slowly:

'We might as well get some things clear at the start. I'm not Contact Section, and I haven't been briefed by Contact Section. I was under the impression that it was Isaacssohn

30

who had dealings with them. I've been doing a very ordinary job in diamond research under Detroit Sector, and I've been pulled in here apparently because they wanted someone in a hurry. I'd hoped you might be able to help me . . . I'm pretty much in the dark all the way round.'

Her eyes had swung to him while he talked. 'Hans had nothing to do with Contact Section. I know that.'

He waited for her to say something further, but she did not oblige. He sighed inwardly. It was going to be very difficult. Whatever he had stepped into was complicated, and even if the complication was no more than an emotional, a romantic one, it was going to take very hard graft to unravel it.

He said, trying to make it delicate: 'It's just those things you know that I'm interested in. Try to see it from my point of view—I'm suddenly pitched into a job like this . . . usually one has the other man's programme to follow. Isaacssohn didn't have time to leave an outline and as far as I can see UC never did know exactly what he was doing. If they did, I can't see why I should have been tossed into it blindfold.'

Her eyes were on the sea again; on the blue-green plain of water stretching up to the sky.

'I'm seeing it,' she said. 'It was most inconsiderate of Hans to get drowned without first leaving you detailed instructions.'

'I'm sorry.' He looked at her averted face, trying to gauge the kind of emotion responsible for the bitterness of her remarks. 'I'm probably not putting things very well. You see, I didn't know Dr Isaacssohn. One can't——'

He thought for a moment she might be going to smile. She said, more gently than she had spoken so far:

'You still aren't putting them very well, are you? You're right that you can't be expected to feel very sorry for some-one you never knew, but at least when you are talking about him you can give him his title—as you finally did.'

He looked at her in astonishment; then he understood.

31

'How long have you been over?' he asked. 'If that isn't another rude question.'

She caught the point. 'Three years.'

'You took your degree in Israel?'

She nodded. 'Jerusalem.'

'And I suppose you have been with—with Dr Isaacssohn all the time? It's a matter of usage. There's no disrespect in not giving a man his title here. Scientific titles are very rarely used, anyway. With Managers and Directors it's a different thing, of course. Apart from that, we just don't bother. There was really no offence meant.' He smiled ruefully. 'In fact, I wasn't even being accidentally rude, though I believe I often am.'

She said: 'I'm sorry.' She studied his face. She had a direct and honest look and for the moment her nervousness had gone. 'I've been rather a fool about that, I suppose.'

He said: 'Perhaps we can get off on the right foot now—both of us.'

She did smile then, but her eyes were still wary. She had eyes that were near the colour the sea was today; they were very striking against her dark-brown hair.

She asked: 'What is it you want to know?'

He looked at her helplessly. 'Primarily, what I am supposed to do. You seem to have a line to follow. It's somewhat embarrassing that I haven't.'

'You mean to tell me, seriously, that they didn't tell you?'

'Seriously.'

The mistrust was there again; and stronger. 'It's hard to swallow—that they should appoint you in Hans' place and not tell you what you were expected to do.'

'All the same,' Charles said, 'I'd like you to make the effort.' He paused. 'It may make a difference that I've been rushed straight here from Detroit. I gather you are implying that Graz know what's up, but that doesn't mean Detroit does. I suppose Graz may finally wake up to the need for telling me. I suppose I could telecall Nikko-Tsi and jog their memories, but in my experience it's always better to get along on your own if you can. Pestering HQ can have unfortunate results.'

She wrinkled her brow. 'Am I being dumb again? Is that a usual sort of thing to happen in a managerial?'

'Not unusual. Why do you think all the original work is now being done in Haifa and Jerusalem?'

She was pleased and surprised. 'You see that, too?'

'They that have eyes can see. Now—this job?'

She still hesitated for a second. He wondered if he could follow her thoughts: some residual doubt, but the comforting reflection that what she was going to tell him was, in any case, no more than Graz knew already.

She said firmly: 'Hans was after a new power source, on a photoelectric basis. I don't know that I can be terribly useful to you. He had reached the stage where he could see things a lot more clearly, but there was still a good deal of work to be done.'

'Power . . .' Charles said. 'Photoelectric . . . ? For the first time I have an inkling. Selenium obviously—germanium and diamond——?'

'Long-term irradiation of type III diamonds induces a fundamental structural change—the refractive index——'

'I saw that report. I thought it was a blind for something else. Type III diamond—that's new on me. And I find it hard to take that refractive index change. It's a startling figure he gives.'

'Type III signifies those stones which *do* respond in that way to prolonged irradiation. There aren't many, but they seem to come indiscriminately from type I and type II groups. The germanium, incidentally, is in because of the structural similarity to diamond. As far as I know it never

B   33 gave anything. But Hans didn't find it easy to explain the lines he was following. He was still working on germanium.'

'And titania?'

'We tried a few things with titania. No soap. The greater refractive index in the raw state doesn't help at all. It's a structural matter.'

'Well,' Charles said thoughtfully. He felt in his pocket. 'Cigarette?' She shook her head. He took one and lit it himself. A breeze was freshening from the ocean; it blew the flame away from his cigarette and pulled a lock of Sarah's hair round her cheek.

'So it's a power source,' Charles said. 'That explains a few things at least. It explains why it was such a rush job getting me down here and also——' He looked at Sarah with attention. 'Did you know the information had got out—outside UC, I mean?'

She said bitterly: 'Does it explain an overturned boat drifting back to shore?'

Gloomily Charles surveyed his cigarette. 'Whatever it is, I'm in it, up to the neck.' The impact of her last words came properly home to him. 'Look, are you suggesting Isaacssohn was murdered?'

She was silent for a moment. 'I talk too much,' she said at last. 'I suppose it doesn't matter now. I've already had my say to Contact Section. It makes no difference—you might as well know what I think. Hans learnt his sailing in the Mediterranean. It's not as placid a sea as you people over here are inclined to imagine. The day he was drowned ... there was a fair swell but nothing that would be likely to worry him unduly.'

'I don't know a thing about sailing or the sea. But accidents do happen. And Ledbetter told me it was a tricky coast.'

34

She said: 'Ledbetter,' as though repeating the name was enough. She added: 'Hans never thought it particularly tricky: he had been sailing it for some years.'

It would be difficult to imagine a seascape more peaceful than the Pacific presented just now. But Charles was not convinced of anything except that his new assistant had been dangerously unsettled by the recent events. He tried to unravel the untidy possibilities.

'If you think that, why the objection to Contact Section? Surely you're not suggesting they had anything to do with it? UC would hardly be likely to kill the goose just when it's getting broody. Why didn't you tell them what you thought about Isaacssohn's death?'

'I did.'

He was surprised. 'And?'

'They would not take it seriously.' Her brows tightened, remembering. 'They reported accidental death.'

'That doesn't make them your enemies. They might just be mistaken—if your view's the right one.'

Her eyes were cold and unfriendly again. 'I was under the impression that the job of Contact Sections was to go into anything that might be to the disadvantage of their managerial.'

He said easily: 'These are slack times, even for Contact Sections. It's rare to find a job done properly nowadays.'

He felt a twofold relief. That there was so simple an explanation of her antipathy to Contact Section, and that the predecessor had, after all, simply got himself drowned. The phantasmagoric mists were clearing, leaving behind a familiar and recognizable world framing an ordinary hysterical girl, instead of a nightmare situation pivoting on murder. It might be unpleasant if she persisted in this point of view—he would not like to have to call in Psycho & Medicine, especially since he had no great faith in their techniques—but at least he could see his way to handling things.

She said: 'And got out—where?'

'Got out?'

Her voice was impatient. 'You said just now—that the information had got out. I suppose, about our work here?'

'That? Yes. It seems to have done. At least, I had the impression that something was known—I don't know how much.'

'Inside UC—or another managerial?'

'Strictly speaking, another managerial. Telecom.'

'And this was in Detroit. Didn't it seem odd to you that Ledbetter should be in the dark, and whoever it was, not?'

'Not really. I didn't mean to imply that he necessarily knew anything more than Ledbetter did. And Ledbetter wasn't entirely in the dark, of course; he knew it was restricted work and had one of Isaacssohn's reports on his desk—not that it conveyed anything to him.'

The interview, he realized, had changed its course. His intention had been to question Sarah; now, with the bit well between her teeth, Sarah was questioning him. The problem was to ease her off the subject without upsetting her further. He would like to keep her well disposed towards him if it were possible; there was certainly a good deal more that might be got out of the complicated jigsaw of Isaacssohn's research intentions. She was welcome to dislike Contact Section; most people did, anyway.

'They make their seedy little plans and whisper secrets in corners, and they haven't any idea what they're dealing with.' She looked at him directly. 'Is there anything at all that can be said in their favour?'

Charles smiled. 'Only that they mean well, really, most of them, most of the time. Well as they see it.'

36

'I don't think so,' Sarah said slowly. 'I did at one time, but I don't any longer.'

He thought he could see how the conversation might be turned; if he could divert the subject from the world at large, which, at the moment, she saw simply as Contact Section's field of operations, to Sarah herself.

He said: 'Why do people—you, for instance, and Isaacssohn—come over from Israel in the first place? Faith in the managerial ideal? Or what? Not just for the fleshpots, I take it?'

'People come over for both those reasons. There are always some students who find the system in operation across the border more attractive than that at home. And the standard of personal comfort is less high in Israel. There's a third reason as well, though. My father came over as a political refugee, and I came with him.'

'Political refugee?' It was hard to get hold of a term that had ceased to be valid, in the major world, a century before. He saw Sarah smile, understanding his bewilderment. 'In what way?'

'It would be difficult to explain. Men conspire as much in Israel as they do here, but in rather different ways. Daddy was in some plot to overthrow the government, and the plot was discovered. He would have been imprisoned if he had stayed.'

Charles said apologetically: 'I'm afraid I don't even know what kind of government you have in Israel. It's not a monarchy, is it?'

'In the true sense of the word, yes. A one-man rule. The President has the advice of the Sanhedrim, but he doesn't need to take the advice.'

Charles thought of asking what the Sanhedrim might be, and then thought better of it. Something else struck him.

37

'Your father was mixed up in a plot against the President? And Isaacssohn?'

'Yes. Hans was in it, too.'

'Then, if there was somehing fishy about his death, might it not be that——?'

She interrupted decisively. 'No. It would only have been imprisonment if they had stayed. We are not a primitive people. And, anyway, it was Daddy who was one of the leaders of the plot; Hans played only a very minor part in it.' Her eyes were on a hydroplane, skimming across the ocean's middle distance. 'It's only here that the innocent are killed, simply because they get in somebody's way.'

Charles saw no advantage in arguing with an obsession. She had been thawing, perceptibly thawing, and his only concern was to have the process continue.

'Your father?' he asked. 'Does he like it over here?'

She shrugged. 'Better than prison. He teaches History at Berkeley.'

'History?'

'Yes.' She smiled. 'There still are some who take it. He has two students at present. He gets paid a little less than'—she gestured towards the laboratory—'than Luke does. But he has modest needs. He seems to enjoy life fairly well.'

Charles got up. 'We could be getting back to see how Luke and Tony are progressing.' He helped Sarah, in turn, to her feet. 'You can't be expected to be greatly impressed by a lot of the things over here, or by the people. I'm not myself. But it would be a help if you could regard me as a—well, as a neutral, anyway. I shall be depending on your help; very much so.'

They were walking up the pebbled path. She said:

'I suppose they gave you a free hand about me?'

'A free hand?'

'You don't have to keep me here if you don't want to?'

38

He hesitated. 'No. But I can think of no reason why I should want to get rid of you.'

She smiled. 'Especially since Hans didn't make the right kind of notes. Well?'

He saw her glance at him. Mischievous as it now was, her face was wholly attractive. He smiled in return.

'There was that, of course. I was prepared to put up with a lot for the sake of the information I need.'

'That's very good of you.'

'*Was* prepared. Since you've shown you can be human and friendly and altogether very nice, I shall expect that as well. Even if you were to put me in the way of the first fundamental discovery in a century, I should want more than that now.'

They both laughed. A moment later her foot slipped on the loose stones, and he had to catch her to prevent her falling. It was precisely the right contact, at the right time.

One of the skills that Charles had bothered to acquire was that of grinding his own diamonds, instead of depending on having the work done outside. He had gone into the matter with a thoroughness that was natural to him, and had found that certain cuts, which for undiscoverable reasons had been allowed to disappear from use, gave a far greater effect of brilliance than the ones currently fashionable. He explained this to Sarah when she showed him one of the stones which had formed the basis of Isaacssohn's report on the refractive index changes in type III diamonds. She held the stone in a narrow pencil of light and they both had to turn their eyes from molten brilliance reflected from it. Charles took the stone and examined it.

'Rose cut. A brilliant cut would give you double the fire. And there was a mid-twentieth-century improvement, the Brown-brilliant, that does even better.'

39

She looked at him with surprise, and with admiration.

'We always had our stones cut in Los Angeles. We asked them to give us the best fire they could.'

'That would be Fransski?' Sarah nodded. 'I once tried to tell him the principles of the brilliant cut, but he very rarely listens to anything. The stones are cut before irradiation, of course? Did you ever try irradiating them first and then cutting?'

'Yes. It goes dead. Whatever form the lattice change takes, it can't be very stable. In fact, there's very likely a natural breakdown, though we haven't come across it yet. That stone I've just demonstrated was our first—about fifteen months ago. It seems all right. Anyway, grinding pressures break it down.'

Charles nodded. 'Not surprising. And the battery—a simple heat—electricity conversion? What about shielding?'

'Sapphire.'

'Yes. Just what was it needed ironing out, Sarah?'

'A lot of things. The shielding's a long way from being perfect, and the mirror system is still primitive. In fact, there's only the idea so far. All the development has to be done.'

Charles turned over the small diamond in his hand, examining it. 'The development . . . yes, I get that.' He looked at Sarah. 'Imagine for a moment that you are running United Chemicals. You get something like this underway. You—lose your research man, but the thing has reached this stage, anyway. What do you do next?'

'Turn it over to the engineers. It's obvious, isn't it?'

Charles nodded. 'Extremely obvious. You certainly don't get another research man in to do what has been done already. So the question remains—why me? Surely not consideration for my health. Can you think of a reason why they haven't turned this over to Design Section?'

'No. I wondered about it while Hans was alive. I asked him what he thought about it.'

'And he said——?'

'He had a poor opinion of the people at Graz. As far as I could gather, he thought they just didn't understand what we were doing. It seems difficult to believe.'

'Quite possible, though, I'm afraid. Hans'—he saw her glance at him with pleasure—'would know more about their reactions than you or I. I suppose you didn't see his confidential reports?'

She pointed towards the microfilm files. 'Only those on work done. Not the actual memoranda to Nikko-Tsi.'

'And the memoranda? Are they on file?'

'They were. Contact Section took them.'

He shook his head. 'Not that it matters a great deal. I don't think there's anything I can do but piece the picture together, and then send it in with a recommendation that they push it through to Detroit or Milan.'

Sarah said slowly: 'I hope you won't make up your mind too quickly.'

'Why?'

'If things have got to the point where they can't even recognize a fundamental job like this when it's thrust under their noses, I'm not sure that it's going to help passing it on to Design Section. I think Hans was quite happy at the prospect of carrying it through here, on our own.'

'We haven't the equipment necessary—or the staff?'

'We could probably do it, though.'

She was not looking at him as she said this, but out of the windows towards the Pacific. He thought with satisfaction: at least, as long as I am here, things aren't going to be too bad. The hostility seemed to have disappeared entirely. But although it was a relief to have the prospect of friendly

41

co-operation in the work, he still did not see how he could do anything but hand over to those people who were really qualified to complete the job. Isaacssohn, like Sarah, would have been imbued with the Israeli individualism, and was probably quite pleased at being left on his own to carry things through. Charles, a managerialist from birth, had a conscience about these things. He put one hand on Sarah's shoulder, and she turned towards him, half-smiling, ready for complicity of the two of them against the huge stupidity of the United Chemicals organization.

'I shan't need to make up my mind for a few days, anyway. I shall have to get the hang of things properly before I can recommend anything.'

She said: 'You could try the irradiation out on a brilliant-cut stone. Do you think you could possibly get some from Saginaw?'

He smiled inwardly at the naïve determination to get him involved in a continuance of research; although it was certainly true that she had dropped on something which he, if anyone, would have to do. The thought of Design Section grinding their own stones was amusing.

'Yes,' he said, 'I imagine Casey will send them on if I ask him. He always thought the importation of a scaife was another sign of my mental instability. In fact, I could have the scaife and the other equipment sent here, too. It will never be used there.'

She said: 'Yes, there wouldn't be any harm in doing that. I'd like you to have a look at the plan for the selenium rectifier. I've had some ideas which I've incorporated into the scheme as Hans left it.'

Without waiting for his reply, she flicked the lights off and dropped a microfilm in the reader. The telescreen on the wall lit up. She demonstrated with a pointer on the small inset screen in the bench, drawing circles round the salient

42

points, circles which, reproduced on the big screen, glowed for perhaps a minute before fading out.

'This is the original scheme. I thought if we made this linkage'—two ellipses joined and became a circle—'and cut out the third stage here . . .'

She pressed a button and a new print appeared on the screen.

'. . . It would look like this. That should boost it.'

Charles said: 'Yes. That's a pretty piece of work. Very pretty. I'm going to have my own work cut out to keep up with you.'

Looking at her as she stood in the shadows beyond the narrow beam of light he thought he saw her flush.

She said: 'Thank you. Hans left most of this side of things to me .'

'I imagine I shall do the same,' Charles said.

Those few of the twenty-first-century managerialists who had the necessary curiosity wondered occasionally why TV should continue to be flat when cinema was so wholeheartedly three-dimensional. The two media were both under Telecom, which made the discrepancy more puzzling. Actually the question had, in the first place, gone right up to the Council of Managerials. The Telecom Directors had wanted three-dimensional TV, but they had lost their case. Psycho & Medicine had put it most forcibly that TV, if given equal advantages with cinema, would drive the latter out, and there were a number of good reasons why the habit of outside and specialized entertainment should be maintained.

So, on the Sunday following his arrival, Charles dropped his gyro into the cinepark in San Miguel, and helped Sarah out. The roof slid to above them, shutting out the driving rain which was, in any case, evaporated by thermo-equipment long before it reached the ground level. Charles could

43

buy tickets for the three highest grades of seats; he got the best and they lay side by side on airfoam cushions in the centre of the bridge balcony that arched midway across the cinema.

While they waited for the film to be shown, Sarah rolled about, pressing herself deep into the airfoam, stretching her limbs against its resilience. Charles watched her with some amusement. She caught his eye.

'I've never been in these before,' she said. 'I came sometimes with Hans, but our natural Israeli frugality made us take the C seats.'

'Then you don't know all their advantages?' Charles suggested. He pressed a button, and the walls dropped down on either side of them, effectively screening them from the sight of people on either side as they were already screened from people in the inferior seats.

Sarah leaned across unhurriedly and pressed the release button; the walls ran up again.

'I know *of* them,' she said.

Charles had proposed the trip to cinema on finding that Sarah was as fond of re-makes as he was himself. Re-makes were the recreation of pictures of historical value with as close a fidelity as was consonant with transposition to 3D-colour-realism. The present programme had two re-makes—*La Femme du Boulanger* and *A Night at the Opera*. They enjoyed the first, but the second bored them. They had both seen originals of the Marx Brothers, on the small postcard screen, and the actors who now scrupulously mimicked them paled by comparison. They had a bond of criticism; they came off the bridge in a warm glow of companionship.

When the gyro lifted through the opened roof, it lifted into a clear sky, whose blue seemed to glisten after the rain. The cloud bank was still visible, a white bar above the inland hills. Visibility was very good, and on the hills themselves small details stood out with surprising clarity. The gyro hovering above the cinepark, Charles pointed them out to Sarah.

She said: 'Yes, wonderful. Can't we run over there?'

He glanced at the electric battery indicator. 'Just under a quarter. Any idea how far it is?'

She said vaguely: 'Five miles. Ten?'

Charles laughed. 'If it is ten, we'll probably have to walk part of the way back. All right?'

She smiled. 'No objection.'

He brought the gyro down on a grassed ledge about four hundred feet above sea-level, looking over the plain towards San Miguel, the laboratory, and the distant frieze of the ocean. The grass was short, probably sheep-cropped, but still wet from the storm; Charles threw a plastic sheet across it and they sat down. He began to offer her a cigarette, and then recollected himself.

'Of course, you don't. What do you take? Mesc?'

She shook her head. 'No. Nothing.'

'Nothing? Wonderful. You don't even bite your finger-nails?'

'Not even that. No credit, though. Remember my puritanical Israeli upbringing. That accounts for it.'

'I'd forgotten. Mesc and tobacco prohibited. You are allowed something, though. Is it——?'

'You're probably thinking of wine.' Sarah was gazing out over the vista which lay before them. 'There's one thing at least which is better on this side. Look at this, and we have it to ourselves. In Israel a spot like this would be packed tight; I doubt if there would even be room to drop a gyro.'

'Overcrowding,' Charles said, 'is one of the few troubles we don't have. In these parts, at any rate.' He got up and went over to the gyro. 'I have an idea——'

He fished in a locker and brought out two beakers and a

45

couple of plasts of red wine. 'Californian, I'm afraid. But better than nothing.' He sliced the corner of one of the plasts and the wine gushed out into the beaker held beneath it. He handed it to Sarah, and helped himself to the other. Tasting it, he said thoughtfully: 'Not too bad.'

'Here's to the solar battery,' Sarah said. Her eyes were on him as he repeated the toast. 'And to our healths.'

He caught the implication. 'I think we're safe enough.'

'So did Hans.'

He turned to look at her fully. It was only three days since they had met, but he could no longer be satisfied simply with having as little trouble as possible in the work they were to do together. It was important that she should not be tormented by false worries.

'Be sensible, Sarah. There's no reason at all why anyone should have killed Hans. It couldn't do any of the managerials any good. Why should UC kill him, since he was working for them? As for the others, I don't pretend that a little judicious murder isn't carried out now and then—but in this case what would be the point? If it were simply a question of eliminating an advantage held by UC, why give UC the chance of putting someone like myself in, and enabling me to pick the threads up from you? If it were that kind of set-up, you would have gone too. Two murders are very little harder than one.'

'It's no good, Charles,' she said. 'I know there's something wrong. That's a conviction.'

'How reached?' he asked with deliberate provocation. 'Through intuition?'

She was stung. 'No, damn you! Through knowing more of the facts than you do—and by knowing I mean really knowing, not just accepting intellectually. It's all right—you take my word for it that Hans was an expert yachtsman and that the sea was calm, but you can't begin to appreciate how

46

expert or how calm. You find the idea of his being killed senseless; I find it just as senseless that it should have been an accident.'

'Your unknowns are more mysterious than mine,' he pointed out. 'The sea has a long record of apparently senseless power and slaughter. The psychology of the managerials is only too predictable, I'm afraid. We know why Leverson didn't try to hang on to the hegemony of Atomics that van Mark had won, but we shall never know why its crew deserted the *Marie Celeste.*'

She smiled. 'I like your argument. You haven't convinced me, though.'

'I didn't expect to so easily. Time will convince you. I hope you realize that, insofar as there's a chance of there being anything in your theory, it lends support to our passing the whole thing over to Design Section?'

She was silent for a moment. 'Caught, I suppose. All right.' She drank from the beaker again. 'To the solar battery, and we'll let our healths look after themselves.'

She laughed. Watching her, Charles reflected that there was no trace now of the nervousness and awkwardness which had been such prominent features of her personality on their first meeting. And in their place, naturalness and charm were very prominent indeed. Especially the charm— he had a conviction of his own, growing all the time, that while it reflected the ease she had begun to feel in their companionship, it reflected something more, too; something that included provocation.

He was far from unwilling to be provoked. It was a long time since he had felt anything resembling his present state of mind; he had thought that state of mind had been adequately canalized in his visits to the P & M Houses. Apparently it had not. Confident of not being unwelcome, he reached leisurely out to embrace her.

47

She pulled her body away, eluding him. Awkwardly he half-rolled, half-plunged after her, and managed to obtain an arm. To his astonishment, she slapped him sharply across the face with her free hand. He sat up and looked at her.

She began laughing, and broke off. 'If you could only see how funny you look, Charles!'

'I can imagine it. What the devil——'

'You've forgotten. Another of our Israeli inhibitions. Like cigarettes and mescalin. We find it very hard to be promiscuous at a moment's notice.'

'How long notice do you require?'

'It's difficult to say. Long enough for you to be able to rule the idea out of your immediate calculations, at any rate. Shall we leave it at that?'

His face felt hot; he rubbed it. He was both annoyed and pleased. He had, in the past, deliberately chosen the Houses in preference to the promiscuity which was available about him, and had, on the whole, been willing to accept the popular view that this represented a perversity on his part. He was not so sure of that now.

'I suppose we must, if you say so.' All the same, it was annoying that his first approach in a very long time should be rebuffed. He looked down into Sarah's demurely smiling face. 'I should have thought that in three years you might have got more—more into the managerial swing.'

'I've led a sheltered life. Remember, I've been with fellow-Israelis all the time—first my father and then Hans. My opportunities have been limited.'

'I'll try not to let them remain so.'

'I suppose you will.' She raised herself on one elbow, and pointed out to the gleaming fringe of sea. 'Hydroplanes. It will be the return in the Guadalupe Chase. Have you

48

any glasses in the locker, Charles? I've got a hundred on Conway.'

He brought the glasses for her. 'A good way of changing the subject. I gather you've got far enough into the swing to be willing to have a flutter on the hydroplane races.'

She sat right up, straining her shoulders back as she focused the glasses on the distant specks in the ocean. The pose set her figure off extremely well; Charles had a suspicion that she knew this, too. The annoyance came back for a moment.

'They bet in Israel, too. And they skip their hydroplanes better, incidentally. That's Ethelgar in the lead. Conway's lying third. I shouldn't think any of them knows how to get the best out of a cross-wind.'

'That isn't the Mediterranean.'

'I told you—the Med is trickier than you people think.' She lowered the glasses and handed them across to Charles. 'Want to look? My hundred's gone. Conway's a good finisher but he'll never make up half a mile.'

Charles took the glasses. 'I've never been interested enough to bet on these affairs.' He glanced casually through them. 'I can't even make the colours out.'

'You don't need to; the superstructure is enough identification. Look.' She came over and took the glasses from him again. She rested her body against him, one of her elbows on his shoulder. He stayed quite still, aware of her warmth and softness. 'Ethelgar—the high bows with the arched carapace. Conway—very low to the water and the wings slightly curved back. That's Spruce second; you can tell by the squareness.'

She shifted away from him a little, lowering the glasses.

He said: 'Carry on. It's more fascinating than I thought. Who's lying fourth?'

She stood up, smiling. 'Enough for one lesson, I think.

49

You might find it too exciting. Shall we think of getting back?'

During the following week they had a couple of other outings together, and Charles was looking forward to the week-end. He made some vague suggestion on the Thursday night when they were flying back from a trip to the Gulf. Sarah shook her head; possibly regretfully, but very firmly.

'This is my Berkeley week. I go up to spend a couple of days with Daddy once a month. Sorry.'

He was not sure whether he was disguising his disappointment. 'Yes, of course.'

She had told him she would be returning fairly late on the Sunday evening, and he had put the gyro at her disposal. He still had the limousine and he got in some practice on it; having graduated to a motorist's status there was no sense in not acquiring the skill. Deliberately he stayed away from the laboratory for Sunday afternoon and evening. He hoped Sarah would be back by the time he returned himself.

It was after twenty-three when he garaged the limousine, and he saw that there was no light from any of Sarah's windows. She might have gone to bed as soon as she got back, of course, but it would be rather surprising if she had. He went to his own suite, but he did not feel like sleep. He buttoned Red League, Cosy Bright, and the local Sunshine Circuit, but found that the offerings of TV corresponded even less than usual to his own needs. He thought of calling Sarah up, but it would be silly if she had in fact gone to bed. He finally played the John Passion records, keeping the volume low and the windows open so that he would be sure to hear the sound of the gyro coming in.

It was in the middle of this that he suddenly remembered there was a simple way of checking whether she had come back or not. He went out to the gyro shed. It was empty.

Everything seemed obvious now. There could be a hundred reasons why she should decide to stay with her father overnight and come back in the morning; he might be ill—anything. Charles went back to his suite, showered, went to bed, and slept until the trumpets of Cosy Bright woke him to a sight of an Alpine dawn sprawled across his bedroom wall.

He called Sarah as soon as he was dressed. She herself had several times casually dropped in on him without warning, but he was not used to that kind of informality. The screen stayed blank. He let the call stay on for five minutes, in case she should be getting dressed or in the shower, and then accepted the fact that she still hadn't got back. He glanced at his finger-watch; it was past eight. Even if she had stayed overnight she should have got back by now, or at least called him up to explain why.

He found her father's frequency in his micro-file, and put the number on call. The call was accepted almost at once. The bronzed, typically Israeli features of a man of about sixty—tall, a little stooped—came into focus. He had a friendly smile, but with a hint of slyness. He spoke with quite a pronounced accent. Presumably he had been a rebel himself from the tradition among aristocratic Israeli families of speaking only German, since he had had Sarah taught English from childhood.

He said: 'Yes? You're Official Grayner. We haven't seen each other before. Wish you well.'

There was a constriction at the back of Charles' throat. He said sharply:

'Is Sarah—your daughter—there? I'd like to speak to her.'

Professor Cohn's face tightened; he seemed to straighten fractionally. He said quietly:

'She left me yesterday—in the early evening—to go back to your laboratory. She has not arrived?'

51

'No.' He was scared, and he rapped the questions out with involuntary sharpness. 'Exactly what time did she leave? Did she say anything about stopping anywhere on the way? Did you notice the battery reading?'

'She left a little after six—eighteen, that is—she wanted to get back early, she told me. She said nothing about stopping anywhere—I told you—that she said she would get back early. The battery was charged. On the Saturday we had it charged, and we did not use it—the gyro.' He paused. 'What should one do, Official?'

'I'll get on to Telecom right away,' Charles said. 'Don't worry. She's probably had to ditch the gyro somewhere in the wilds. You can sleep in a gyro quite comfortably. I'll call you back as soon as I get hold of something.'

He broke off without waiting for more than the beginning of Professor Cohn's reply: 'Yes. I hope——' He got through to the Telecom Recovery Section. The screen showed a yawning fat woman, clearly interested in nothing but the arrival of the day relief shift.

He said brusquely: 'UC Laboratory 719, San Miguel. Official Grayner. We have a member of staff missing. Assistant Sarah Cohn. Missing between Berkeley and here last evening on a gyro flight. Have you anything in on her?'

She looked at him with bored and drooping eyes. 'Almost swear not. Haven't had a gyro pick-up in a month. Hold it, anyways. I'll check Field.'

He watched her while she turned sideways and got the Field group on another screen; he could just see a corner of that screen: a portion of a distorted male face. He could hear the reply she got, too. She flicked off, and came back to Charles.

'Nothing. I'll send it out on a rescue call. Berkeley, you said? To San Miguel?'

'Yes. You'll send a report in as soon as you get hold of something?'

She nodded. 'You better flash her record-film to us, just in case. You got it there?'

'It's not here. I'll get it. I'll call you again.'

'Do that.'

She had turned away to watch the entertainment screen even before she broke contact. Charles stared at the faintly-glowing screen for a moment or two before breaking contact himself. Then he went out to the office to find Sarah's record-film. He brought it back to his living-suite. To check, he ran it through the projector. The particulars considered relevant to Assistant Sarah Cohn filled the top half of the screen; on the lower half was projected Sarah herself—three Sarahs: head-and-shoulders, front view and profile, and full figure. The fear, the pain, gripped him more sharply as he gazed at it.

He made the call to Telecom again, and the fat woman answered.

'You weren't long. Got the R.F.? Put it through.'

The screen blanked for a minute or two while the auto-matic took over, photographing the record-film. Then the woman came through again.

'That's O.K.' She smiled; a hint of malice. 'Now I dig the rush. We'll try and locate her for you. It's a story for the telezine boys at that—beautiful girl scientist lost in gyro. You'll have them round fast.'

Telecom always carried more weight than they were worth; Charles resented the woman but he kept the resent-ment to himself. In any case he must rely on Telecom for letting him have any news that came in promptly.

He said only : 'We're restricted. Would you tell them that?'

'Never mind. They'll de-restrict you. You under Mettrill? They'll make him unlock.'

53

He said: 'Please let me have anything that comes in as soon as it does, will you.'

As she said: 'Surely,' he switched off.

His next call was to Mettrill; it was a necessary notification. He had been through to Mettrill only once before; a formal call on his taking over the laboratory. Mettrill was the avuncular type—slow, friendly, eager-to-help surface, masking, Charles was sure, a typical file-and-forget lazy mind. This news made him sit up, though, and look irritated. It was something that was going to demand action.

Mettrill said: 'You checked with her father?'

'Yes. She left with a full battery, just after eighteen.'

Mettrill looked at him thoughtfully. 'How did she come to be using a gyro?'

'I loaned her mine.'

'Why?'

'I wasn't using it—to save her trouble. Otherwise it would have meant a taxi into San Diego and meeting the air schedules and the rest of it. She's a qualified flyer.'

'Was, anyway.' It was the casualness rather than the finality of the remark that made Charles want to hit him. 'I advise you to stick to regulations, Official Grayner. It saves everybody trouble in the end, even if it means a little extra trouble in the short run.'

'Yes.'

Mettrill stirred in his chair. 'What's her file number?'

Charles gave it to him. He watched Mettrill scrawl it down. He said: 'I was wondering . . .'

Mettrill said: 'Yes?' without looking up.

'. . . If I could have another gyro sent up. I thought I might go out and have a look for her myself.'

Mettrill looked up now. He fixed his gaze thoughtfully on Charles.

54

'We'll see about the gyro replacement. But stay where you are. Contact will have to drop in on you.'

'I could make an appointment for them and still have time——'

'Stay where you are. You have work to do. We'll see about the gyro replacement—the other replacement, too.'

'The other replacement' could only refer to Sarah. Charles said, with a rising of anger: 'Won't you at least say: "But we hope it won't be necessary?"'

Mettrill continued to stare at him. 'Two thirds of the direct route between your place and Berkeley is over the ocean. I don't see any point whatsoever in making your suggested addition to my original remark. Stay on hand, Official Grayner. Contact will be seeing you.'

Mettrill's hand came forward to break, and then stopped. 'And don't get in touch with anyone else about this. Telecom, for instance.'

Charles tightened his lips. 'The first call I made after hearing from Professor Cohn was to Telecom, to see if she had been picked up.'

Mettrill leaned back and clasped his hands behind his balding head. For a moment he was silent. Then he said:

'When I was a young man, I did one thing thoroughly. I learned the regulations. It was the most useful thing I ever did, and I suggest it's not too late for you to do the same. Under 29 you will find a stipulation—no one—Supervisor, Official, Manager or Director—will communicate anything concerning managerial personnel to any outside source until after the matter has been referred to the next higher authority within the managerial. Words to that effect. There's always a reason for the regulations.'

'This might have been a matter of life and death.'

Mettrill glanced away. 'I'll note that as your excuse. What did you get at Telecom—Recovery?'

'Yes.' He didn't give a damn, at that moment, about anything except savaging Mettrill. 'They had Assistant Cohn's record-film. I gathered they were putting it through to TV. I informed them this place was restricted. They were going to contact you.'

'Official Grayner,' Mettrill said, 'you're an incompetent fool. I'm breaking off. Stay where you are.'

Charles put his callscreen on alarm before he went out. He went to the laboratory first. Luke and Tony were on some routine work Sarah had put in hand. He told them what had happened. Then, not able to concentrate on the work he himself was supposed to be doing, he went outside. A robot tree-tender was trundling away into the orange grove. It was a grey sullen day, with a sharp damp wind coming in off the sea. He walked slowly down the path to the shore. Although remaining within earshot of the callscreen alarm, he was out of the noise range of the generators. It was very quiet. There was no sound but that of the sea, washing without haste against the rocks.

He stayed there for more than an hour. There was nothing from the alarm. What eventually made him retrace his steps was the gyro, its noise first heard above the heavy whisper of the waves and then the sight of it, side-slipping down towards the back of the laboratory. He walked quickly; there was even a faint hope that it might be Sarah.

There were two men. They wore the usual plastoleather jerkins and the tag, Contact Section, beneath their UC badges. One was very short and bandy; the other was of average build, with red hair forming a fiery halo round a conspicuously bald top. It was this one who nodded amiably towards Charles.

'You Grayner? My name's Caston. This is Stenner.'

Stenner produced a punctilious version of the UC salute,

and Charles gave a sloppy one in return. It was almost the first time he had been confronted with that kind of etiquette since he had graduated. Caston grinned.

'Somewhere we can talk?'

Charles took them into his living-suite. Caston looked around openly and casually, Stenner with covert attention.

'What happened to all the water-colours of the Sea of Galilee and Mount Hebron?' Caston inquired.

Charles said slowly: 'They're in my assistant's rooms.' He added: 'There hasn't been any news?'

'I gather you passed it on to Telecom Recovery,' Caston said. 'We're leaving it to them. Anyway, they're better equipped for that kind of thing.'

'Mettrill seemed rather annoyed about my passing it on.'

'Mettrill,' Caston observed, 'is so eager to avoid trouble that he goes around inventing it. He's weak-willed, too. He had to get us to put the blinkers on the telezine boys. I guess you won't be bothered by them—unless you had been looking forward to the publicity?'

'No,' Charles said, 'I hadn't.' He looked at Caston. 'You know this country better than I do. Tell me, what do you think the chances are?'

Caston looked puzzled. 'Chances?'

'Of my assistant being safe.'

Caston shrugged. 'I guess there's an outside chance. She might be knocked out somewhere, alive but too injured to get clear. Slim, though. The sea's more likely. She was a nice wench at that.'

Charles said tensely: 'But why? Why should she have crashed? The gyro was in good order, battery fully charged, no storms or anything else. What could go wrong?'

'In my experience,' Caston said, 'there's always something that can go wrong—generally three or four things Height gauge, maybe. Showing two thousand and then—

57

wham!—you hit the ocean. Or a blackout—people have blackouts. Then again, she may have had her reasons.' He glanced obliquely at Charles. 'Seemed she was quite a bit cut up about the accident your predecessor had. I don't know what was in it, of course, but——'

'I can tell you,' Charles said. 'Nothing. And she was very far from being the suicidal type.'

Stenner spoke. He had a voice that gave an impression of being parched.

'The suicidal type is the type that commits suicide. Otherwise unclassifiable.' He gazed out of the window with what might have been an air of profundity in someone with a different physique. 'You hadn't known this woman long. There is often a poor correlation between outer and inner lives. She was a nervous type.'

'With strangers she was,' Charles said. 'She could relax.'

Caston said: 'Not that it matters. It was just a thought. Could have been the height gauge—anything.'

There was a brief silence. Charles said:

'I suppose it's occurred to you that, whatever happened, the accident rate for personnel in this establishment has taken a very sharp upward jump?'

'Well,' Caston said, 'if you allow the suicide possibility in, it's still only one incident. If you rule it out—lightning may not strike twice in the same spot but it has a pretty habit of hitting the next tree in line. You know when you strike it lucky and hit five balls in a row on the Randomator? Lady Luck works in reverse sometimes.'

'Let's get it straight and on the table,' Charles said. 'I don't allow the suicide possibility in at all. And it still looks like a remarkable coincidence to me that peculiar accidents should happen to both a Research Official and his Assistant within a two-week period—and the blame on the sea each time.'

58

Caston seemed to be bored. 'You got a better solution?'

'This place is restricted.'

Caston walked across and examined the books Charles had on a shelf. He said over his shoulder:

'You read books? My old man used to read books. Tried one or two myself once, but it never seemed worth the trouble. Restricted? Just about every goddam tinpot laboratory in this half of the continent is restricted.'

Stenner's dry voice said: 'Are you suggesting that another managerial has—taken action against Isaacssohn and Cohn. Is the work you are doing here of that order of importance?'

Charles hesitated. 'The importance or otherwise of the work seems less important than the coincidence.'

'In our line,' Caston said, 'we can't afford to be impressed by coincidence. If another managerial did think it might be a good idea to write those two off—why not both together? Why wait till you move in before completing the job?'

'I don't know.' Charles paused. 'They might have thought it would be more convincing this way.'

Stenner smiled austerely. 'We can assure you that there would be no difficulty about making a double disposal look like a single accident; no trouble at all.'

Caston shook his head. 'No. Nothing in it.'

'Any two accidents, occurring within so short a time, would seem odd, but when you can't see a natural explanation for either of them——'

'Come and have a look at it from where we're standing,' Caston invited. 'There's nothing funny about a yachtsman getting himself drowned; you should see the figures for Key Largo last season. Damned if I can see how the things ever stay upright, anyway. As for this latest business, it's all very well for you to rule suicide out, but it covers the facts. You can't get away from that.'

Charles said: 'I understand that there was no more than an average swell the day Isaacssohn was drowned; also that he was an exceptionally skilled yachtsman.'

'In my experience,' Caston said, 'it's the exceptionally skilled man and the bungling amateur who are most likely to have accidents—whatever the trade. The exceptionally skilled man becomes careless. He gets big ideas, and then one day he trips over them. My way of looking at it, Israelis do that more than most. We had the Telecom Met report on the area for that day—gusty winds up to force 8. Tricky enough for any expert.'

'You said "I understand," ' Stenner remarked. 'Might we know—who gave you to understand?'

'My assistant was not at all happy about the circumstances surrounding his death. She thought it was murder.'

Stenner smiled; a thin resigned cynical smile.

Caston said: 'Tell me, Grayner. In your own experience, would you expect a really balanced person to go around seeing murder in the fact that a guy gets drowned at sea? You're upset, of course, when it's someone you know, but why drag murder in? We're the police: we were satisfied. You might as well know that it was just this attitude on the girl's part which made the latest news less of a surprise to us than it might have been otherwise. We didn't realize she had been talking to you on those lines, but if she was, doesn't that chalk up a couple more points? I bet she threw it at you first time you talked with her.'

Charles said reluctantly: 'Yes. She did. I thought she was crazy, too.'

'If she did have suspicions,' Caston insisted, 'why should she blurt them out that way? If she didn't like the way we handled the case—and we could see damn well she didn't— she knew the procedure. She only had to make a complaint to Mettrill and he would have had to send checking Officials down. She didn't do that—she spun a yarn to you, though. Why?'

'A stranger,' Charles said, 'in a strange land. She wasn't born into managerialism, remember. I can see what it looks like, all right. It looked that way to me at first, as I've told you. Then, working with her, I got to know her better. She wasn't crazy.' He looked from one of them to the other. 'And she wasn't suicidal.'

Caston shrugged. 'Feelings about people—convictions, even—don't tell anyone much. A suicidal paranoiac is a very convincing person. In our profession we meet quite a few of them, and we're still fooled sometimes. You—maybe you never met a paranoiac close up all your life. You've been working in a little lab like this nearly all the time—that right?'

'All the time,' Charles said. His mind was not far from being won over; there was something even more compelling about the things Stenner didn't say than about those Caston said. It was true that he knew very little about human beings; he had never, until so very recently, thought it worth while learning. And he could have been wrong about Sarah . . . But when the point was put to him as plainly as that, he would not accept it.

Stenner broke the silence that had held for some moments.

'Did Assistant Cohn suggest any reason why Contact Section should be derelict of duty—assuming that her strange suspicions were justified? We're more prone to acquire a reputation for excessive meddling than for the reverse.'

That, after all, had been one of his own points. Charles hesitated. He said then:

'You may be right, of course. It is your job, not mine. If they don't—don't find my assistant, then, you will simply write the case off? You aren't going into it at all?'

'Contact Section,' Caston said, 'works on a solid routine.

61

At least, in UC we do. We'll check the other end naturally. It may be her father will be able to give us something—some clue on the mental state. With nothing else in line, we have to concentrate on that.'

'I should like to meet Professor Cohn, too,' Charles said. 'Would there be any objection to my coming up to Berkeley with you?'

The two Contact Section men exchanged glances. It confirmed the view Charles had already formed of their relations when Stenner replied. Stenner said:

'It isn't altogether usual, but I don't see any real objection. From our point of view, that is. As far as your being away from the laboratory is concerned ... I suppose Mettrill would not object to that?'

The hell with Mettrill, Charles thought. He said flatly: 'No. There will be no objection from that quarter.'

Stenner picked up his gauntlets. 'In that case——'

'I thought I might call Professor Cohn first—if you were thinking of going right up there? And I should like to see if there's anything from Telecom Recovery.'

'Go ahead,' Stenner told him. He went over to the window, pulling his gauntlets on. Caston, with an air of being fascinated, had gone back to studying Charles' row of books. Charles went across to the control panel, and called Telecom.

The girl on Recovery Inquiries was a little more prepossessing, but just as uninterested.

'Nothing in. We'll call you if something turns up.'

'I'm leaving here.' He gave her Professor Cohn's number. 'Send any news you get through there, will you? And gently, please. It's her father.'

The girl yawned. 'We are trained in public relations.'

She broke off, and he put through the call to Berkeley.

'Wish you well,' Professor Cohn said. 'You have not had any news?'

'Not yet.' Charles jerked his head back, indicating the two figures in the background of the room. 'These two gentlemen I have with me are from Contact Section. They propose coming up to Berkeley to see you, and I've begged a place in their gyro. It will be all right, I take it?'

Professor Cohn nodded. 'That is all right.' He hesitated, as though searching for words or for an effect; he had the kind of face that provoked cynicism, though probably unjustifiably. He went on to speak now with an exaggerated despair:

'For me, you will understand, there is nothing that matters now. When such blows are dealt and one is young, there is perhaps good to be gained from them. At my age, not. My dear friend and my daughter.'

He broke off, perhaps at a loss. Charles said helplessly:

'I'm sorry. But there may yet be news——'

The Professor shook his head. 'One hopes, but one comes to know when hope has lost its meaning.'

'We could put our visit off till tomorrow, perhaps.'

The head shaking again—too dramatically? 'No. It doesn't matter. It doesn't matter.'

Caston and Stenner made no comment. On the trip north they were simply two Contact Officials on a routine job, with an extra passenger. Stenner said practically nothing; Caston talked a great deal about anything that came into his mind. They stopped for a meal at Los Angeles, and it was late afternoon before they began slipping down through the grey sky to the sprawl of Berkeley. To the north of the campus, smoke drifted away from the rocket-pits—the inassimilable residue of blasting. The sky flamed orange red at another rocket take-off, and then faded back to grey. The gyro dropped to the roof of the lodge where Professor Cohn had his suite. The three of them climbed out stiffly, and found the lift.

Cohn was second floor. Caston buttoned the callscreen panel. There was no reply. He buttoned again, and then, without waiting any longer, produced a whistle-master from one of his pockets. He whistled a complicated series of notes, breaking off when the door slid open before them.

The two Contact men moved purposefully into the suite, Charles following them. Caston came up with the note, inside a couple of minutes. It was on the permapad beside the callscreen panel in the living-room. He gestured, and Charles and Stenner came over.

The note was badly scrawled. It read:

'I am sorry. Perhaps I should have waited. But with age one becomes selfish—at least in small things.'

Caston said: 'Clear enough. But how? You checked the bathroom, didn't you?'

Stenner was buttoning on the panel. He said: 'How? The usual. What do you expect in a place like Berkeley?'

Caston's face cleared in understanding as the screen showed the long Inquiry counter with the Interplanetary motif running along the backwall. 'I guess so,' he said.

Stenner said sharply: 'Contact Section, United Chemicals. Put me on to the Pits Manager. It's urgent.'

The order was obeyed with Interplanetary's usual efficiency. The Pits Manager was a small round anxious-looking man.

'Contact Section, United Chemicals,' Stenner introduced himself again. 'Will you please check the pits at once for a potential suicide? Professor Cohn, of this University.'

'Herman? My God!'

He was already busy putting the call through on his sidescreen. Stenner asked: 'You know him?'

'Quite well. And he's been round here this afternoon.'

'We'll come right over,' Stenner said. 'Breaking off.'

The Pits Manager had gone down to Pit 17, and they were taken there to join him. When he saw them he pointed mutely into the pit; the super-refractory base and sides were still smouldering, and the heat, rising thirty feet to the pit lip, was unbearable.

Caston said: 'Well? Too late?'

'The JA 9 blasted twenty minutes ago. He was here not long before; the Supervisor saw him.'

Caston nodded. Charles said: 'Any traces——?'

Caston laughed. 'That a UC man should ask that! You know what the temperatures are down there, at blasting? Maybe a spectroscope would show some surface impurities in the refractory; and maybe again it wouldn't.' He swung to the Manager. 'How did he get down there?'

The Manager pointed along the pit; a service-crane was now swung clear of the pit.

The Manager said: 'The Supervisor found it swung into the pit. He thought the last service crew had left it that way; they shouldn't, but they do. So he simply had it swung out again, and approved the blasting in the usual way.'

Stenner spoke. 'I was under the impression that you people had put additional safeguards into operation, following the Mura-Ti report. You know these places are suicides' delights.'

He used a stinging tone of voice, and the little man seemed stung by it. He said:

'We have safeguards. Anyone coming into here has to be known or vouched for. We can't put mechanical safeguards in. The rockets have got to go off on schedule.'

'Who vouched for Cohn?' Caston asked.

'I would have done, if I'd been asked. I used to play chess with him. I wasn't asked because the Supervisor knew him, too. He was known all over Berkeley. If he'd asked anyone for an open knife, a poison phial, a Klaberg pistol—they would have given them to him. I still don't get it. He wasn't the kind to act like this.'

Caston said: 'Did he tell you that his daughter was missing on her gyro flight back to San Miguel?'

The Manager did not look at them; he looked instead down to the smouldering pit. He said slowly:

'So that was it. No, he didn't tell me that. You don't imagine that if he had——'

Stenner said incisively: 'We shan't keep you any longer. You will have your report to make out.' His thin smile barely hinted of derision. 'That will require some care in preparation, I imagine. We shall be at the Cohn apartments'—he looked at his finger-watch—'until seventeen thirty.' He brought out a small plastic card. 'This refers you to us.'

Caston was chattering on the way back to the campus, mainly about what he saw as the slipshod reality behind the efficiency façade of Interplanetary. 'You got that? Known or vouched for—hell, just about everybody in town's known one way or another. It's not the first time they've shown up that way, either. Remember that smuggling two years back? Why should rockets be checked—who was going to smuggle drugs to Luna City? Never occurred to them that the boats drop at a different city every trip back. And they still stick their tails in the air.'

Stenner was silent as usual, and Charles paid no attention either. He was thinking about Professor Cohn, and yet again admitting his own limitations as a judge of character. He had imagined he was acting his grief; now the stark realization of the man's sincerity came home to him, and brought another and even starker realization with it. Part of his mind had clung to the hope of Sarah being found—injured, perhaps, but alive. Seeing the extent of her father's despair, it was no longer possible to keep even the flicker of hope alive in his own consciousness. That had to be faced, too.

The two Contact men moved quickly and efficiently around the suite. Charles looked round himself in a desultory way; he found a microfilm labelled 'Sarah—Two to Twenty,' and slipped it into his pocket. He was glancing through the Professor's small library—with little advantage since the books were all in German—when a call came through. Half an hour before he would have gone to the control panel with some renewal of hope, but there was none now. The panel flashed:

COHN FROM ALLIED ELECTRICAL—BERKELEY REPAIR & SERVICE . . . COHN FROM ALLIED ELECTRICAL—BERKELEY RE——

Charles accepted the call automatically. A young man.

'Call for Cohn,' the young man said.

Charles looked at him. 'Not available.'

'Not Professor Cohn. His daughter. Assistant Cohn.'

'Not available.' To hide the pain, from himself as much as from the face on the screen, he said: 'Do you want her for any particular reason?'

The young man shrugged. 'Routine notification. We always notify forty-eight hours after receipt of servicing jobs. She left a watch for recharging on Saturday. Said she would pick it up from the automat delivery on Sunday morning. It's still with us. Can you inform her? It starts collecting storage charges from today.'

Charles said quietly: 'May I see the watch?'

'I don't see why, but then again, I don't see why not.' He held up a small, familiar finger-watch. 'Well?'

The relief, the happiness, was welling up and would not be controlled. Charles laughed, to the young man's astonishment.

'I'll try to get your message through to her,' he told him. 'Breaking off now.'

He called, and Caston came in from the next room, Stenner following. Caston said:

'You found something good? A pornofilm?'

Charles told them of the call that had come through. Stenner listened attentively. Caston said disgustedly:

'That all? I thought you'd got on to the old boy's ex-mistress at the least. So the girl put her finger-watch in for charging. I knew one suicide who ordered almost every goddam commodity in New York just before he took a pill. We got to his place through a traffic jam two blocks long. Two hundredweight of dog biscuits was one item. With a sense of humour like that, I guess he died happy.'

Stenner said, ignoring Caston: 'You find something significant in this?'

Charles said: 'Assume—just for a moment assume—that she isn't dead.'

'If she isn't dead, where is she?' Caston demanded.

'Assume you are Contact in another managerial—Atomics, for the sake of argument—and you're told to kidnap the girl. You make it look like a gyro crash—suicide, maybe—and you put up a good show. You cover all the facts that you could reasonably be expected to cover—but there's something you can't cover.'

'And that is?' Stenner asked.

'The little items you don't know about. The fact that her watch may have needed recharging, and that she may have put it in for service without mentioning it to anyone. Without mentioning it even to her father. According to him, she left quite normally on Sunday evening on her way, as he thought, to my lab. But if she left on Sunday evening, why didn't she pick the watch up from automat delivery on Sunday morning, as she had told the Service people she would?'

'Because she forgot,' Caston said promptly. 'People forget

all kinds of things. I knew a guy once used to forget to put his contacts on when he went to the pictures.'

'She had my gyro,' Charles said. 'The clock's been broken since before I took it over. Do you take a several hundred mile trip without having the time on you?'

'This guy I'm talking about,' Caston said, '—he found out what he'd forgotten as soon as the screen lit up.'

Stenner said: 'I get your point, Grayner. But you are forgetting something. Our guess is suicide in the girl's case as well as her father's. If you check that note Cohn left on the pad with his other writing, I shouldn't be at all surprised if you found it graphologically inconsistent. The mind that has set itself on suicide is necessarily a confused one. The girl forgot to collect the watch. Or perhaps she even remembered, and realized that for her time had ceased to be important.'

'If time had ceased to be important, why put the watch in for recharging?'

'We haven't,' Stenner pointed out, 'established the point at which suicide was determined on. It could very easily lie between the time of putting her watch in and the time when she should have taken it out again. It was that kind of information we wanted to get from her father.'

'She didn't tell him she was going to commit suicide,' Charles said. 'He would have mentioned it.'

Stenner said patiently: 'We are not supposing that her father knew of the decision, or even of the state of her mind. But there's always some little thing that you can understand, after the event, if you're trained in this kind of thing. This business of the watch in fact—I take it that kind of forgetfulness is out of character, in your experience? From her psychoplan it certainly is.'

'No more than suicide is.'

'Psychoplans,' Stenner said, 'are not much use for suicide

predictions except in the matter of psychopaths. On the other hand, they give a lot on normal behaviour patterns. Assistant Cohn's showed a high degree of attentiveness to small details; that is why forgetting to pick up the watch is significant.'

'Assistant Cohn,' Charles said flatly, 'did not commit suicide. There is no reason to think she is dead. If it comes to that, there is no reason to think her father is dead. Or my predecessor, Isaacssohn. You are recording three deaths, and you haven't got a single body—not even a trace of a body.'

Caston began to say something, but Stenner silenced him with a small gesture. Stenner said:

'This idea of yours of kidnapping—you are taking that seriously?'

Charles said defensively: 'It strikes me as at least as plausible as this multiplication of suicide. I should most certainly say it was worth looking into.'

Stenner smiled: 'Addition, not multiplication. Very simple addition, too—one and one. Any theory is worth looking into. On the other hand, no theory is worth retaining if it lets the rain in. Let's have a look at yours. Three people have been kidnapped—the first made to look like accidental death and the other two dressed up as suicides. Points in favour first.

'As you have pointed out, we haven't got a single body. We could take a spectroscopic test of the floor of the rocket-pit, but it wouldn't be conclusive if it didn't show anything, and if it did someone could always have managed to toss the necessary chemicals down there before the blasting. It's a valid point—the absence of bodies. The other point, I gather, is your own personal conviction that Assistant Cohn would not have committed suicide. I'll come back to that later.

'Now let's see what the waterproofing is like. The lack of bodies—a hydroplane was lost in the Caribbean ten days ago; twenty people on board; no survivors and no bodies recovered. The sea doesn't often leave traces, and the supposition is that two of our cases went into the sea. The third went, on our theory, into the launching pit, and that certainly doesn't leave traces. I think we must take the absence of bodies as a neutral factor.

'Before going on to your feeling about the woman, there is something else I should like you to have a look at. If it were a kidnapping business, the time schedules are rather odd. Quite apart from the long gap between Isaacssohn and the girl, there's the further gap between the girl and her father. And that leads us to an interesting point. If the girl was kidnapped from here, then your watch factor puts the kidnapping between Saturday afternoon and Sunday morning. That makes her father privy to the matter, since he told you she left on her return journey on Sunday afternoon. Well? Did he arrange for his daughter's kidnapping?'

Stenner's eyes were on him; Charles did not say anything. He was aware of the cogency with which the Contact man was showing his theory to be so much the more fantastic of the two, and he could find nothing to produce as rebuttal.

Stenner went on: 'Now there's the matter of your feeling about the case. We've met this before, remember. Assistant Cohn told us, just about flatly, that Isaacssohn could not have been drowned in the way the evidence pointed, and took it badly when we refused to pay a great deal of attention. We had her psychoplan, and we were not very surprised by the way she acted. Whether or not there was a deep emotional tie-up with the dead man, she would have had some similar kind of reaction. Her mind was of the unaccommodating type—in that respect, typically Israeli.

'You now. You are not an Israeli, of course, but your

71

mental patterns are interesting. By error you were fixed in a dead-end research post, and it could not be expected that there would not be traces of this in your subsequent behaviour. Some reaction was inevitable, and in fact your reaction was anti-social.' Charles stiffened, and Stenner looked at him. 'Only mildly so. You did your job efficiently. On the other hand, you developed no friendships; most significantly, no close relations with women. You patronized the Houses, although you had no sexual abnormality and could have had affairs with women in the normal way. You began to read and collect books—books, moreover, that were unconnected with your own subject. You collected gramophone records of the pre-managerial era. You viewed Channel KF, and in other respects showed an unmistakable psychological resistance to TV.'

Stenner paused. Charles, considering the weight of the indictment levelled against him, still said nothing.

'It is interesting,' Stenner continued, 'that in the majority of these things you were conforming to a pattern of intellectualism that is typically Israeli and, to that extent, reactionary. The accident of Isaacssohn's death and the need for replacing with another diamond man brought you into a typically Israeli circle—where your predecessor had been and your assistant was ex-Israeli. In parentheses, I find it a little surprising that two ex-Israelis should have been allowed to work together like that; we've nothing particular against them, but they represent a factor that's more easily assimilated in isolation. Anyway, that wasn't my concern.

'You, Grayner, were bound to have a subconscious orientation both towards your dead predecessor and towards the girl. The latter, since you are heterosexual, would attract more powerfully. I think I can say, on the basis of your psychoplan and hers, that in another month, at the outside, you would have become infatuated by her. As it is, the attraction has been so strong that you are powerfully influenced towards a refusal to accept the fact of her death. Detroit Contact should never have passed you for Isaacssohn's job.'

Charles said: 'Infatuated? I am in love with her, if that's what you mean. I've come to realize that during the course of the day.'

Caston, moving restlessly about the room, pulled at one of Professor Cohn's books and a dozen of them cascaded to the floor. He stared at them, poking one with his foot.

'Books,' Caston said. 'What a set-up. This is the biggest nest of queers we've had this year.' The remark was clearly enough directed at Charles, although he did not look at him. Stenner was watching for both of them, presumably.

Stenner said: 'The shock probably precipitated your new state of mind. You know what the sensible thing to do is— go to Psycho & Med. They can put you on the high-mesc course, and a holiday trip.'

Charles said: 'Thanks. I'll think about it. I take it you have quite made up your mind that my belief that Sarah is still alive is a sign of lack of mental balance? As far as you are concerned, she's dead?'

'Missing,' Stenner said. 'Presumed dead.'

'Will you do something for me?'

'Anything,' Stenner said, 'within the regulations.'

'I should like to put my view to a higher echelon. I could go to Mettrill, of course, but I doubt if he would be sympathetic—I've rubbed him badly already. I should prefer to see my old Manager—Ledbetter at Detroit.'

Charles caught a glimpse of Caston's face, registering surprise and annoyance. Stenner was expressionless.

'I think we can manage that for you,' Stenner said. 'I very much doubt whether Ledbetter will query our findings, but it may help your own orientation to see him.'

'Fairly soon?'

'Tomorrow. Will that suit you?'

'Very well. Just one other thing, then. It's hardly worth my going south to the lab for the night. Can you give me an authorization to stay on here?'

Stenner looked at him thoughtfully. 'Here—in the Cohn apartment?' Charles nodded. 'I guess so. You appreciate it goes down in your record as another symptom of irrational fixation on this group of ex-Israelis?'

'I shall have to live that down,' Charles said. 'Or learn to live with it.'

Some of his confidence went when the two Contact men left him. He walked round the small suite of rooms as restlessly as Caston had done, picking things up and putting them down in much the same way. There was wine in the old Colonial sideboard—Israeli wine. How could the Professor have managed that kind of luxury on his salary at the University? But Sarah probably bought it for him, or one of his local friends. He seemed to have made plenty.

Pouring wine into a glass, his mind reverted to the problem of the disappearances. There seemed to be no way round Stenner's objection: the watch question, which had first given him hope again, pointed to Sarah having been kidnapped—if she had been kidnapped—from this suite. And that meant, with her father's complicity. It seemed ridiculous.

And yet he would not, a second time, resign himself to the thought of Sarah's death. He smiled ruefully to himself: chalk up another point to the obsessive infatuation.

In the end he embarked on a final search of the rooms, in the hope of finding some clue to a forcible abduction. It was a slender hope—Stenner and Caston had given every sign of knowing the routine of their job at any rate—and it showed no results. He gave up finally; by now he was hungry, and he buttoned for bread and cheese and olives. He ate them with more of the Professor's wine. Should Cohn re-appear, he would be more than glad to make it up for him.

He slept that night in the small room, looking over the lawns, that had been Sarah's on her visits; there were touching signs of the occasional feminine occupancy. A china doll, somewhat battered by the years, sat on the bedside table; presumably it had watched over a much smaller Sarah, years ago, in a distant land. His eyes were on it as he drifted into sleep. Obsessive infatuation, was his last conscious thought.

Stenner called him up in the morning and gave him the authorization to see Ledbetter. His face on the screen was as remote and ironical as ever.

'Mettrill had to be told, of course,' he said. 'You are most certainly not his candidate. If Ledbetter shows any disposition towards taking you back for work at Detroit, I recommend you give it earnest consideration.'

Charles said: 'Thank you. I'll remember that.'

'Anyway, you weren't kidnapped during the night. What a mess it would have made of our report if you had been.'

'I'm glad for your sake.'

Stenner's smile faded. 'I have to tell you, by the way, that Telecom Recovery are calling off the search for Assistant Cohn at midday today. The comparatively small land area concerned has been well covered, and there's nothing to be hoped for from the sea.'

'Thank you.'

'I hope you weren't upset at all by my analysis yesterday; you had made it necessary, of course, by persisting in this theory of yours.'

'It is I who should apologize for getting in your way—and for adding one to the nest of queers.'

Stenner smiled again. 'Caston is a good man in his way, but something of a fool. Confidentially, I read Shakespeare myself; I like the feel of paper. Breaking off. Enjoy yourself in Detroit.'

He took the stratoliner, and was in Detroit by eleven. He took a gyro-taxi direct to the UC building, and made himself known at Inquiries. The girl looked at her record board.

'Official Grayner? For the Manager. You're to go down right away. I'll call you a page.'

He followed the pageboy with some surprise and not a little uneasiness; he had expected to be left cooling his heels for some time as a reward for his awkwardness in coming back here to Detroit. Over the boy's shoulder, as he made contact on the callscreen panel, he saw the familiar interior— Ledbetter's desk and Ledbetter behind it. He heard Ledbetter's voice, small and scratchy from the screen: 'Yes. Send him right in.'

Ledbetter rose to meet him as he entered the room, and waved him to a chair. 'You smoke, I remember.' The cigarette box slid across the desk again, and again the two men bent together to light from the steady flame. It was difficult to realize that less than a fortnight ago this had been happening the first time. Ledbetter was smiling. Charles relaxed in his chair. Relaxed physically; mentally he was alert for the change in mood which he was sure must come.

Ledbetter said: 'Well, for such a short stay, you've managed to run into plenty of trouble.'

'A certain amount of death and vanishment.'

Ledbetter looked startled. 'What? Oh, I see. No, I wasn't thinking of that.' He held up a couple of reports. 'I meant these. "Failure to comply with Regulations 29 (iii) and 42 (vii). Breach of Regulation 29 (ix). Unnecessary invocation of Regulation 112 (i)." Shall I translate? You notified the fact of your assistant being missing to an outside source before getting in touch with Mettrill, after previously giving her the use of your gyro, again without higher confirmation. You left your lab without getting in touch with Mettrill. And you insisted on bypassing Mettrill to give me your views on the situation, a course which is only justifiable in Regulations when a real suspicion of victimization can be established.'

Ledbetter put down the reports and looked at Charles across the desk. His face was expressionless.

'There's another report from Contact which refers to your mental attitude; I gather that at least some of this has already been explained to you.'

Ledbetter paused; there was an obvious implication that Charles should launch into some kind of explanation or defence. He refused the chance, and remained silent. Ledbetter gave him a little longer, while he tossed the reports back into his file tray. Then his blank expression broke, and he grinned.

'I told you you would like Mettrill. No reason why you two shouldn't have got on together, except that a minor crisis blew up. Mettrill isn't good in a crisis; hence this bumph and what I imagine was an unfavourable impression when you called him up. You did the right thing in coming to me. I can sort this lot out fairly easily.'

Ledbetter leaned back and looked at his cigarette. 'It's the future we have to consider. I'm not promising anything, but there's a chance I may be able to swing something useful there.'

Charles said: 'Useful?'

'It's a little out of the ordinary, but there's a chance I may be able to acquire extraterritorial rights in your Pacific Coast place. That would make you directly answerable to me for admin—reports would go through to Nikko-Tsi, of course, as before.' Ledbetter grinned again. 'There's an incidental advantage—I could use that tie-up for the odd trip to see you out there, and get a little yachting in. Well? How does it strike you?'

Charles said: 'Favourably. You're being very helpful. But it wasn't precisely my future that I came to talk about— my future in that sense, anyway.'

'No?' Ledbetter said. 'All right. I've had Stenner's report. I've got some of it. You might as well let me have the rest.'

Charles went through it for him, carefully and slowly, detailing Sarah's original dissatisfaction with the result of the inquiry on Isaacssohn's supposed death, and his own growing awareness that something was wrong with the superficial appearances of Sarah's own disappearance and her father's suicide. When he had finished, Ledbetter commented: 'That all?'

'That's all.'

Ledbetter smiled. 'What about your Israeli fixation?'

Charles smiled himself. 'It didn't seem relevant. For that matter, you have to assume your own objectiveness—it's up to the outsider to examine it.'

Ledbetter nodded amusedly. 'With the invaluable aid of Official Stenner, who seems to have a few unfulfilled yearnings of his own—towards a job in Psycho & Med, maybe. I don't hold a brief for Contact Section; specifically not for Caston and Stenner. Caston does a fair job as long as no deep thinking is necessary—better if no thinking at all is necessary. Stenner is shrewder, but not very flexible mentally. A man prone to guess his result and then cut his orbit to make the proof fit.'

Ledbetter leaned forward slightly, and made a motion of spreading a deck in front of him.

'Cards on the table. I've got their report, and I've told you what I think of them. Now I've heard your interpretation of the facts. Will you take me as impartial?'

78

Charles said warily: 'I've no reason to suspect you of not being impartial.'

'I hope you won't have, either.' Ledbetter stubbed his cigarette out, half-smoked, and began to play with his aromofact. On the wall another wall, of giant pines, began to unroll steadily towards a clouded sunset; their scent came in gusts, mixed with a dozen other bucolic perfumes. Ledbetter watched for a moment or two. He returned his gaze at last to Charles.

He said abruptly: 'I've thought a good deal about this. I had Stenner's report in last night; as you may guess, he mentions your theory only to damn it. That's a thing that always gets my back up. I began with a prejudice in favour of your views. The case you have just stated would have confirmed that. Fixations or not, you put it logically.'

Charles caught at a phrase. ' "Would have confirmed it?" '

Ledbetter nodded. 'There are some inconsistencies in your theory. I imagine Stenner has pointed them out already. The odd time intervals between the "kidnappings," especially in relation to the Cohn girl and her father. The failure to take Isaacssohn and the girl at the same time, presuming they were both "wanted." But those are mechanical objections, and I don't propose making them.

'No, it's the picture as a whole that I'm inclined to accept or reject, and I find it very difficult to accept it. You say that your predecessor, your assistant and her father have been abducted by Contact Section of some other managerial. My automatic reaction is to look for motive. If it were true it would represent a large-scale measure in any managerial's terms. Then, why? What reason could there be that would justify the risks involved?'

Charles studied Ledbetter closely. His lanky form was stretched back now in his chair, and he looked entirely and genuinely curious as to the answer to his question.

Charles said: 'When I was here before, you seemed very uncertain as to the kind of work I would be called on to do at the new place. Are you still as uncertain?'

'It's interesting you should say that. Naturally the report from Stenner made me curious about the set-up. I sent a flip to Nikko-Tsi. I explained the situation briefly, and put a question to him: could I be told what work it was Isaacssohn had been doing and which you were to continue—or if the information was top restricted, could I pass you on to Graz for their handling as I did not feel I would be competent to handle things myself. I had the reply printed. Would you care to see it?'

Charles nodded. Ledbetter brought out a sheet of paper, and passed it across the desk. Charles took it. It ran:

REFERENCE LABORATORY 719, SAN MIGUEL. ESTABLISH-MENT ENGAGED ON ROUTINE WORK INTO POSSIBILITY OF NEW POWER SOURCE CONNECTED WITH IRRADIATED DIAMOND. RESTRICTED ON BASIS OF INITIAL REPORTS FROM ISAACSSOHN. SUBSEQUENT REPORTS HAVE NOT DEVELOPED PROMISE OF FIRST. QUESTION OF CONTINU-ANCE OR RE-ROUTING OF THIS RESEARCH WILL COME UP AT NEXT APPROPRIATE COUNCIL MEETING. GRAYNER TO BE RETURNED TO POST PENDING FULL CONSIDERATION OF POSITION. YOUR DISCRETION TO HANDLE. NIKKO-TSI FOR PRESTON.

Charles read the message through two or three times, while he collected his thoughts. 'Subsequent reports have not developed promise of first.' Something was wrong; badly wrong. There were three possibilities. That Isaacssohn had somehow, for some reason, not submitted correct reports to Graz. That Graz was engaged in some tortuous course of deceit which involved putting one of their own Managers off the scent. Or that the flip from Nikko-Tsi was a private

80

forgery of Ledbetter's. The second possibility seemed much the most likely. In any case, since two out of the three possibilities involved trickery within United Chemicals, the obvious thing for him to do was to watch his step. He pushed the message back to Ledbetter.

Ledbetter said: 'Well?'

And something else was wrong. Ledbetter was too amiable, too anxious *not* to embarrass him. He tried fitting himself into Ledbetter's position, an imaginative exercise more difficult for him than it would have been for many others, because so infrequently practised. Ledbetter had wondered whether there might not be some truth in his suspicions, and had got in touch with Graz—with the clear intention of ducking the problem should it offer any major difficulties. Having got this kind of reply it was reasonable enough that he should have rejected Charles' theory, but surely there was another implication to be drawn as well? Immediately before Ledbetter showed him the message from Graz, Charles had referred to the work of the laboratory in veiled but portentous terms. Ledbetter had known—on the basis of his information—that there could be nothing in such a claim. His obvious move should be to put a disaffected and self-important subordinate in his place. Instead, he was watching Charles with friendly sympathy.

Charles said, striving to be non-committal: 'The flip seems clear enough. Your view then is——?'

Ledbetter shrugged. 'You've seen something of one of the missing three, so you're at an advantage there. But in my experience human beings can be very deceptive in that respect. I prefer to stick to the big picture. And that takes me back to the original question—what reason could there be to justify the kind of thing you have suggested? I'm not blinking the fact that there are several managerials who would stick at very little if they thought there really was something that would give them the advantage. I haven't forgotten the little shot Atomics had at—shall we say, centralization?—a few years ago. Or the Hydroponics—Agriculture combination in the '36 famine. But what is there in this for anyone? Can you see anything?'

The solicitude was wrong, altogether wrong. There was one possibility, he reflected wrily, that might account for it. Stenner seemed to have had some doubts as to his mental balance. It might be that Ledbetter had them, to an even greater degree. Some people were naturally polite and considerate to the insane.

Temporizing, he said: 'I suppose you must be right.' He hesitated, summoning up words that would deceive the tall friendly man opposite him. 'I won't conceal the fact that my assistant—Sarah Cohn—made a very great impression on me.' He smiled. 'I couldn't conceal it, anyway, could I? It's in Stenner's report. I found it hard to recognize that she might be dead; harder that her death had been of her own volition.' He looked at Ledbetter, his embarrassment producing a good effect of honesty. 'I still do.'

'Naturally you do,' Ledbetter said. 'I don't think we need to call in Stenner's amateur psycho-analysis. Whether the affections are conditioned or free, one feels them—and damned painfully at times. This has been a bad business, even if an innocent one. Of course you would be inclined to see things the way you did. Anyone would. And it can't be much consolation to you now to be told that you will get over it—though you will. Work is a useful thing in that respect. I hope the flip I showed you won't put you off the work, just because it hints at the possibility of things being changed. Actually, they will probably carry on under their inertia; you would be surprised if you knew some of the lines of research that have been automatically O.K.'d, year after year.'

Charles said: 'You want me to go back to the lab?'

Ledbetter said: 'I'm pretty sure I can swing you under my jurisdiction. Mettrill is not the kind to stand on a question of prestige if he sees a chance of less work or less trouble. You will be O.K.'

'Stenner's advice,' Charles said, 'was to visit Psycho & Med. He went so far as to suggest the prescription, too—a high-mesc course and a holiday trip.'

'You can disregard Stenner. You are as sane as he is, and considerably more intelligent.'

'As a matter of fact, I don't find the suggestion altogether repulsive. I could do without the mesc, but there is something about the holiday trip that appeals.'

Leadbetter said emphatically: 'Take my advice—work is the best remedy. A holiday trip is no good except to a mind already contented. You've got to learn to live with things. Work provides the best way of doing that.'

He was, Charles reflected, surrounded by well-wishers—Stenner, Ledbetter ... Ledbetter especially was rather curiously benevolent—there was an emphasis behind his words which it was difficult to believe stemmed entirely from his concern for Charles. Ledbetter wanted him back at the lab.

Charles said: 'I guess it takes different people different ways. I'm not sure that it takes me that way. I have an idea a holiday trip would be quite attractive.' He glanced across at Ledbetter. 'The change of scene, for one thing. The lab has acquired a few memories even in so short a time.'

'Face them,' Ledbetter said. 'It's the only way to get on top of them; they would hit you with much more force when you finally got back.'

'But then,' Charles said, 'I would be better able to cope with them. Or so I think. I take it there wouldn't be any actual *objection* to my consulting P & M and asking for the break?'

Ledbetter said, with obvious reluctance: 'No. Of course you can. How long had you thought of asking for?'

'I hadn't thought. But with my grade and record, and with Stenner's report, I think I could probably get six months if I asked, don't you? And it happens that I have another six months' holiday furlough to my credit. I could take a year off.'

Ledbetter was startled. 'A year? What about the work?'

Charles shrugged. 'It doesn't seem to have any urgency, as you and Nikko-Tsi have both pointed out.' Ledbetter looked as though he were going to say something, and then thought better of it. Charles let a pause rest between them, to encourage him, but without effect. Then he relented. 'I don't imagine I should want anything like that time, though. I've never had much pleasure out of furloughs in the past, and I don't suppose this will be any exception.'

Ledbetter looked as though he had just thought of something. He said brightly: 'I hope you won't take too long, for personal reasons. I'm looking forward to your hospitality to let me get those yachting trips in.'

'I'll try not to make you wait too long,' Charles said.

The KF studio had at one time been a brewery; long low-ceilinged rooms were broken at intervals by peculiar vertical shafts. Charles found Dinkuhl watching the interior of Room 17 through the glass partition. He came and stood beside him. There was a peculiar little man—almost a dwarf —in the room, reciting with a melancholy air. From the muted speaker by Dinkuhl's elbow his voice issued:

'Nine seven one three seven . . .'

Charles touched Dinkuhl's arm; he looked round.

'Charlie! I heard you'd joined a procession to the morgue.'

Charles said: 'I've come for some more of your excellent

advice, Hiram. And for permission to listen in on your grapevine.'

Dinkuhl performed his characteristic mocking grin. 'Advice is something we always have available. As for the grapevine, I'm not so sure. Come on upstairs, anyway, and I'll get you a drink.' He jerked his head towards Room 17. 'What do you think of my new interval transmission?'

The sad monotonous voice was still continuing:

'. . . eight five three seven three one . . .'

'Can I be told what it is?' Charles asked.

'Pi,' Dinkuhl said with satisfaction, 'to the first fifteen hundred places. I've got a blonde to read the next fifteen hundred. Anything to drive the paying customers mad.'

'Where did you get your figures from?'

'I did a good turn once,' Dinkuhl said, 'for an electronic brain. Straight up the stairs—straight up for three flights, as a matter of fact. They kill me—these goddam stairs. I'd move my office down to ground floor if it weren't for the fact that they kill the pale lilies from Telecom even more—those who still visit me, that is.'

Charles was breathing heavily himself by the time they reached the top, but Dinkuhl showed no signs of the physical exertion. Charles received another grin as they turned in through the heavy old oak door to his office. He felt oddly reassured. Dinkuhl's malice was totally unlike Ledbetter's geniality, and just as he had come now to suspect Ledbetter of having other motives so he had a feeling that Dinkuhl's malice was barely skin deep.

There were two comfortable chairs. Dinkuhl directed him to one, and went across to a spindly top-heavy Welsh dresser that just about covered one wall. He opened up a cupboard.

'Take what comes?'

'Within reason.' He watched Dinkuhl pour two glasses and

85

bring them over, together with the bottle, on a tray. 'Turnip and tomato again?'

Dinkuhl shook his head. 'The real stuff. Plum brandy. Well now. How've you been missing KF?'

'To tell you the truth, I hadn't given it a thought.'

'You're a lucky man.' Dinkuhl let his nose rest for a moment against the edge of his glass. 'Ah. That's a bad business you landed in.'

'What do you know about it?'

'Nothing,' Dinkuhl said blandly. 'You tell me.'

Charles told him. When he had finished, Dinkuhl replenished their glasses. Charles looked at him. 'Well?'

'And your good friends in UC haven't quite succeeded in persuading you that you are a promising psychotic?' Dinkuhl asked.

'I had my doubts at times, but I have none now.'

'Good boy. It has long been a fixed principle of mine to assume that the world around me was populated by mugs and fleecers; I never take any man's word unless I know he has an axe to grind, and know just what the axe is. Then I can make allowances.'

'What axe have you got?'

'An interesting point. Two principally—to further anything that looks as though it may sabotage, in the least degree, the managerial world in which we live; and to save my own skin.'

Charles grinned. 'All right. I'll settle for them.'

'Not yet you won't. First I have to justify my seditious attitude.' He finished his own glass. 'You're not drinking.'

'Not at your pace. I don't think I need the justification. I'm more concerned with getting some advice.'

Dinkuhl filled his own glass. 'The advice can wait. It won't be of an order to require your urgent attention—urgent within the next half-hour at any rate. Why do I wish to destroy this world-wide fatherly society of managerials in whose bosom we live? Why indeed?'

Charles resigned himself to the situation. 'Because the end is in sight—the end of KF?'

'Partly, partly. But a few other things as well. Tell me— what anniversary falls two years from now?'

'I don't know. Should I?'

'It's the anniversary of the War. What do you know about the War—about the way the society of today came into being? I'll ask you another question. Professor Cohn taught History at Berkeley, one of the very few academic institutions which provide tuition in that subject. How many students did he have?'

'Before his disappearance? Two.'

'You surprise me. Yes. Two. I doubt if there are a score of students reading History in continental North America. Although you could not be expected to appreciate it, this is—historically speaking—an extraordinary state of affairs. Other decadent periods have misread and distorted the history of their origins; ours is the first to have succeeded in ignoring it altogether.'

'Decadent?'

Dinkuhl sighed. 'I hoped I shouldn't have to argue about that. You must have been viewing Red League. Man conquering the last barrier—twenty-first-century Man grasping for a new heritage among the Stars—Conquering the Chill Lunar Wastes. But tell me: how long is it since the lunar base was established? You don't remember. It was there when you were a child. Perhaps you can remember when the last attempts were made at Mars and Venus? You should remember them.'

Charles thought. 'The Del Marro expedition——'

'Over twenty years ago.' Dinkuhl glanced at him sardonically. 'You were a young man, then, settling down into your niche at Saginaw. That was Mars. They had ruled Venus out ten years before that.'

'The difficulties are very great.'

'Not as great as they were for the first trip to the Moon. But in any case, we aren't trying any longer. The work has been abandoned. Not worth the risk.'

'The Moon,' Charles pointed out, 'hasn't been worth it. Except possibly in terms of astronomical research.'

'By which,' Dinkuhl said, 'you display yourself as a true child of your age. If you are going to calculate that kind of endeavour in terms of profit and loss, then you have failed before you start. No, that is decadence. But, of course, it's a long way from being the only sign. Look at the arts. True enough, the last days of capitalism produced nothing that was worth inheriting, but at least they produced *something*. And today we haven't even the saving grace of discrimination to tell us that their stuff isn't worth inheriting. What do you hear on Honey and Cosy Bright? *The Rhapsody in Blue* . . . *The Blue Danube* . . . *Chattanooga Chu-Chu* . . . or, if your taste is for the rarefied heights of Red League—Elgar, Stravinsky, Sibelius and Gilbert and Sullivan. And they ring the changes by a series of gimmicks, and even there they repeat themselves. That adaptation of the Sibelius *Violin Concerto* to the mouth-organ—there was a run of that kind of foolery when I was a boy.

'People are still surrounded by mid-twentieth-century neo-Scandinavian furniture, and what few painters there are slavishly follow one or another of the twentieth-century schools—neo-Impressionists, Cubists, Fauvists—we've got them all. Leisure Group still turn out chunks of stone with holes in them by the thousand.'

'Perhaps it's the right kind of art.'

'There is no right kind of art. And if there were, it certainly wouldn't be this prosaic and unimaginative rubbish.

Decadence involves a loss of creative energy in the first place, and eventually a loss of taste. We've touched rock bottom.'

'All right,' Charles said. 'I see why you would like to put a bomb under it all.'

Dinkuhl ignored him. 'How did things get like this?' He reached for the bottle without pausing and refilled his own glass and—over his gestured protest—Charles'. 'In the twentieth century they knew—those of them that could see any further than their noses—that they were heading for a crash. And they got it, of course. They got the lot—atom bombs, hydrogen bombs, breakdown, disease, famine—the Four Horsemen and a posse of others trailing behind them. It was the end. They sniped at each other from behind the chunks of stone that had been their major cities, and developed very fine talents in choosing which portions of their best friends would barbecue really well. I suppose those who had time to think about things must have been quite sure it was all over—the whole business of civilization was over, from commercial television to bath-tubs and canasta parties. The world's dark age beginning anew.

'And yet, before they had even had time to attune themselves to the new conditions—while they were still eating each other in order to stay alive and not for any pleasure in the taste of human flesh—the breakdown was over. The incredible was happening, and a new society was rising, lifting itself, as far as they could see, by its own bootstraps, and bringing bath-tubs and canasta parties with it, and television, though not commercial television.

'Even though people today have succeeded so well in obliterating the memory of their origins, it is generally remembered that Atomics was the first of the managerials, the resurgent centre about which the forces of reconstruction

89

gathered. From Philadelphia the call went out, and across the world, after a brief hesitation, came the response.

'It wasn't a matter of the world lifting itself by its bootstraps, of course. The fact is that communications had become so good that, short of wiping out every small centre of population, civilization was bound to recover. And not even all the large centres were wiped out, though few escaped quite as happily as Philadelphia. Atomics provided the nucleus of the new grouping of society, and the other managerials grew up round them; under their wing. The obvious ones first—United Chemicals, Agriculture, Hydroponics, Lignin Industries, Telecom, Steel, Mining and the rest; and after them the secondaries: Psycho & Med, Genetics Division, Leisure Group, and so on.

'There was a time when Atomics tried to centralize—no, not the recent squeeze : right at the beginning. Had they been whole-hearted enough they might have got away with a world dictatorship then, but the opportunity passed and the Council of Managerials was set up and now, as you know, in theory all managerials are independent and equal and with full sovereign rights. A balance of power.'

'One thing I've never understood,' Charles said. 'How did Israel come to be left out?'

'That,' Dinkuhl said, 'is part of the larger question—how did men come to abandon their old-established national sovereignties for the new managerial ones? Principally because they felt their national sovereignties had let them down; their old loyalties were dead and so they could cleave to a new one. But Israel was a different matter. The Israelis had spent nearly nineteen hundred years clutching a nationalism in exile. The managerial world had nothing in it they could possibly prefer to the concept of the Holy Land. They made good use of the interregnum to expand down to the Nile and up to the Euphrates, and after that they stayed put.'

90

'Isn't that,' Charles asked, 'something of a flaw in your anti-managerialism? The Israelis haven't got to Mars or Venus—they haven't even got to the Moon except as passengers through the courtesy of Interplanetary.'

'Before the War, when they first got back to Israel, they were a tribe in a desert, and a vastly overpopulated tribe at that. Their conquests during the interregnum were for the most part more desert, and already carrying quite a high indigenous population. Their religious views have required them to continue multiplying and being fruitful. As a result they have spent the last century contemplating the most basic of human needs: the means by which they could continue to fill their bellies.

'Today their country is cultivated up to the hilt and for the time being they have caught up with their population increase. Now, unless I am badly mistaken, you will see them go ahead.'

'With the aid and comfort of Channel KF?'

'That,' said Dinkuhl, 'is my problem.' He paused in the act of filling the glasses again. 'I had almost forgotten that you had a problem too. Tell me, what objective precisely have you got in view?'

'I should like to establish to my own satisfaction that my view of the recent happenings is the right one. More to the point, I should like to find Sarah Cohn and ask her to marry me.'

'Ah,' Dinkuhl remarked, 'the human side! You do right to bring such little problems to your Uncle Hiram. And what if it should prove that Stenner and Ledbetter happen to have been right for once—what if Sarah Cohn is dead, along with Herman Cohn and Hans Isaacssohn? You retire to your little UC niche, and stay a respected and valuable managerial citizen for the remainder of your days?'

After three glasses of plum brandy, Charles was in a

condition which he would have described as relaxed. 'Yes, I imagine so. I'm no crusader, Hiram.'

'You need not be so damned complacent about it, at any rate. I'm not either, but I have the grace to be ashamed of it. Well, I suppose we shall have to do what we can for you. Even though, like myself, you are unwilling to risk inconvenience and danger for the sake of humanity, you are willing for the reasons you have given me—right?'

Charles nodded. 'I think so.'

'What's the situation about leave?'

'I've been to P & M. They've given me up to six months' leave, and a number of containers of mescalin which I tipped down a drain.'

'What are you doing with the leave—officially?'

'A trip to the Pacific Islands.'

'Got the tickets?'

Charles patted his notecase pocket.

'Hand them over.' Dinkuhl took the transparent plastic envelope containing the small coloured plastic cards. 'I know someone who will quite enjoy this trip. I would go myself if I didn't have something else to do.' He glanced at Charles. 'It is important that the tickets should have been used, just in case someone inquires.'

'And me,' Charles said. 'What do I do?'

Dinkuhl shook the bottle. 'Help me to finish this off first.' He poured the remains into the glasses, and lifted his own. 'Here's to managerialism, the lordly heir to all the societies of Man. Or failing that, to Sarah, and her safe return to the bosom of United Chemicals. Now then, we're ready for off. First to my place, for a little plastic make-up and then elsewhere.'

'Elsewhere?'

'To see a man,' Dinkuhl said, 'about a dog-tag.'

*   *   *

Two hours later, Charles inspected himself in a long mirror. In place of his own features—pale, thin, with straight dark hair and, as he had always privately thought, an intellectual cast—he confronted someone with light auburn curly hair and fuller high-coloured cheeks.

Dinkuhl said complacently: 'I believe in the satisfied customer; quite an improvement. That fill-in on the cheeks will go six months, but don't wash it too violently. You can wash the hair. I know a tailor who will pad you out suitably, and you'll look fine. How do you feel?'

'I don't know. Comfortable. I think I prefer my old self.'

'Voice,' Dinkuhl said. 'Voice and bad taste we can't do anything about. All right, let's go.'

3

A MANAGERIAL world had no uniquely capital cities, but it had happened, by accident or design, that each managerial had developed a head, an organizing centre, based on some particular locality. Thus you had Atomics at Philadelphia, United Chemicals at Graz in what had been Austria, Lignin Industries at Stockholm, Steel at Detroit. But none of those cities was held in any way exclusively by the managerial which happened to have its central organization there. Here, at Detroit, the badges of Steel were predominant, but nearly all the other managerials were represented in varying degrees; some of them, like United Chemicals, with a major centre and others, like Interplanetary and Genetics, with no more than a branch office.

The Genetics branch office was a four-storey building on the corner of Cadillac and 17th. In the Genetics tradition it was a good deal smarter than the other buildings around, and the interior more luxuriously appointed. Dinkuhl and Charles went through to the central shaft, Dinkuhl bypassing the doorkeeper with a nod and a grin, and took one of the three airspheres that rested there.

Fiddling with the controls, Dinkuhl said: 'Another touch of decadence—preoccupation with the ridiculous. What's wrong with elevators? But no, they have to bring these damn

94

silly things in. The height of twenty-first-century achievement
—the Sokije valve!'

Under his direction the Sokije valve decompressed the
helium inside the double skin of polystyrene plastic and
evacuated the air that had been admitted for weight. The
transparent plastic bubble rose, with the two men inside it.
At the landing platform on the third floor, Dinkuhl jiggled
frantically to get the sphere into equilibrium. At last it
rested, bobbing only slightly against the platform, and they
got out.

'Such trouble,' Dinkuhl commented. 'I suppose they will
persist until someone really important misses his footing and
breaks his exalted neck.'

They found a private room; the legend stencilled on
the door was Official Awkright. Official Awkright was a
short sandy-haired man who had something of Dinkuhl's
own temperamental appearance. He pressed a button and
the door closed behind them. Only then did he grin at
Dinkuhl.

'How's it go, Hiram?'

'Moderately. Very moderately. Burt, this is Charlie.
Charlie Grayner as was; now Charlie Macintosh.'

Awkright nodded. He put a hand out and Charles took it.
'Glad to know you, Official Macintosh. I've heard about you,
Charlie.'

Charles said: 'Is there anyone who hasn't?' He glanced
at Dinkuhl. 'I should keep the same first name?'

Dinkuhl said gravely: 'You are still inexperienced in the
arts of deception. Yes, you keep your first name. It's not
all that uncommon, and it is useful for you to be able to turn
round naturally if anyone calls it in the street.' He sat down
in an airfoam chair and motioned Charles to take another.
He rested his elbows on Awkright's desk, and addressed
him.

'How's it with you? Who's in the lead now—Nature or Genetics Division?'

'Births in the Ganges and Oxus areas are down several per cent on the previous year. On the other hand, Bang-Kok and Sumatra are up about the same amount. You might say it's a knock-down ding-dong tie up to the present. As you know, though, this venerable organization doesn't give in without a struggle.'

'What's the latest move?'

'Through from Edinburgh this morning. We are forming a series of mobile Birth-Reducing Units.'

'You've been peddling contraceptives for years,' Dinkuhl said. 'What makes you think they're going to start buying now?'

'This time they don't have the option. Our brilliant scientists have developed an anti-fertility factor that can be added to the local water supply. From what I've seen of the figures, there will be some deaths, but not above one or two per cent, and the majority among the women.'

'A wonderfully humane measure.' Dinkuhl glanced at Charles. 'Don't you agree, Charlie?'

Charles had been disturbed by Awkright's account, but more by the fact of it being given than by the content. He could not help being offended by the realization that Awkright was passing confidential information to two men from different managerials. It was impossible not to be affronted by this; he viewed Awkright with combined amazement and mistrust.

Dinkuhl, apparently sensing the trend of his thought, said to Awkright: 'Charlie's a rebel by force of circumstance, not by nature. Your disloyalty worries him.'

Awkright shook his head. 'I thought you'd brought a convert. What did you bring him for, if it comes to that?'

'For his GD card, in the first place. You can do that!'

96

'I can.' Awkright stared at Charles, examining him with attention. 'It might be useful to know what he's going underground for.' Directly to Charles, he said: 'I hear you got an adverse report from Stenner—you want to avoid a discipline? If you're not the rebellious type, it might be better to take whatever they gave you. There are difficulties in creating and maintaining a new personality.'

Dinkuhl spoke for him: 'No, not to avoid a discipline. Charlie is still well regarded in these parts. In fact, they are keen on his getting back to work as soon as possible. Some of them are. Officially he's got six months' leave on medical grounds, and officially he's going to the South Pacific Islands. Here are the tickets.' Dinkuhl tossed the little envelope over. 'Can you get these used today?'

Awkright looked at them. 'They're for tomorrow.'

'I know. Get them used today. It would not surprise me if Manager Ledbetter found a way of cancelling them by tomorrow.'

Charles said: 'Cancelling them? Why?'

'It's not unknown for Psycho & Med to call cases back for review, even within twenty-four hours. They might change their minds and decide you are fit for duty.'

'I have six months' furlough to my credit,' Charles said. 'I could always use that to get away.'

'I couldn't say precisely where it is in the UC regulations, but I'll lay any money there's a loophole on that, too,' Dinkuhl said. 'Anyway, you would be wiser not to risk it.'

'I'll do it today,' Awkright said. 'I still don't know why he wants to get away, though.'

'It's a private matter,' Dinkuhl said. 'He wants to find Sarah Cohn.'

Awkright smiled. He said to Charles: 'So they didn't convince you?'

The web of conspiracy was becoming increasingly irritating. Charles successfully fought an impulse to be rude. After all, of his own decision he had rejected not only the advice of his Manager but, in a sense, his membership of the managerial. He had resolved on the apparently hopeless but certainly wilful course of making his own search for Sarah. He had put himself outside the ranks of normal society, and that being so he must regard it as a stroke of fortune that he had so soon happened on a group who would be able to further his plans. To an extent he was to be identified with them, but he could still limit the identification.

'No,' he said. 'They didn't convince me.' He hesitated. 'I don't quite know how you people can help me. Apart from the new identity and so on. And I'm not even certain that the new identity is essential.'

Awkright said: 'Well, that can wait for a few hours.' To Dinkuhl, he continued: 'Bring him along this evening, will you, Hiram? I'll have the card ready.'

The gyro slipped down towards a typical Agricultural outpost, the cluster of squat buildings which one saw universally from the air. Detroit was twenty miles away. The land here was flat and empty; it was not an area scheduled for night as well as daylight operation. Everything seemed deserted.

When the gyro touched down, Dinkuhl checked Charles' move to get out. Instead he rolled the gyro along, on the ground, towards the largest of the buildings that faced them. As they reached it, the doors slid open and the gyro nudged its way inside.

Charles looked around. Full lights were on; the place looked like a gyrotaxi hangar—he counted a score of gyros before he gave up counting. Dinkuhl got out, and he followed him.

Dinkuhl said: 'Fair gathering tonight.'

'Am I to know what it is yet?'

'Follow me,' Dinkuhl said. 'All shall be made clear.'

They went through another long shed packed with gyros, and from that, through a connecting corridor, to a third shed, more square in shape. The people from the gyros were here, sitting in rows of chairs but also standing, in overflow, behind them. At the far end of the room a rough dais had been put up. There was a table on it, and a man standing behind the table. He was not particularly unusual except that he was bearded—although that in itself was unusual enough. He was in full flow of rhetoric; Charles disregarded this for the moment while he surveyed the audience.

At first glance they, too, were a very ordinary assembly; they comprised a well-varied set of age-groups between early twenties and sixties. The first thing to surprise him was that badges of the different managerials were scattered indiscriminately among them—it was not a question of a bloc of Atomics, a bloc of Mining, and so on; they were entirely mixed. Then he noted their faces more carefully. One could read the everyday features that they must normally show, but they were clouded now by something else—a concentration, a passion, which he never remembered seeing anywhere. He looked back to the speaker: it was there, too, and in a more powerful and vivid form.

He listened to what the speaker was saying.

'. . . for time must have a stop! Time that was endless must end! All must be fulfilled! What comfort do I give you? No comfort but that of knowing and being prepared. For the sky will brighten and it will seem that day has come in the night, but I tell you that that day will be more terrible than any night. It will be flames that brighten the sky, and the flames will be the flames of hell!'

When he paused, Charles felt rather than heard the sigh

99

of indrawn breath from his hearers. He began to speak more softly, his words carefully brought out and speciously reasonable.

'Why do you come here, my friends? Why do you leave those airfoam seats in the cinemas, that TV screen, the air-sphering and the lascivious picnics? Why do you leave all those pleasures and come here, to listen to me, a poor prophet of the Last Word that shall be Spoken? Is it because you are tired of your follies and your ill-doings, tired of your back-slidings and your fornications? Is it because your minds at last are turned towards the Right?'

His eyes rested on them, caressing, despising.

'No! It is not that which brings you here. In your hearts you are as vile as ever you were, and Jahweh knows how vile that is. You come because you cannot help coming. You cannot help coming any more than you can help wallowing in your wickedness, writhing in the clutch of your own iniquities. My friends!' The words, Charles noted, were a lash. 'My friends, you come because you are in Hell! Now—at this instant—you are in Hell! The Pit is all about you, the flames are prepared around you, the Demons dance at your heels! All that is necessary is that your eyes should be opened to see where you are and what your sufferings are to be. And Jahweh shall cause them to be opened! The time approaches! The hour must strike!'

Dinkuhl touched Charles lightly on the shoulder. He spoke softly in his ear:

'Not getting carried away, I hope?'

Charles looked at him, aware that his gaze left the man on the dais with a kind of reluctance.

'What in hell is all this?' he asked.

Dinkuhl jerked his head. 'This way.'

He led the way to a side door, and whistled it open. It

100

closed behind them, cutting off the vibrant eloquence in the hall they had left. They were in another corridor.

Dinkuhl said: 'Didn't you know about the Cometeers? They aren't featured on TV, of course—not even on KF— but I thought the news had got around. The big boys know about them, and think they're unimportant. And that suppressing them wouldn't help, anyway—in which they are certainly right. Meanwhile, they provide a useful cover.'

Through a second door they passed into quite a small room. There were half a dozen people in it; Charles recognized Awkright. Dinkuhl introduced him to the rest; he was confused and failed to take in their names, but he noted that one was from Atomics, one from Steel, one from Mining, and the other two from minor managerials—Psycho & Med and Interplanetary.

Awkright said: 'You managed to get him here O.K.? The wanted man?'

Charles said: 'Wanted?' Dinkuhl said: 'Already?'

'The alarm went out late this afternoon. We got our own man through on to the Tonga stratoliner, but only just in time.'

Dinkuhl said quickly: 'Checking through to Tonga?'

'We've had the message mislaid for the night. It will get through in the morning. He will have got clear on a hydroplane before they can do anything about it. After that...' Awkright shrugged. '... There are a lot of islands in those parts, and plenty of places where a man who doesn't want company can hole up. With the help of a few wrong clues it should be a couple of months before they even suspect they're not going to find him. And then they can never be sure why—the sea, as their own official reports have pointed out, holds on to the bodies it picks up.'

Dinkuhl said: 'That's all very satisfactory. Charlie boy, there's nothing to stop you going ahead with your plans.'

'Nothing,' Charles said. 'Except that you haven't told me what they are yet.'

Dinkuhl grinned. 'Slack of me.'

Charles looked round the little group. 'I would feel a lot more at ease if I had some idea of what the whole gang of you were up to.'

The man with the Atomics badge—Blain or Baines?—was a lean sardonic individual. He spoke in an English drawl:

'Hiram should have introduced us collectively as well as one by one. This is the Society of Individualists, Charles, Headquarters Branch and General Assembly combined. We lift our helping hands to any little lame dog that looks like he's having trouble with his climbing apparatus. We don't amount to nothing, but we like to think we do.'

Charles said: 'I haven't made any secret of the fact that I have no quarrel with society myself. I suppose you have thought of the possibility that I might talk about your little group in the wrong quarters. You don't mind putting yourselves up for Remedials—you risk that out of the goodness of your hearts?'

Dinkuhl said: 'Well taken. Mark it, though, Charlie, that I have been with you from the time you came to my studio until now. You could only have been a danger in the way you suggest up to the point where you accepted your new identity at our hands and used our resources to fool your own Manager on the holiday trip. Once you did that, you put yourself in a position where you stand to get a Remedial two or three times as heavy as ours, should matters come out. Because we—those of us who belong to managerials and, of course, I don't—can only be picked up on such minor infringements as communicating information and illegal consorting. You are high, wide and handsome on a point of open rebellion against your own managerial.'

102

Awkright said: 'And don't think pull would help you. We would certainly blow the whole case wide open, with Hiram's help.'

Charles shook his head. 'I still don't get it. Why should you——? Well, I'll take it on trust for now. What do you want me to do?'

Dinkuhl said: 'It's your angle from which we are looking at things. You want Sarah Cohn. You have come to the conclusion—and it is our considered view that you are very possibly right—that she did not commit suicide or get herself killed by accident, but that she, and probably her father and Isaacssohn as well, were picked up by someone for some reason not unconnected with the kind of work that was being done at your laboratory. Well, who picked her up, and where is she now?'

Dinkuhl gestured round the small room. 'We have a fair selection here, as you can see. Half a dozen different managerials represented. Unfortunately you can't rule that half a dozen out for that reason. We hear a lot of things, but we don't hear everything, and whoever is holding these people will be exercising a certain amount of care in keeping the news from spreading. So the kidnapping could be the work of any one. Even Telecom. Beneath that bland front you see all round you, things are reaching a point of heavy stress. The wheel is getting ready to run loose.'

Awkright interrupted. 'Hiram,' he said, 'we have heard your platitudes before.'

Dinkuhl said: 'Just for the present I can't think why I waste my time on you people. All right. The point was that we have nothing to go on, as far as suspicion of some particular managerial is concerned. We all know Atomics made a bid for centralized control a few years ago. But Agriculture and Hydroponics had a try before that, and even innocent little Genetics Division have tried their hand—in

103

their case a shot at producing super-geniuses who could do the rest of the work for them. In this case it might even be United Chemicals who had kidnapped their own people, though I can't think why they should—or why they should let Charlie here loose even for a few hours if they had done.

'O.K., I'll come to it. In my view, the only thing to do is try picking up the trail where the last scent showed. That means going back to Berkeley.'

Charles said: 'I stayed the night in Professor Cohn's suite. I went over it pretty thoroughly; so did Caston and Stenner. I doubt if anything will turn up there.'

'There's more to Berkeley than Cohn's suite. There's his room at college. There's the chance that someone saw him in that crucial time immediately after he was last seen at the Interplanetary rocket pits.'

One of the group objected: 'Berkeley's not all that big a place, and everyone knows everyone in those campus towns. What excuse is Macintosh going to have for being there— he'll be noticed as a stranger, sure as H-bombs.'

Charles felt a slight twitch of surprise at the use of his new name. It was used very casually; he hoped he would be able to use it as casually himself.

Dinkuhl said: 'Charlie will have two authorizations along with his GD card. One will be a routine authorization of furlough. The other, specially fixed for the trip to Berkeley, will be an arrangement to stay over at Berkeley as a visiting student working on idiopathic decalcification in certain Outer Mongolian tribes. It so happens that they have some stuff on that at Berkeley that isn't available elsewhere on this continent.'

Charles had started. 'What,' he asked, 'is idiopathic decalcification in——?'

'Their teeth drop out early,' Dinkuhl said briefly. 'We will hope you don't happen on another GD man working in that line—I think it unlikely. Anyway, that's the scheme. Once at Berkeley, it's up to you, Charlie. We'll try to keep in touch with you, but essentially you're on your own.'

Charles nodded. The Atomics man said: 'Sounds all right. I can think of about fifty things likely to go wrong.'

'We'll hope they don't,' Dinkuhl said. 'All right, then. I'll run Charlie here back to Detroit and ship him on the strato-liner to Berkeley. See you boys at the next meeting.'

They retraced their steps, the others following behind them. The room where the big meeting had been in progress was empty. Dinkuhl explained:

'Gone out to bay at the moon. They always wind up that way. We'd better go join them for the last few minutes.'

They had taken the speaker's dais out for him. He was standing on it, addressing the silent crowd that surrounded him. There was a bare sliver of moon, but the skies were clear and the starlight threw a dim uncertain light on them all; complete darkness had fallen since Charles' and Dinkuhl's arrival.

The speaker was saying: '... let the air be filled with the jangling of chains and lamentations that cannot be ended because the grief and the pain is endless! Let the great serpent wind about the earth and . . .' He hesitated frac-tionally, and when he spoke again his voice was lower but charged with venom, '... and *crush* it! Look up, look up!'

In the darkness, their faces turning as of one accord towards the night sky were like a lake flickering suddenly into view. They stared towards a point perhaps fifteen degrees above the horizon. Looking with them, Charles saw the pale smudge of the comet.

The speaker said, his voice soft but carrying:

'See it. See it.' The sibilance was like a sharp-edged breeze

105

in the night. 'The Finger of Jahweh! The Finger that points to a world of doom! The Finger that poises to strike a people given over to iniquities! The Finger that marks the cattle for the slaughter! It approaches! It approaches! And when it strikes, the Voice of Jahweh will be a thunder from the mountains, a quake from the bowels of the earth! None shall escape the words of judgment—none shall escape!'

Charles was conscious of the same almost corporate shuddering sigh that he had been aware of within the building. For perhaps half a minute there was silence after that. Their gaze was still fixed on the heavens. Then the speaker broke the calm, his voice a shout that became a shriek.

'Down! Kneel! You dogs, you bitches! Down, down, down!' They were falling to their knees like corn before the reaper, but his voice shrilled on. 'Down to your damnation! Down on your knees, and cry, cry to Jahweh the Eternal: "Lord Jahweh, we are damned! Send us your whips, your scorpions, your fires to sear our tenderest flesh!"'

The words came back, a hideous echo. 'Lord Jahweh, we are damned! Send us your whips, your scorpions, your fires to sear our tenderest flesh!'

'Unleash your demons!' exhorted the speaker.

'Unleash your demons!' came the murmuring echo.

'One mercy only, Lord Jahweh, one mercy only we ask.'

'One mercy only, Lord Jahweh, one mercy only we ask.'

'After a million years of torment, grant us oblivion.'

'After a million years of torment, grant us oblivion.'

'We, your damned, kneel before you, Lord Jahweh!'

'We, your damned, kneel before you, Lord Jahweh!'

A silence followed. The speaker stood erect, his arms outstretched over the grovelling mass before him. Charles, with Dinkuhl and the others, stood a few yards away from the main body. Charles wondered whether they might not be in

106

some danger, but he realized that all attention was the other way, towards the dais and towards the tiny blur of the comet.

The bearded man stepped off the dais, and the crowd began to struggle to its feet. Dinkuhl nudged Charles.

'O.K., we can move now.'

Charles did not say anything until they were in the gyro and clear of the buildings. Dinkuhl started the engine, and Charles spoke above the soft rhythmic purr.

'I can't really believe what I've just been watching.'

'Cultivate your imagination,' Dinkuhl said abstractedly. 'One impossible thing before breakfast every morning.'

'They seemed such an ordinary set of people. It's incredible to think they could be capable of changing into that kind of rabble.'

The gyro lifted into the dim night sky, towards the scattered brilliance of the Milky Way. Dinkuhl said:

'One kind of rabble is very like another. They were quite respectable tonight. You should see them when they really go to town.'

'But how can a normal person——?'

'A normal person is a person reasonably well adjusted to his environment. I could make a good case for saying that that is precisely what that lot back there are: the well-adjusted human beings of the twenty-first century. Adjusted to a life that has lost its meaning, to a decadence, to a stagnation. Adjusted to managerial society.'

'As far as I know,' Charles said, 'I've never had the remotest inclination to behave like that.'

The stars always seemed very close, night-flying in a gyro. Tonight they seemed not far out of plucking distance.

Dinkuhl said: 'But you wouldn't consider yourself a normal person, would you—normal for your day and age, at any rate? That's just what I've been telling you. Normality

107

isn't an absolute. They're normal. I bet they're all ex-clients of Cosy Bright and Red League. Not of KF, anyway.'

A thought struck Charles. 'Are there more of them?'

'Hell, yes! That was only a minor branch meeting. Plenty of other preachers, too, though that guy tonight was one of the best I've heard.'

'Where did it start?'

'Different stories say different places. Some say New England, some say France. One story said India. It started before the comet came in view, but the comet's the main feature now—as you saw.'

'Then when the comet goes——'

'It will die out? Maybe. I don't think so, though. When something gets wound up the way this has got wound up, a little thing like a prophecy not coming off doesn't prevent it breaking loose. No, I think the fun's still in its early stages.'

'And you're in favour,' Charles said.

Dinkuhl laughed. 'I'm all for normalcy.'

They dropped at last towards the lights of Detroit, and to Dinkuhl's house by the edge of the lake. Dinkuhl brought the vanes into vertical and switched on the landing light; the gyro dropped effortlessly on to its grounding strip.

Dinkuhl said: 'I'll shove this in its kennel. You know your way about the house by now.' He handed Charles the whistle-key. 'Find yourself a drink. I'll be right up.'

Dinkuhl had put on the path-lights; Charles walked along a narrow strip of light towards the dark house. He reached the door, and whistled it open; the inside lights went on automatically. He made his way up to the first floor, and into the lounge. There was a whiff of some kind of perfume in the air; it was oddly familiar.

He knew what it was when his knees began to buckle:

108

astarate, the nerve gas. He slumped to the floor with his head towards the threshold––so it was that he saw Dinkuhl appear and stand the other side of it, looking into the room. He was wishing he could read Dinkuhl's expression when consciousness went.

4

THE room in which Charles awoke—cell would be a more appropriate description—was windowless and approximately a cube, with sides of perhaps nine feet. There were two gratings facing each other in opposite walls—small square patches of mesh in a bare expanse of pastel yellow plastic. Ventilation ducts. A door was set in another wall. It was much too centrally placed; in point of fact the bottom of the door-frame was over a foot off the floor of the room, and there was the same gap between the lintel top and the ceiling.

Charles had a shattering headache; as he knew, an inevitable after-effect of astarate. He could remember an experiment with the stuff, back at college. But he had deliberately taken a minor dose then, and the hangover had been less severe; his head now ached with a recurring throb of pain that reached a climax every half minute or so. He knew it would gradually lessen, but without knowing how much he had inhaled it was impossible to hazard a guess as to how long it would be before existence became anything but an agony again.

He raised his head very gingerly, to complete the survey of his surroundings. He himself was lying on the floor, on an airfoam mattress. There was a very curiously shaped airfoam chair in one corner, and what appeared to be a rolled hammock, attached to a hook. In the wall facing the door was the ubiquitous TV screen, but he looked in vain for any control panel. He was feeling thirsty, but there was nothing to drink. He thought of getting up and trying the door, but the waves of pain were too much for him. He let his head fall back, and closed his eyes.

Dinkuhl's face. He was visualizing it again, as he had seen it in the shadows beyond the door, peering into the room where he lay crumpled on the floor. The expression—had it been surprise, anxiety—or satisfaction? He thought angrily to himself: admitted he was no great judge of character, but if he had been wrong about Dinkuhl, he might as well give up. And yet there was the oddness of the set-up; Dinkuhl's membership of this group of subversives, who were willing to take risks to help him for no other reason than that he was rebelling against his managerial. That had worried him before. It worried him now.

A fortnight ago his life had been a routine long known and practised, a secure niche from which he could look out on a sane and ordinary world with slight resentment and a good deal of superiority. Now he was in this whirlpool, and all the landmarks were gone. Presumably this new world had not sprung suddenly into being. It had existed before. All the time he had been doing his usual job at Saginaw this turmoil had been going on—a dozen or more Contact Sections at each other's throats—Dinkuhl and his circle of saboteurs—the Cometeers joyfully lashing themselves with whips of despair. It must have been there already; it had simply been his bad luck to fall into the maelstrom.

And Sarah, too. That thought checked him, with a pain that mastered the mere physical pain from the astarate. In its wake his determination was re-aroused. However

111

confused and incapable of being resolved the situation might seem, he still had an objective. And for that matter, everything that contributed to the complexity around him made it more certain that he had been right in his suspicions of Stenner's explanation, and more probable that Sarah was still alive, somewhere.

The pain was a little less acute, and he made up his mind to disregard it. He got to his feet and walked unsteadily across to the door. Dinkuhl's whistle-key had disappeared, but he could remember a few standard combinations of notes. He tried them out, despite the dryness of his throat. There was no response; the door remained closed. He pressed his shoulder against it, too, but it remained firm. He went over and sat down in the airfoam chair to think things out. It folded persuasively about him, and he saw that there were straps by which he could fasten himself in. He couldn't think why they should be needed.

He heard the usual mounting purr, and looked up to see the TV screen on the wall coming to life. A middle-aged man at a desk. A desk bare of anything that might identify it. And the man wore no managerial badge.

He was fat, red-faced, with a long thin nose and a remote sly look. He spoke with a slight lisp.

'How are you, Official Grayner? Is there anything you need?'

Charles said: 'Yes. Water, a pain-killer, and an explanation. In that order, if it doesn't inconvenience you.'

The man nodded. He called, to someone out of camera range: 'Water and neurasp for Official Grayner.' To Charles, he added: 'You wouldn't prefer brandy?'

'Water will do.'

'Let me introduce myself. My name is Ellecott.'

'Of . . . ?'

Ellecott smiled; it was a dreamy unpleasant smile. 'Don't

112

think I want to be awkward. But I would prefer it if you did not press that question—not right at the moment.'

The door opened. Charles went across and took a flask of water and two neurasp pills from a tall silent man, again unidentifiable as to managerial. He nodded to the figure in the screen. 'Excuse me.' While he was taking the pills and drinking from the flask, the door closed again.

There was an almost immediate lifting of pain. Feeling a great deal more comfortable, Charles dragged the chair over to a position more directly facing the screen, and sat down.

'You were saying?'

Ellecott said: 'Simply expressing a hope that you would not object to my retaining my incognito. In a delicate matter like this . . . I'm sure you'll understand.'

He could think more clearly and quickly now that the ache in his head was subsiding. The important thing was to establish some kind of advantage, however slight, to help balance the altogether disadvantageous position in which he found himself. It must be something not entirely unreasonable; something which these people would not be obliged to refuse—a point on which they would be inclined to relax.

'Where's Dinkuhl?' Charles asked.

Ellecott pursed his lips. 'Dinkuhl?'

'I can't see any point in your pretending not to know who Dinkuhl is. You kidnapped me from his house.'

'I was not trying to deceive you. I know of Dinkuhl, of course. But that doesn't mean I know his present whereabouts.'

The equivocality of the reply was, Charles guessed, deliberate. He thought he knew why, too. They were not sure whether he had classified Dinkuhl as a friend or an enemy. It would help them, if they could establish that, to know what kind of a front to put on for him. He thought hard. Whatever his motives, Dinkuhl represented a link with

113

the old familiar world that had existed so short a time ago; Dinkuhl was a lifeline. It wasn't necessary to trust him.

'I want to see Dinkuhl,' Charles said.

Ellecott shrugged. 'And if we haven't got him?'

'Then get him. He was standing just outside the door when I passed out. I can't believe you would have left him behind to use the story on KF.'

'I don't know.' Ellecott tried to look disarming. 'The—the picking-up wasn't my affair. I don't know about Dinkuhl. He hesitated. 'Accidents sometimes happen at these affairs.'

Charles said: 'In the circumstances, you have been treating me fairly well. I gather my goodwill is not completely unimportant. If there has been that kind of accident, you can rule the goodwill out. Now and permanently.'

Ellecott shook his head with what seemed to be an attempt at roguishness. 'We'll have to see what we can do. I don't know what's happened about Dinkuhl, but I'll try to find out for you. Like to have TV while you wait? You must find it boring in there.'

There was one way of checking whether he was still on the North American continent, although he had no reason to think he wasn't. He said casually:

'Thank you. Red League will do. Unless you can get me KF?'

'I *believe*,' Ellecott said, 'that KF is temporarily off transmission. Red League coming up.'

It was on the cards that Ellecott was telling the truth about KF—it was so much a one-man affair that Dinkuhl's absence for more than twelve hours would probably knock it out. But in any case they would hardly have been likely to give him information that would tell him explicitly that he was or was not in the Detroit area. He watched the closing stages of a Red League melodrama apathetically. He was still in North America, anyway. Somewhere overhead the fixed

114

space station, rotating precisely with the rotation of the earth, was beaming its message of placid security from eastern to western seaboard, from the North West Passage to the Mexican deserts.

The play ended, and there was a newscast. It was Henry Millheim, warm, solid, grave with the fleeting touch of jocularity—the Red League archetype. The news, too, was as usual—a window on to a reassuring world. Manager Vautrin had been appointed Director of Steel—a flash of the complacent Vautrin transfixed in mock-modesty. United Chemicals announced the opening of a new branch on the Moon—the stark lunar mountains reached their craggy fingers against a black sky powdered with diamanté stars. Something shifted in Charles' memory at this, but he could not hold the link. The first results were in of the Adirondacks airsphering handicap—the plastic bubbles danced elegantly across the screen as Millheim's steady voice rolled out the names: 'Kapell—Edwards—Burgoicz . . .'

Charles' attention left the screen as the link of memory snapped into place. The new UC lunar branch . . . he remembered now: the Tycho branch, closed down probably ten years earlier. There had been no publicity about the close-down, but one of the staff had been drafted to Saginaw; that was how he had known of it. Now the re-opening was hailed as an achievement, an extension of frontiers. He wondered how many other extensions of frontiers, blazoned on the TV networks, had been of that kind.

His eye was brought back to the screen by a familiar march tune—the UC signature-tune. On the screen the serried ranks stood on a wide expanse of parade ground. At signals, blocks broke away and marched forward to salute the UC flag. That told him the date—November 21st. Graduation day. He watched the marching squads with something of nostalgia, something of pity. He knew what they were. With the aid of

115

Psycho & Med, their minds had been sifted, their psycho-plans prepared. And so they advanced—Squads A and B destined for leadership, the administrators and rulers of the future—Squads C, D and E for research and development work—Squads F, G, H and I for foremen and generally supervisory jobs—and at the end all those other squads who were now embarking on an adult life of routine and security and Cosy Bright in steady doses. The workers. Charles watched the gaily-coloured standard flap in a sharp north-easterly breeze. He had been a Squad D man. He wondered . . . Dinkuhl's view that the managerial world was breaking down . . . could the explanation lie somehow in these neat military formations and the billowing flag?

The screen clicked to emptiness, and then the emptiness gave way to Ellecott's face again. Ellecott was still smiling.

'Good news for you, Official Grayner. We've got Dinkuhl. We can arrange for you to be quartered with him for the period of your—for the period while we are fixing things up. We're putting you into rather more comfortable quarters, too. I imagine you will be finding your present place on the cramped side.'

Charles said warily: 'That's very good of you.'

'Two of our men are coming along to collect you now. I know you will co-operate.'

Charles said: 'Of course. I wouldn't want to put you to unreasonable expense—and I know the cost of astarate.'

'A sense of humour,' Ellecott said, 'can help to make the whole present situation more comfortable all round. We do appreciate the way you are taking things. We really do.'

It was when, at the bidding of the two men, he climbed through the door into a peculiar tunnel-shaped passage that he realized what his surroundings were. The original cell, of course, should have put him on the track—the functional bareness, the door equidistant between floor and ceiling, the

116

chair with straps and the hammock. Now the convoluting corridor, the evidence of bulkhead construction, and, above all, the handrails for manœuvring in non-gravity conditions, made things quite unmistakable. He was in a spaceship. A spaceship at rest, it was true, since gravity was the normal gravity, not the artificial variety, and there was nothing of the inevitable background vibration. But a spaceship nevertheless. He glanced at his two badgeless guardians with private satisfaction. So it was Interplanetary who had him. More encouraging still, they were fools enough to try concealing their identity while holding him on a spaceship. His new knowledge gave a definite fillip to his morale.

He recognized the room into which he was shown as one of the messrooms, converted hastily for his own and Dinkuhl's accommodation. The fine seams in the walls were indicators of the presence of pop-out tables, and there was the hatch in one corner, through which food would normally arrive. The TV screens on facing walls were messroom style, too.

A certain amount of odd furniture had been brought in, including, he was surprised and pleased to see, a bookcase. Dinkuhl was standing behind this with a book in his hand. He looked up when Charles came in, and waved.

'Glad to see you, Charlie. They've already written me off as a big-mouthed recalcitrant so I will begin with a word or two of warning. Those TV screens may be blank, but don't think they aren't registering. And I know enough about modern microphones to be able to assure you that if you or I whisper loud enough for the other to hear, we are whispering loud enough for our friends to listen too. That being so, I think they should be warned that we are taking the reasonable precaution of not discussing anything that in our view is likely to help them in any way.'

Charles said: 'Fair enough. How did they get you by the way?'

'Astarate—but a milder dose than you, I gather. At any rate I have been awake for a few hours, and I took it you were newly risen. They told me you had insisted on our being reunited before you answered any questions.'

Charles watched Dinkuhl, trying to probe whatever might underlie the familiar sardonic friendliness. 'I thought it a good idea.'

Dinkuhl nodded. 'Very sound. I can't say what they planned to do with me—I was presumably picked up in the first place because I could hardly be left behind in the circumstances. But I take it I am dispensable. And that is something else that I think we must have out in the open, where we can see it as well as the eyes that watch, the ears that harken. To what extent are you to trust me? It's an interesting point altogether. I could quite easily be a stooge, planted on you by our friends. The fact that you asked to see me doesn't signify, except insofar as it makes things easier for them—supposing I am on their side.'

Charles said: 'I had thought of that.'

'Naturally. Frankly, I don't see there is anything we can do about it. I would prefer to have relations between us on a level of mutual confidence, but there is only one way in which I think it *might* be done, and to my view the fact of our being in a goldfish bowl is against that line. I'm not sure it would be a conclusive piece of evidence, anyway. No, Charlie, much as you may dislike the thought, I must counsel you to keep your mind in its present mood of suspicion. And, of course, the fact that I give you this advice doesn't mean anything, either. I would naturally expect you to be suspicious, and to discuss your suspicions quite openly would be one good way of allaying them. And then to discuss the fact that I was discussing . . . well, we won't pursue things too far.'

Charles grinned. 'The company is welcome, anyway. You restore my morale, Hiram.'

'And that, too, can work both ways. But this seems a good time to tackle a point that I imagine may have begun to worry you—the question of your own importance.'

'I have wondered. Both Ledbetter and yourself . . . and now this present lot—presuming they aren't related to you.'

'Presuming,' Dinkuhl said. He glanced casually at the TV screen. 'I imagine we are allowed to talk about this; they must have guessed I was likely to say something. Your importance, then. You will have realized that quite a number of people are more interested than a little in the work that was being done at the UC laboratory where you had so short and eventful a stay. That opens up the interesting speculation—which I offer you for what it's worth—that Isaacssohn and the Cohns may not have been captured by the same managerial. There is no reason to assume they were, and if they weren't, some of the apparent confusion in leaving Sarah Cohn for a fortnight after Isaacssohn's apparent death is removed.'

Charles nodded towards the TV screen. 'Making this Number Three?'

'Very possibly. Now, is there anything that still strikes you as odd?'

Charles hesitated. Dinkuhl waved an expansive hand at the blank screen. He said encouragingly:

'Go on. I don't think you are giving anything away. It's an obvious point, after all.'

'The lab wasn't particularly well protected. All Isaacssohn's reports were on file there. I admit I was a bit confused at first, but as soon as Sarah explained what Isaacssohn had been after, the pieces clicked together. Now these people who are showing such an interest in the whole business—I take it they must know what it is they are interested in. So in that case, why not simply pick up the reports? The work is straightforward. They could do it themselves. As far as

I am concerned personally, I only had a week of following the lines Isaacssohn had laid down. Why grab me?'

'That,' Dinkuhl said, 'is, of course, the crux of the matter. Why are you important—important enough to be treated with such circumspection by your own managerial, to be offered substantial aid and comfort by my own little group of subversives, and now to find yourself benevolently but firmly held as a prisoner by Interplanetary?'

Charles jerked a glance at him. Dinkuhl said calmly:

'There's no need to let ourselves be branded entirely as fools. I can't think why they are so concerned at having no insignia on show, but it can hardly be more than a temporary measure of confusion. We could not be expected to be blind for very long to the obvious explanation of our surroundings. Type 7 freighter, for my guess, but that's unimportant.'

'But still in the pits,' Charles said. 'And I don't quite see the point. Interplanetary have offices and suites of their own. We could have easily been taken to one of those, where we should not have been able to draw the conclusion you have just mentioned. Why stick us in a grounded spaceship, where our suspicions were bound to be aroused?'

'Why indeed?' Dinkuhl said. 'I can think of only one reason, but that's a good one. The spaceship is not to remain grounded. On my guess, preparations for blasting are going ahead at the moment. And it's a fairly obvious move. You are a valuable property; the best place to store you is where Interplanetary is by far the strongest managerial—in Luna City. Since the Earth-Moon traffic is their monopoly, they can be reasonably certain that you will remain there just as long as they want you to——'

It was eminently reasonable, but a sobering thought all the same. The man who had been on the UC Tycho station had painted a grim enough picture of life on the Moon, and he had not been a prisoner. There would be no yearly

120

furloughs for Charles while Interplanetary wanted to hold him.

Dinkuhl interrupted his line of thought. 'But we are getting away from the question of your importance. It is obvious that you are important and also, as you have pointed out, obvious that your importance doesn't lie in any one thing that you know. What does that leave us?'

Charles said : 'What indeed?'

'The general, not the particular. Your mind and its skills. In fact, you're the O'Reilly they talk of so highly.' Dinkuhl grinned faintly. 'Gorblimey, O'Reilly, you are looking well!'

'I'm afraid that's nonsense. Sixteen years of a routine lab job don't make for indispensability. And it isn't as though the problem is a particularly stiff one. I can't see it offering insurmountable difficulties to anyone.'

'Point one,' Dinkuhl said. 'The sixteen years were an error. I'll come back to that in a minute. Point two. I could show you a neat little problem in mike and camera handling which would leave you blank and wondering. It's not an exceptionally difficult problem, but you wouldn't get to first base on it, because you haven't got the basic orientation. Problems look easy to those who can see a way of cracking them; if you haven't the right kind of mind and the right kind of background, they're insuperable.'

Charles said tolerantly: 'And I'm the blue-eyed boy—the only one who can crack the nut? An odd coincidence that there should have been three of us linked together—Isaacssohn and Sarah and myself.'

'Isaacssohn and Sarah Cohn,' Dinkuhl said, 'were Israelis. In a way it was a coincidence that you should have been sent to take Isaacssohn's place, but the coincidence was a limited one only. Now we come back to the question of those sixteen years in routine research at Saginaw. The coincidence was that after P & M had made their blunder and routed you

121

into D Squad at graduation—what a lot we all know about you, Charlie!—you should have been shoved, entirely by chance, into work on the substance, diamond, that Isaacssohn was going to do big things with fifteen years later.'

Dinkuhl glanced at him speculatively. 'I wonder why you didn't do anything big yourself?'

Charles said: 'My procedure was mapped out for me. As far as I can see, Isaacssohn was given a free hand. It's the only way you can hope to get anything valuable 'done.'

'And, apart from Isaacssohn, do you know of anyone who has been given a free hand in research?'

'I only know Saginaw. There were no free hands there.'

'There are no free hands anywhere, Charlie. But it wouldn't matter a nickel if they were free, because they would not do anything. Yes, you might have done, but you were the exception—you were P & M's prize error. If your psychoplan had been properly prepared you wouldn't have been in research in the first place. You would have been fulfilling your rightful duties as an administrator. Along with Ledbetter and the rest of the boys.'

Charles said: 'I suppose so. You mean——'

'I've been trying to tell you for a long time,' Dinkuhl said. 'The managerial state is dead. *Felo de se.* And to a certain extent, killed by its merits. It evolved a neat system for picking out its better brains and giving them the plum jobs, but it broke its neck on a minor anomaly—that the plum jobs, whatever form of society you base your ideas on, are going to be the administrative jobs, the jobs involving power of men over men. Science doesn't fit into that pretty scheme; it never has done. At its best, under the later capitalism, it developed a hierarchy which meshed in with the real society around it. Scientists did their good work while they were young, and landed the plum jobs in later life. The man who was a brilliant physicist at thirty or thirty-five had retired

122

from physics by the time he was fifty into a front-office job.

'All very satisfactory—because you always had the younger generation coming along to take up the places left by promotion—to do the real work which kept science on the move, in fact. And they in their turn did their stint and passed on to a well-paid bureaucracy, with a knighthood or some similar meaningless but eagerly grasped honour. But observe the managerial arrangements: a basic and largely disciplinary and conditioning training up to the point of graduation. Followed by specialization. Very efficient. Too efficient. Because to the managerial world it would seem pointless to train a man in the sciences unless he were going to spend the remainder of his life in those fields; and once he had been trained in a scientific discipline, then they made sure that he did that, and nothing else. You get it?'

Charles said: 'It might work, providing the rewards were assessed fairly.'

'And who,' asked Dinkuhl, 'assesses the rewards? The administrators. People always tend to see their own job as peculiarly important and valuable, but when the job involves telling other people to do things, there's no checking their self-approval. A reason why capitalism was so fruitful was that under capitalism the administrators did not form a cohesive governing body. Money, and money-power, sprouted from all kinds of odd corners. We've got the flow controlled today, and although the managerials may differ among themselves, they all have the same set-up. The administrators are firmly in the saddle, and naturally they perpetuate their own supremacy.

'Their own children make Squad A, of course, even if their psychoplans show them to be on the verge of imbecilic. But the standard of intelligence handed on is naturally above average in any case, and being an assured ruling class they

123

have smaller families than the rest. The rest of Squad A along with Squad B is made up of the high IQ's drawn from the population at large. Show anything above average intelligence and you're an administrator. Except, of course, when P & M slips up.'

Charles said: 'We were always told that the psychoplans tested aptitudes.'

'They do that, too. But aptitudes are very conditional things. The man who would make a first-class scientist will also make a first-class administrator, granted the proper training. Don't underrate the administrative genius. I wouldn't like to give you the impression that the present situation could be made good simply by reversing the top layers—making the bright boys scientists and development engineers, and the not-so-bright boys government officials. The situation thus produced would be very likely even more horrifying than the one around us.'

'There's one thing,' Charles said. 'You've been analysing the situation. I imagine the rulers of the managerials must have made similar analyses in the past. Why didn't they do something about it? Why wait until something like this crops up, and then rush around scraping the bottom of the barrel, trying to find someone to cope with it?'

Dinkuhl brought out a pack of cigarettes, took one himself and tossed one over to Charles. His eyes roamed briefly round the room. Then he fished in his pocket and brought out an automatic lighter. They lit up.

'Why didn't they do something about it?' Dinkuhl echoed. 'Because it's a human reaction not to. Every single one of the crises that have convulsed the human race in the past has been evident in advance. The writing was there to read, but even when people were willing to read it, they treated it as unimportant. In this case, the *status quo* was particularly comfortable. Managerialism held a secure and untroubled

124

world. Individual managerials may have had moments in which they were distracted by tempting thoughts of world power, and the thought may even have been expressed at one or another Managers' Conference that a different selection policy at graduation might be the means of giving one managerial the boost that would enable it to dominate and swallow the others.

'But, apart from that fact that there are natural difficulties, the temptation was never worth the trouble and the certainty of change that it would entail. There are social as well as managerial loyalties, and they can be at odds. I remember noting your disgust, Charlie, when you saw people from different managerials sitting side by side at the Cometeers' meeting. A conditioned reflex, as I imagine you would be willing to admit. But the conditioning doesn't apply to the really big people; they get on very nicely together.

'You can find something of the same divided loyalty in the stress period of late capitalism. There nationalism was the primary and official loyalty, and different sets of national rulers would contemplate going to war with each other, with equanimity and even with enthusiasm. But the more likely it became that the wars would have the incidental effects of bringing about major social changes, the more their enthusiasm dwindled. In the end they were being dragooned into wars from below, where the conditioning had been sounder.'

Charles said: 'And now they will have to do something about it—about science, anyway?'

'Now,' Dinkuhl said, 'they are doing only one thing—scrambling for the means of domination that's been tossed into the arena. What's the answer? One will get it, or more than one will get it. If the former, you have your centralized world control. If the latter, you either have a smaller, tighter hierarchy, or else a bloody struggle which one may win.

125

Give managerialism credit for political astuteness—I think they will arrange it peaceably in the long run.'

'And then?'

'Then the Managers will settle down to enjoy themselves again. The crisis will be over. Why should they make changes in so satisfactory a set-up?'

'Satisfactory!'

Dinkuhl glanced at him shrewdly. 'You found it so.'

Charles grinned ruefully: 'Under conditioning.'

'We're all conditioned—them, too. Nine-tenths of what they do is on the unconscious level. When a form of society has become moribund, only a fool would hope to revive it. The kindest thing to do is to stick a knife between its ribs. You may have to do it more than once to get through the excess fat, but every stab drains a little more blood. In the end, it dies—perhaps in some different way, but your contribution will have helped.'

'And then?'

Dinkuhl shrugged. 'I'm not God. Another form of society. The runs have been getting shorter. Slave economies for God knows how long. Feudalism about eight hundred years. Capitalism about four. And now not much more than a century sees managerialism on the way out. I don't know what comes next. Maybe the deluge.'

'But why destroy, without having anything to offer?'

'Some things need destroying. We should put them out of their misery.' Dinkuhl smiled. 'That's why I like you, Charlie. You're the kind of time-bomb they can't stop happening. You and Isaacssohn and Sarah Cohn. For that matter, they will have to do something about Israel sooner or later. I guess it is beginning to dawn on them that they have a nice little focus of infection there, now that the Israelis are beginning to find time for something else apart from food production. But it won't matter if they do. There will always

126

be the odd one like you, anyway, and it's the odd one that grits up those nice smooth bearings.'

'Grit in the bearings. I can think of more comfortable rôles to have.'

Dinkuhl looked round for a moment, and then bent down and stubbed his cigarette out against the TV screen control panel.

'Yes, you do have your personal situation to consider. Well, our Interplanetary friends, who have permitted me to get indignant at such length about the world at large, will presumably be coming through with a nice warm offer for you. You will understand that—could they be sure of knocking out Isaacssohn and Sarah Cohn as well—it might be more convenient for them simply to eliminate you. Short-sighted, but then, they are all incorrigibly myopic, as I have been trying to make clear. Well, they can't. At the moment, anyway.'

Dinkuhl glanced thoughtfully in the direction of the TV screen on the nearer wall. 'It would be more cheering, of course, if you could eliminate the possibility that the hierarchy will be formed *before* the weapon materializes. From their point of view—Interplanetary and whoever hold the remaining two—that might be a simpler solution. It must have occurred to them. In that case you would all become dispens——'

Dinkuhl broke off speaking. The TV screen was glowing into life. Dinkuhl chuckled.

'I thought that might fetch them.'

Ellecott's expression, on the screen, was somewhat ruffled. He made an evident effort at self-control; the same thin smile on the same fat features.

He said: 'I may say that my remarks, unless otherwise specified, will be addressed to you, Official Grayner. You

127

wanted to see Dinkuhl again, and your wishes rank very high on our priority list. Dinkuhl himself is entirely unimportant.'

Dinkuhl made a slight bow in acknowledgment. 'Lacking a managerial membership card, I must be. Nevertheless——'

Ellecott cut across his words. 'Dinkuhl has been talking a little sense and a lot of nonsense. I won't apologize for our eavesdropping; I am quite confident that you will appreciate how necessary it was in the circumstances. It is quite true that you are now in the hands of Interplanetary.' Ellecott flickered with one finger the small rocket-badge on his chest. 'We left these off before, as a routine precaution until the possibilities of your being—recovered—had been entirely excluded. You are in a type 7 freighter, as Dinkuhl observed.'

'At which pits?' Charles asked.

Ellecott hesitated. 'I imagine there can be no harm in telling you that, too. Toledo.'

'Home, sweet home,' Dinkuhl murmured. 'Still in the poison belt.'

'The points that Dinkuhl made about your importance,' Ellecott went on, 'were quite valid ones. You will see, Official Grayner, that we are being quite frank with you. We permitted Dinkuhl to tell you all this, although you will understand that we need not have done so, and we are now confirming it. You are of very great importance, not only to us in Interplanetary, but to the whole world.'

'Where are Isaacssohn, and Sarah Cohn?' Charles asked.

'We don't know—yet. We have formed the impression—largely owing to that odd time-lag in their disappearances—that they are not in the same hands. We have a good Contact Section, and they are working on it. It will be a help when we have you safely at Luna City. We can then allow the rumour that we have you to get around. That may bring in something.'

128

'I am not impressed by the prospect of Luna City,' Charles said. 'Is that essential?'

'Unfortunately. Luna City is our stronghold. We are the only managerial based outside the planet, and I put it to you as evidence of our fundamentally non-aggressive and responsible outlook that Interplanetary has never attempted to use the power given by that fact. We could withdraw our relatively small bases on the planet and destroy every major city within twenty-four hours, from the space stations. It has never been considered.'

Dinkuhl murmured: 'I wonder if the fact that the other managerials keep Interplanetary's vital supplies on rather a hand-to-mouth basis could have anything to do with that?'

Ellecott ignored him. 'Interplanetary was founded to carry man to the stars. We have long been perturbed by the trend of events, and we propose to use our influence to change them. But the immediate and urgent problem is the question of the diamond solar power-source. This can be used as a small portable but very powerful battery, as you know. It can also be used as a weapon, with some minor modifications.'

'That hadn't escaped me,' Charles said.

Ellecott leaned forward towards the cameras, emphasizing the importance of what he was going to say.

'There are some managerials who would misuse such a power source and such a weapon. One of those may have either Isaacssohn or Sarah Cohn, or both. We need your help, Official Grayner, to enable us to keep abreast of this other, or others. With your help, we can maintain peace. Without it, there is the prospect of a confused and barbarous civil war, and perhaps at last of tyranny.'

'The offer,' Dinkuhl said impatiently. 'Out with it, man. Let's have the smell of the money.'

'The continued safety of Dinkuhl is a minor part of it,' Ellecott said. 'A man charged with acts subversive to the managerial may claim immunity by reference to his own managerial; an immunity which does not, of course, hold for Dinkuhl who has no managerial. Normally there are good reasons for not invoking that clause, but it is different when matters can be arranged in private.'

Ellecott's small deep-set eyes rested on Dinkuhl while he spoke; the thin smile twisted his lips upwards.

'Do not trust them,' Dinkuhl said. 'The gipsy's warning. This is not antique Roman gallantry on my part, but realism.'

Ellecott's attention returned to Charles. 'A minor part. As far as your future status is concerned, it is proposed to confirm you as a Director of this managerial, and a member of the Board. You will be given a free hand in your work, in the first place on Luna City but before too long, we hope, under your own choice of conditions here on Earth. Once the present crisis has been got under control you will be in charge of scientific development—and it is inevitable, you understand, that Interplanetary will have risen to a commanding position among managerials by that time.'

'Charlie boy,' Dinkuhl said, 'it's an offer in a thousand. Everything you want, and when it's all over you join the administrators. Will you put your kids into science? There's a lovely little problem for you!'

Ellecott said: 'We are being very forbearing with Dinkuhl, but you will understand that there must be limits to this patience on our part. I think our offer is a fair one, and not unattractive. I hope you will agree to accept it.'

'And if I don't?'

Ellecott smiled. 'As an academic point, we'll consider that. You will still go to Luna City, of course, because in addition to our major concern of having you work for us, there is the minor concern of making sure you don't work for anyone

130

else. There would be no question of treating you vindictively. You would be regarded like the prisoners-of-war in the old days. That means, of course, that you would be in restraint, and with no privileges. It would be our hope that you would eventually resign yourself to the commonsense outlook, and change your mind.'

'I doubt if I would,' Charles said. 'I don't want to seem dogmatic about this, but I think you might be unlucky. I retain some odd and awkward feelings of loyalty. It would not be easy for me to feel at home in another managerial, and I have an idea that the discomforts of guilt would be likely to outweigh those of imprisonment.'

'Attaboy the lower classes,' Dinkuhl said.

Ellecott rested his fat head back on heavy shoulders.

'Have you anything in view that you think might help to nullify your potential guilt feelings? We are prepared to go to considerable lengths to help you, if we can.'

They didn't know where Sarah was. Doubtless they would promise to get her if he were to co-operate; but they would be putting all their effort into the search for her and Isaacs-sohn anyway, for their own purposes. He thought about Ellecott's remark, analysing the tone and the recurring sly smile that had accompanied it. If you have vices, prepare to indulge them now. He would not deny all powers of attraction to the suggestion; the trouble was that he was too old, or too conscience-ridden, to accept his vices as amiable play-mates rather than fawning enemies. And, besides, he was in love.

'Nothing that I can think of,' Charles said. He hesitated. Presumably it was always a good principle to stall an unpromising situation. 'Any reason why I shouldn't have time to consider things?'

'As long as you like,' Ellecott said. He lifted his finger and looked at it. 'Purely as a point of information, this ship blasts in three hours. But of course you will have the whole time of the journey to the Moon in which to think things over.'

It was Ellecott's blandness as much as anything else which irritated Charles. They were not going to be budged from the path they had laid out for themselves. And they were certain that, in the end, he would come round.

He said curtly: 'Never mind. I don't need time. The answer is no. I don't care for being forced into a membership.'

Ellecott shook his head. 'It was better when you weren't being dogmatic. I know an old fellow on Luna City, name of Morrison. He was stationed on the Development Project. They gave him the routine medical before he returned to Earth and found he had developed a heart condition quite unusual for one of his age. P & M wouldn't pass him for the return—they couldn't. He didn't have a chance in ten million of surviving the take-off. Otherwise he was all right; as you know, bad hearts function better up there.'

Ellecott smiled his thin unpleasant smile. 'That was forty-six years ago—he was only twenty-five when it happened. Forty-six years. Forty-six years of an underground city, about a quarter of a mile square, and surrounded by airlessness and death. Forty-six years of food concentrates, and that sick and straggly group of trees which most people find worse than no vegetation at all.'

The story was horrible enough; Charles had heard of Morrison from the UC man who had been at Tycho. But even more horrible was Ellecott's pleasure in being able, at last, to exercise his sadism to a limited degree. He must have been under quite a restraint during the previous conversation.

Finding Charles made no reply, Ellecott went on:

'And he's still fit today, you know—physically fit. The only trouble is that he's been mad for over twenty years. They found out when he went for the trees with an axe.'

132

Dinkuhl said: 'And that ends Uncle's bedtime story for tonight. I could use you on KF, Ellecott.'

Ellecott agreed to notice him again. 'Dinkuhl,' he said, almost gently, 'there is no KF. If I were you I should occupy the next few days in using your well-known arts of persuasion on your friend here. For both your sakes.'

'If you were me,' Dinkuhl said pleasantly, 'you would spit in your eye, given the opportunity.'

Ellecott was undisturbed; probably, Charles thought, because he had been able to indulge himself and was visualizing the occasions when he would be able to do so again.

Ellecott said: 'I propose leaving you alone now. You will be under surveillance, either by me or one of my assistants. The door in the corner is not locked, and leads to the toilet room. The microphones and cameras installed there will not be put into operation unless you are ill-advised enough to repair there together for private consultation. And do not try taking anything in there on which one of you might leave a message for the other. I think that's all. You will have food and drink sent along shortly. Anything else?'

Charles patted the fuller cheeks which he now had. 'There seems little point in my continuing to look like someone else. Can you send the fixings for Hiram to get these off me, and wash my hair back to normal?'

Ellecott laughed briefly, his voice rising approximately an octave when he did so.

'What a pity! I think your new appearance suits you better altogether. Charles Macintosh—what a treat Genetics were getting unawares. No guilt feelings?'

'I had a purpose,' Charles said. 'And the arrangement was temporary. Can we have the stuff?'

'We'll have it done for you; we have a good cosmetics staff.

133

I'll send an escort to pick you up.' He smiled. *'This* arrangement is permanent.'

When Charles got back from having his make-up removed, Dinkuhl was watching TV. He switched the sound off, but left the pictures flickering on the wall.

'In Luna City,' he observed, 'they have only one TV link. A canned composite of Red League, Honey, Cosy Bright, and whatever is particularly banal in the local networks. Run by a guy called Schmidt. He applied to KF once—I guess someone put him on to us for a joke. He wanted to have a look at the programmes we had scheduled. I sent them, too, for the hell of it. He flipped back that there was only one title he found interesting—"The Cocktail Party." But as he did not remember seeing the author's name in programmes on the major networks, would I give him some idea as to the kind of thing Official Eliot wrote. Was it a leg show, for instance?'

'What did you tell him?'

'I didn't tell him anything. Sent him the play canned, without comment. I got it back by the next rocket. It wasn't quite what he wanted . . . if I *did* have any leg shows——'

'Cheer up. You may find yourself running Luna City TV yet; if you live long enough.'

Dinkuhl groaned. 'Pioneers, O pioneers! I don't think I will somehow. Well, let's have a proper look at you, Charlie. You know, I still think you looked better the way I fixed you up. I guess there's no accounting for tastes, though.'

'It may have been decorative. It didn't serve any useful purpose though, did it? For that matter, it would be interesting to know how Interplanetary got on to my tracks so easily.'

'Interesting, but not evidential, as one or another of the

134

great detectives used to say. You'll have to ask Ellecott some time. There'll be plenty of time for it.'

'Time.' Charles looked at his finger-watch. 'We're due to blast in an hour and a half. I suppose Ellecott will come through and give us some final instructions before then. I don't even know how to fix those damned hammocks up.'

'Blasting,' Dinkuhl said thoughtfully. 'I wonder how they will manage that? Tricky.'

Charles echoed: 'Tricky? What's tricky in it? It's a job they're used to.'

Dinkuhl said: 'Forget it. Sometimes my mind wanders. Yes, I think Ellecott will get through to us in the next ninety minutes. Meanwhile, let's make the most of things by seeing what Red League has to offer as a valedictory message from the planet Earth.'

He switched the sound up. It was a play. The ramifications of what had gone before were quite quickly apparent: She, the daughter of an Atomics Manager, and He, the son of a Manager of Steel. They had met on an airsphering picnic and soon, being young, had fancied themselves in love. Their respective parents were tolerant, but shook their heads. And when the point came of the hard facts being put to the couple themselves; to him that he should cut off from his family and all his friends, forfeit his Assistantship in the new tungsten reduction plant and go begging to Atomics for a place . . . to her that she should hand in the Atomics badge which her great grandfather had accepted from the hands of van Mark himself . . . then it seemed that there was nothing for them but misery all round.

Fortunately their happinesses were to be preserved. She, wildly airsphering to overcome her grief, found herself, with her sphere disabled, lost in the wild hills of Connecticut. Her radio had gone, too . . . it would soon be night. Then, his

135

sphere bursting like a golden bubble out of the sunset, came her rescuer. He was taller than the Steel man had been, and his hair was well suited to the blonde knot style which was currently fashionable. And, as he walked towards her, the cameras moved in for a close-up on his right breast—on an Atomics badge.

As for He, his worries took him not to airsphering but to a psychiatrist. And the psychiatrist's nurse was small and dark and sympathetic. (Psycho & Medicine being, to some extent, all things to all managerials, presented one of the few exceptions to the ban on intermarriages.) It was not long before he had exchanged the airfoam rubber of the psychiatrist's couch for the nurse's breasts, as a resting place for his troubled young head.

'From airfoam to airfoam,' Dinkuhl remarked cynically. 'I happen to know that wench.'

'Switch it off?' Charles suggested.

'No. Leave it. It's always been one of my favourite pastimes, torturing myself by watching this stuff. When I think of the money they spend in putting over the kind of things they put over, it makes my stomach turn but it fascinates me all the same. That girl now, the nurse. I used to have her on KF when she was only a spare-time actress; funny thing, she was in P & M then—as a clerk. She had it in her to be good. I used her in *Romeo and Juliet* a couple of years ago.'

'I saw it,' Charles said. 'It was good. That isn't the girl who was Juliet?'

'None other. And now look at her—trading on a false bust and a syruppy note in her voice which I spent God knows how many hours trying to get rid of. And doing this kind of thing.'

'It's what the public wants.'

'Don't!' Dinkuhl urged him. 'Don't drive me from my

136

usual jaundiced misery to real despair by reminding me of that.'

The screen clicked off, and Ellecott's face appeared a few seconds later. He looked distraught.

'It's necessary to make some changes. Blasting will take place sooner than we expected; almost immediately, in fact. Get into your hammocks.'

Charles shook his head. 'We don't know how to rig them.'

'I'll send someone down to——'

Charles and Dinkuhl saw Ellecott's face transfixed, the open mouth, the eyes staring, for some moments before his head slid forward to his desk. The screen showed the top of his head, with an incongruous bald spot in the centre.

'Here we go again,' Dinkuhl said.

'What the——'

'Don't talk. Take deep breaths. Keep on taking them. With astarate, the quicker you go out the less hangover you have later. I wonder who's got us now?'

5

FROM being aware of the coolness of sheets and a background of muffled speech, Charles awoke more fully to the sound of a familiar voice.

Ledbetter was saying: 'Yes, I think he's coming round now. Have you the neurasp ready, Nurse? Help me lift him up.'

Raised into sitting position, he blinked in the bright glare of sunlight through plaspex walls. The nurse gave him the neurasp pills and he swallowed them with water. The pain began to ebb. He said to Ledbetter: 'Dinkuhl?'

Ledbetter smiled. 'Right beside you. He's not come out of it yet. I think there are signs of activity now, though. Neurasp again, Nurse.'

Dinkuhl looked about him. 'I'm still wondering . . . Ledbetter! Well, I'm damned!'

Ledbetter said: 'I must apologize to both of you for putting you under with astarate, especially since I understand it was the second time in twenty-four hours. There wasn't any alternative, though. We had to act quickly.'

'They were getting ready to blast ahead of time,' Charles said. 'I take it that means they were aware a rescue party was on the way.'

'But not how far on the way it was,' Ledbetter said. 'Even

138

the notorious Interplanetary efficiency doesn't always deliver the goods. We managed to get through and break a few astarate capsules into the air intake. Not before time. If they were getting ready to blast they would have been going on to internal air control at any moment.'

Dinkuhl was staring at Ledbetter with a puzzled expression on his face. Ledbetter caught sight of it.

'Something bothering you?'

Dinkuhl hesitated, and then grinned and shook his head. 'I guess my brain's taken a beating from those two helpings of astarate. What did you do with Ellecott and the rest of the boys?'

'We left them. There are good reasons why we don't want to make an open issue of all this. I don't think they will want to, either.'

'No,' Dinkuhl said. 'I suppose not.'

'Where are we now, anyway?' Charles asked.

'Vermont. Place called Pasquin.'

'Long way from Detroit,' Dinkuhl observed.

'You slept the journey.'

Charles had been looking out of the plaspex walls of the room they were in. The view gave on to an ornamental garden, with a lake and what looked like a waterfall away up on the left. Beyond the garden's edge the ground fell away to a wide valley, bearing the marks of Agriculture's careful husbandry. In the distance there were gently rolling hills.

'What kind of an establishment is this?' Charles asked. 'It doesn't have much of the UC stamp about it.'

'It *was* a Director's mansion. You will like the layout, I fancy. I do. Marble saucepans in the kitchen and gold spittoons in the lounge. All the hooey and whatzis. I hope you like it, anyway. You'll have to put up with it for some time.'

Charles' relief at seeing Ledbetter and finding himself in the hands of his own managerial again had blinded him to

139

the circumstances which had led up to his capture by Interplanetary. He remembered now.

He said mildly: 'There was a matter of six months' sick leave that is due to me. I feel I need it more than ever.'

'Cancelled.' Ledbetter smiled. 'You'll find this a real rest home. It's called The Cottage, by the by.'

Charles said: 'I was under the impression sick leave was not subject to cancellation. Regulation—I've forgotten the number.'

'I haven't. But there's always a regulation which cancels the regulation. It's an academic point. If you were tested by P & M again I have an idea they might find you fit for duty. But I don't think we need bother with that. You broke one or two regulations yourself in this business of taking tickets for the South Pacific, and getting yourself fixed up with a new face and a GD card.'

'Is that a threat?'

Ledbetter shook his head in mock despair. 'For heaven's sake—we're not Interplanetary! You're home again, in UC. There's no need for threats, or anything else. You're amongst your own people.'

Dinkuhl said: 'Excuse me if I turn my back on this touching family scene.'

Dinkuhl got up from his bed, and went across to the plaspex wall to get a clearer view of the grounds. He was wearing a night-smock, and Charles realized that he had been fitted into one, too, while he was unconscious.

Charles said: 'I haven't noticed all that much of trust and honesty from my own people in the recent past. You weren't doing badly at persuading me the work Isaacssohn and Sarah had been doing—the work I was supposed to take over—was unimportant. And then—wham! I find myself important enough to be astarated twice in one day.'

'All right, we tried to fool you,' Ledbetter said. 'But it was for your own good. Our judgment was that your peace of mind would best be secured if you could be made to believe that Sarah Cohn was dead, and that you were simply to carry on a routine job which your superiors were too dumb to evaluate. We figured that you had already shown more than enough initiative in going after her, and we didn't see how we could keep you on the job—a vital job—if you thought there was anything to be gained in continuing the search. Meanwhile, of course, we had put Contact Section on to looking for her, and her father and Isaacssohn.'

'Have you any clues yet?'

Ledbetter shook his head. 'It's only been a couple of days, remember. You were never meant to have sick leave in the first place. I had to let you go to P & M to stall you, but we had already arranged for it to be cancelled. That was a neat business with the tickets!'

Ledbetter's face broke into a lean smile.

Charles said: 'I was wondering, a while back, how Interplanetary managed to get on to my tracks as easily as they did. The same applies to UC. How did you manage to pick up the trail?'

'Contact Sections,' said Ledbetter, 'are not always as inefficient as they generally seem. As for their methods, I'm afraid that's one regulation I have to take seriously myself— Regulation 73: Detailed information on Contact Section activities is most expressly secret and not to be divulged even within the managerial—even to a superior at the superior's request. You can just take it that anything Interplanetary can do, we can do better.'

'Now you surprise me,' Dinkuhl called from the other side of the room.

Ledbetter glanced in Dinkuhl's direction—he had his back to them—and winked at Charles. It was a wink designed to convey a lot: amusement and tolerance and complicity

141

against someone who after all was not UC. A regular guy, but not UC. It was difficult not to respond to it. It was part, after all, of the entire difference of atmosphere, of the heart-felt relief—not only at being rescued and being spared Luna City, but also, more subtly, of being back: a confirmation that the world was not quite as bad as all that.

Charles grinned in return.

Dinkuhl came over and sat on the edge of his bed, his knees spread under his night-smock.

'Well,' he remarked. 'Have we got it on the deck now? Charlie is still the guest who mustn't leave? You wouldn't have a little lab fitted up for him out back?'

Ledbetter and Charles both laughed. Ledbetter said:

'It so happens ... the stuff isn't here yet, but there's a good suite of rooms that can be used. The Director used to have a model layout of the old train systems in them. Very good light. We shall look after you, Charles.'

It was the first time Ledbetter had used his given name. Charles was not disposed to think much about that because he was still too amazed by the fact that Ledbetter was treating what he had thought to be Dinkuhl's joke seriously.

Charles said: 'You mean that? I'm not to go back to San Miguel?'

Ledbetter made a gesture of negation.

'But the idea was that I should go back there.'

'Shall we put it this way?' Ledbetter said. 'That this recent affair has given us something of a shock. Naturally we had woken up to the fact that some managerial or managerials had wanted the other two badly enough to take some trouble about getting hold of them. As a result we were prepared to have to look after you very very carefully indeed. But we now realize that we must be a lot more careful even than we had planned. San Miguel is out. It would be like putting the honey back in the hollow tree once the bears had found it.'

'So instead of San Miguel there's Pasquin. We think we have covered our tracks this time. There'll be ample guard on, just in case we haven't. Incidentally, I'm afraid I have to be just a little awkward. The garden and grounds—you will be able to use them as soon as our security plans are fully fixed, but that won't be for two or three days. Till then, we'd like you to stay home.'

Dinkuhl looked up, succeeding in wrinkling his bald patch; it was a physical mannerism he had exploited on KF, generally when he was being satirical about something.

'I take it I'm not out of line in assuming that everything you say to Charlie—anyway, on the negative side—applies to me equally.'

Ledbetter nodded. 'That's right.'

Dinkuhl said: 'So. Charlie may be home with Momma, but it looks like I'm still prisoner. Different base, but still prisoner.'

'Could be worse,' Ledbetter suggested. Dinkuhl looked at him. 'Could be Luna City. This is your tough luck, Dinkuhl. You just happened to have got mixed up with something big, and I'm afraid you'll have to sit in on it for the duration.' He glanced at Dinkuhl speculatively. 'You walked in on your own two feet.'

Dinkuhl smiled. *Touché!* All right then, no complaints. You'll do one little thing for me?'

'Within reason and ability.'

'I've got an assistant. No cap on that "a." He's not what I would pick for my successor, not by some distance, but he should be able to keep the flag flying for—for the duration I think you said? If I give you a message with some elementary instructions—mostly operating guff and so on—will you get it through to him for me?'

'Don't see why not. Provided it's in English.'

'You set my anxious mind at rest,' Dinkuhl said. 'Now

143

that I have done my duty, I guess I can take it easy. I don't land any chores here, do I? Prisoner's rights?'

'No chores. I wouldn't mind the life.'

'One little thing. So small it embarrasses me to mention it. I suffer mildly from satyriasis.'

Ledbetter smiled. 'See what we can do.'

Dinkuhl raised his hand. 'I'm not asking you to prostitute the virgins of United Chemicals. This is a horse that works for its feed, and likes it that way. Just so it isn't an exclusively male staff, I'll manage O.K.'

'Set your mind at rest,' Ledbetter said. 'But right at rest. We shall do what we can to make this a happy and profitable stay for both of you. The only difference is that we shall expect Charles to do a little real work now and then.'

'The ties of home,' Dinkuhl said. 'A homeless wanderer like me must sometimes think of them with a pang. Charlie now, looking cheerful about the prospect of sorting out his bag of tricks, for the glory of UC and the use of a gold spittoon. And a little while back he was spurning a Directorship.'

'We put first things first,' Ledbetter said. 'The important thing is the job.' He looked at Charles. 'There will be a Directorship afterwards. You can take that for granted. Just now we've got to keep you here and under supervision, for reasons you appreciate as well as we do. You have already been promoted Manager, but it would be pointless to create you a Director until you can be one in fact as well as name. You see that?'

Charles nodded. It was odd, being told so casually of the Managership he had abandoned as out of reach more than ten years ago. Odd, and unimportant.

Dinkuhl said: 'Whatever goldfish bowl they put you in, Charlie, you just bob right up to the top. Mind you don't pop right out of the water.'

The words were as trivial-sounding as Dinkuhl's generally

were, but Charles wondered whether there was not a little more edge to his voice. He wasn't going to worry over it, anyway.

Ledbetter said: 'It's been quite a rush job, and I've got a few things to look after. You have a four-room suite here, with a sun-terrace leading from the next room. But that's just for your privacy—you are at liberty to roam all over The Cottage, and incidentally there's a very nice bar on the other side of the house. I'll probably be seeing you there later.'

'If not sooner,' Dinkuhl suggested.

'Button for service. The buttons are marked, but the one that says "2nd Chambermaid" brings you the nurse—just in case you have any after-effects from your double astarating.' He glanced at Dinkuhl. 'She's here for the duration, too, but since she's P & M we are rather more responsible for her than for the rest.'

Dinkuhl nodded gravely. 'I shall treat her with the reverence due to a Ming saucer, providing I can find the odd plastitasse to cool my coffee in.'

'Well, that's that.' To Charles, Ledbetter said: 'We're getting the stuff through for the lab as quickly as possible, but it will take a few days. Take it easy till then.' He paused slightly. 'I hope you will be able to take it easy. We know how concerned you are over Sarah Cohn. But you do realize, don't you, that by yourself you could never have hoped to rescue her? All you could do would be to put yourself in jeopardy of capture—as you did, of course.

'At least you know now that UC Contact Section is on the job, and I think it's as good a Contact Section as any you are likely to find. If anyone can get her, they will. And meanwhile you have the consolation of knowing that whoever has her will be looking after her. She is as valuable a piece of property to them as you were to Interplanetary.'

145

Charles said : 'I suppose so.'

'An added incentive when we have the lab fitted up! The sooner this business is over, the sooner things get back to normal.'

'Providing, of course,' Dinkuhl said, 'that as good a Contact Section as any you are likely to find doesn't turn the goods up even sooner.'

'Exactly,' Ledbetter said. He glanced from his finger-watch to Charles, including him again in that managerial warmth from which Dinkuhl, with all his many qualities, had excluded himself. 'I must streak. Have a good time.'

When they were left alone, Charles and Dinkuhl explored the remainder of the suite that had been allotted them. The room in which they had woken up was one of the bedrooms; there was a similar one at the other end of the suite. In between there were good-sized rooms for diner and lounge, which could be thrown together. The lounge gave on to the sun-terrace Ledbetter had mentioned; it presented much the same view as had been visible through the bedroom's plaspex wall, but took in a wider expanse. They were on the east side of the house, and there was some fitful sunlight on it now. But in any case the little artificial sunlets hung overhead—three of them—only waiting the touch of the actuating button.

The furnishings were twentieth-century Scandinavian in the bedrooms and Louis XIV in the remainder of the suite; the former had at least the advantage of emphasizing the grace and elegance of the latter. In the lounge even the TV screen on the wall was covered, when not in use, by an Aubusson; the tapestry slid away from view while the valves were picking up. Dinkuhl tried this, and hurriedly buttoned the Aubusson back into place at the sight of Loulou del Keith's mouth stretched in agonized sensual song. He went across to the gilt-inlaid sideboard and found drinks for both of them.

146

'Brandy,' Dinkuhl said. He sniffed. 'And not half bad brandy, at that. You know, Charlie, this is a very pleasant set-up altogether. Had I but known you did yourself so well in UC, I might have tossed my anti-managerialism over my shoulder and applied for membership. Too late now, I guess.'

Charles said: 'You forget my new and exalted position. I suppose it's always good at the top.'

'Not managerial-wise, it isn't. Just bigger and broader scope for bad taste. The guy who fixed this place up must have been an exception. I think I am going to enjoy myself for as long as the good Ledbetter feels obliged to keep me.'

Charles said: 'There's something about Ledbetter. You notice anything? He looks as though he specializes in putting people at ease, but I never feel properly at ease with him. There's a feeling that there's something else behind everything he's saying so simply and straightforwardly. You feel anything like that?'

Dinkuhl looked at him quizzically for a moment; then he shook his head. 'Can't say I've noticed anything. Maybe it's because you weren't trained in the diplomatic arts that the old syrup doesn't taste the way it should. And then—you will be inclined to look critically at anything Ledbetter says because you found he was giving you the old malarkey once before. But he's explained why he had to do that. It all seems to be on the level this time. He didn't even promise you they would get Sarah Cohn; he could have invented the odd clue to keep your nose stretching after the carrot. He only told you the UC Contact Section is after her, and that it's as good a section as any other managerial can offer. And that doesn't seem an unreasonable claim in view of the way they got us out of our recent predicament.'

Charles sipped the brandy. He had got into the habit of expecting iconoclasm from Dinkuhl, and for that reason he

147

was faintly astonished to find him now an apologist for Ledbetter and UC. But he saw that there was no real basis for his astonishment. Apart from the time immediately after their capture by Interplanetary, when his mind had been in a confusion in which everyone, even Dinkuhl, was likely to be part of the monstrous hostile forces leagued against him, he had found Dinkuhl an honest ally. And it was the function of an honest ally to discern and approve his good fortunes, as well as help fight against the bad.

All the same, there was something that didn't chime.

Charles said: 'I thought I was the bomb that was going to blow things higher than sky-high. You don't seem worried that the bomb's back in its old rack again.'

'Should I be?' Dinkuhl asked. 'There are more bombs than one. You go right ahead and do as you're told, Charlie. I'm the disruptive element but as long as things are disrupting nicely on their own I don't mind sitting back and enjoying my creature comforts. And I've got sufficient old-fashioned horse-sense to see that it's better to be on this sideline than one that stretches up to Luna City. They make their own hooch up there, from a concentrate.' He sipped his brandy. 'I'm told it tastes like nothing on earth, which I suppose is only reasonable.'

'So that's O.K.,' Charles said. 'So long as you have your creature comforts.'

'Relax,' Dinkuhl advised him. 'You're still keyed up. That reminds me.' He walked across to the service panel, which was set alongside the TV control panel. '2nd Chambermaid is out. We could try 1st, I guess.'

He pressed the button, and looked expectantly towards the door. Charles watched him with amusement.

The girl who came in was a young and magnificent blonde of height rather above average and figure to match; she was dressed in a well-designed uniform in the UC colours of green and gold, and with the UC monogram in appropriate places.

She addressed herself to Charles: 'At your service, Manager.'

Charles jerked his head towards Dinkuhl. 'His need is greater than mine. He buttoned you, at any rate.'

Dinkuhl looked at her in open admiration. 'I'm trying to remember what it was I wanted. Honey, you've driven every single thought right out of my head.'

She smiled thoughtfully. 'I guess amnesia comes under Lydia's department—she's the nurse. 2nd Chambermaid's button, or I'll get her for you, if you like.'

'Don't go,' Dinkuhl said. 'I'm beginning to recover, in part. What did you say your name was, sunlet?'

'I didn't. Myra.'

'Myra, I'm your admirer. Call me Hiram, Myra.'

Gradually, over the next few days, Charles began to make himself at home, as Dinkuhl had done from the beginning. The Cottage was an extensive and well-appointed mansion, and there was an atmosphere surprisingly free from the consciousness of grade that Charles had previously accepted as part of the natural order of managerial life. Although, with the exception of Ledbetter and himself, there was none who seemed to have any higher appointment than Assistant, and the majority were not even of that level, they did not show any particular deference in their attitudes. Ledbetter, as well as Charles and Dinkuhl, was treated in a way that made the difference in rank appear relatively unimportant, and that contributed to the establishment of a kind of holiday spirit.

Ledbetter, Charles knew, functioned best in an atmosphere of this kind—there had been the case of Paulton, on that first visit of his to Ledbetter, which now seemed so long ago.

149

But Paulton had been an Official, and Ledbetter's personal aide. The surprising thing was not that Ledbetter tolerated, or even encouraged this kind of attitude, but that the people themselves were capable of adopting it. Perhaps Saginaw had not been typical; and his experience had, after all, been confined largely to Saginaw.

Whatever the reasons, it made life pleasant. The whole project—everyone appeared to know that The Cottage was to house a laboratory from which, with Charles' help, great things were expected—was treated jocularly but with no suggestion of carelessness. Charles spent about an hour each morning in checking the fittings of the lab itself, but that was mainly a question of making suggestions on layout, and approving the previous day's work. Things were dropping into place with remarkable smoothness and efficiency. A fair part of the remainder of the day came to be spent in the bar, on the west side, which was a very good bar indeed, or in the library adjoining. To someone who had been used to associating the term library with a collection of two or three dozen tattered volumes, there was something awesome about a room lined with shelves that were solidly packed with books, and mostly in first-class condition. Two of his earliest discoveries were a Shakespeare First Folio, in calf, and a Thurber—*Leave Your Mind Alone*—which had been marked "Probably lost" in Marantovich's critical assessment and bibliography.

Dinkuhl accepted and shared his enthusiasm, but Dinkuhl was consumed by other enthusiasms as well. Myra proved to be only one of a number of comely females around the house, although they saw more of her than most, since they were more directly her concern. It was an odd thing that they conformed to a physical pattern. They were, with one exception, tall blondes, and they were affably extrovert in disposition. It was Dinkuhl who drew Charles' attention to

150

this while they were in the bar one evening, drinking lager before dinner.

'Blonde and big, big and blonde, a type of which I'm more than fond,' he remarked. 'Tennyson, I believe.'

Charles looked around. There was Susie, polishing a glass behind the bar, and Anthea, who had something to do with the catering arrangements and who was just now buffing her nails over a dry Martini. He thought of the rest.

'It's a funny thing,' he said. 'There does seem to be something of a concentration. Except——'

Dinkuhl glanced at him. 'Except Lydia. What type would you say she was?'

It was a point that Charles had considered before. For Lydia was very much the same physical type as Sarah—dark, not very tall, rather squarely built. She also gave an appearance of being shy; friendly enough, but reluctant to initiate conversations. It was not the nervous shyness Sarah had shown to him when they first met, but it was effective in marking her out as different from the rest.

Charles said: 'She reminds me a little . . . but how do you know that? You never saw Sarah.'

'Jot it down to my remarkable intuition. When I see so stately an array of blondes, I have two thoughts. The second is: these are hand-picked—why? One good reason would be to set off someone quite different, and Ledbetter did take the trouble to warn me off one particular track. So that makes Lydia the nigger in the woodpile.' Dinkuhl shrugged. 'Since so many other things around here are contrived for your delight, and you are the monogamous type, it was a fairly reasonable deduction to make.'

'Well I'm damned! They couldn't have thought that would work?'

'On my guess, it's a P & M proposition. It has all the earmarks. Don't forget Stenner's neat little behaviouristic

151

explanation of your conduct. People think people work that way. And they're not altogether wrong. Lydia's a nice kid. If our present arrangements were to last some considerable length of time, you would be bound to appreciate that more and more forcibly. Especially from seeing me cavort with these blondes, who are also nice kids but of an emphatically different type.'

'Do you think she's in on the scheme, too—Lydia?'

Dinkuhl shook his head. 'I told you—she's a nice kid.'

'Do you . . . does that mean that they aren't really looking for Sarah, after all?'

'Don't worry about that. They want Sarah, and they want Isaacssohn, too. Meanwhile they want you to be happy. It should have occurred to you that—supposing you three are now split between three managerials—everything probably depends on who can settle their genius in best. In that respect UC have an advantage over the others—your natural attachment of your managerial. You will be likely to put your back into the job; it's arguable whether whoever has Isaacssohn or Sarah will be getting results as good. It might have taken Interplanetary quite some time to settle you down in that Luna City lab.'

'Quite some time.' Charles thought a moment. 'Ledbetter must have worked fast, fixing all this.'

'Ledbetter,' Dinkuhl commented, 'commands admiration.'

It was impossible, after his conversation with Dinkuhl, to avoid paying rather more attention to Lydia. It was true that he found her refreshing after the off-handed breeziness of the other women around the place. But closer acquaintance did not bring home the resemblance to Sarah; the reverse, in fact. There was a softness about her which was not unpleasant, but which was most unlike Sarah's spirited sturdiness. He was amused to note how Ledbetter, casually but with care, fostered the friendship between them.

One afternoon Charles had been sitting with Ledbetter in the roof-garden; it was a *tour-de-force*, a tropical garden in New England, in November. Overhead more than a dozen sunlets dripped their light and heat on to the luxuriance of plants that surrounded the central pool in which curious fishes from the Barrier Reef swam over brilliant matching corals. It was a popular resort for the people in The Cottage, but this afternoon, there were only Charles and Ledbetter. And Ledbetter, after chatting for a while, got up and left; he was due back in Detroit to check the routing arrangements for the new electrobombard.

Left alone, Charles lay back in the airfoam summer-seat and watched the angry November clouds drift past, high above the pattern of sunlets which provided this exotic warmth in which he was relaxing. He was in swim-trunks, but he could not summon up the energy to plunge into the pool. He wondered if it would rain. It made no difference if it did; a servomechanism was arranged to react to the first drops and operate the two halves of the plaspex shell which would rise from either side of the house's circular top and join overhead. Charles had never seen this in operation. He was speculating on the chances this afternoon, and looking forward to the possibility with a natural schoolboy's anticipation in the mechanical novelty, when he heard the sound of feminine shoes clipping along the path towards him. He raised himself on one shoulder. It was Lydia.

He made room for her on the summer-seat, at the same time easing it forward into a more upright and respectable position. She remained standing, though. She had her small P & M satchel over one shoulder.

'George said you wanted me,' she told him.

153

He had learned to call Ledbetter 'George' himself, though not very easily. The others seemed to do it naturally.

Charles said disbelievingly: 'George said that?'

Lydia said primly: 'He said something about your being over-tired; he mentioned a vit pick-me-up. I brought some in my bag.'

Charles saw the point now. He said gravely:

'He misunderstood me. It was laziness, not fatigue. You could help all the same, I imagine. I need someone to encourage me into some kind of physical activity. If you haven't anything better to do you could lead me into the pool.'

She hesitated, and then smiled. 'I'll go down for my swim-suit.'

Charles pointed to the plastic robing cubicle, neatly camouflaged by palms. 'Why bother?'

'I've never tried them.'

There was a wistful note in her voice.

'Now's a good time to try, then.'

She let herself be persuaded, and he watched her disappear behind the palms. He had tried the plastic rober himself a few days before, but found that he preferred more ordinary swim-trunks. It was an expensive gadget, and it was not surprising that he had not encountered it before, although it was featured often enough on TV swimming programmes.

The person wishing to be robed stood naked on a small mat in the centre of the cubicle. Mechanical caliper arms went over the body first, checking the measurements. Then the applicator arms followed the course laid down, applying an opaque plastic that fitted closely to the body and dried on contact. An adjustment for different heights of costume was possible, and for different colours and textures within a limited range. After use, the plastic swim-suit was ripped along a weaker seam at the front, and discarded.

154

It was not particularly popular. Most men found, as Charles had done, something unpleasant about the procedure. Some women affected to find it so, too, or with more subtlety complained of the poor range of choice offered. Another possible reason was that the device only flattered a naturally good figure; it was pitiless to a bad one.

Charles was pleased to find that Lydia came unhesitatingly into the first category. She had chosen a silky texture and a bright red colour which set off her dark hair and rather dusky skin. It was also evident that she had followed the instructional advice for women in clasping her hands behind her head and bracing her head back. Unnecessarily in her case; the lily was a little over-gilded—and such an unawareness of her own physical excellence was pleasant and unusual in itself. She walked along the side of the pool and stood in front of him, waiting for his comment.

'Very nice,' he said. 'It suits you.'

'Do you think so?' She shuddered. 'Horrible feeling, though—those rubber arms! I don't think I'll use it again.'

Charles nodded. 'To be used once, just for the experience. I should think one would always have the lurking fear that it might go berserk, and spin one into some great cocoon of plastic like a spider with a fly.'

She laughed. 'Well? Ready to be led in?'

They plunged into the pool, startling a small shoal of rainbow-coloured fish, about the size of trout, and sending them fleeting across towards the other side. They chased them for a short time, but soon lost them. The water was warm and buoyant. It was very pleasant swimming lazily around with Lydia; so pleasant that he could not avoid picturing Sarah on some goddess-like eminence, watching them with cynical amusement. It also occurred to him that if UC were trying such blandishment on him, it was not unlikely that whatever managerial had Sarah might be plying her with young Adonises—probably, since they had no reason to suspect her of the attachment which in his own case had become so notorious, with Adonises whose features had an Israeli cast.

For that matter, he had no real reason to think that Sarah reciprocated in any way his own feelings. Because she was fundamentally so honest a person he had been able to see that she did not dislike him—that she had actually come to like him, in fact. But that was a far cry from being in love. There was a good chance that Sarah, whose antagonism to managerialism had only been less pronounced than Dinkuhl's because she was less concerned, had settled tolerantly and equably into her new surroundings, whatever they were. In which case one of the theoretical Adonises might well have taken his place. He grinned, remembering. At least he had learned that, as an Israeli, she did not approve of promiscuity!

Lydia drew herself up on to the flat stones which made an island in the centre of the pool, and he followed her. You approached the stones through an umbrella of spray from a fountain which cast its drops well clear of their origin. On the stones you could look up and see the small perfect rainbow formed between spray and sunlets. The sunlets' rays, filtered through this shifting curtain, were tempered but still warm.

Charles lay on his back. Lydia was sitting on a flat stone eminence close by him. The water rolled in large droplets from the surface of the plastic that covered her.

Charles said drowsily: 'Much better than Luna City. I believe they have to ration the water there.'

The fountain rustled somnolently overhead. A large blue fish nosed up curiously towards the stones and then, with a whisk, darted back into the recesses of the pool.

Lydia said: 'There's a feeling of being cut off, here. Do you notice that, Charles?'

156

Her voice was pleasantly modulated; without the vigour of Sarah's but also without the impression, that Sarah's gave, of a possible sharp edge just beneath the surface.

'So we are cut off,' Charles said. 'Cut off from the managerial world, here on the roof of The Cottage. All very paradoxical.'

'The fountain,' she said. 'And I suppose the sound of it more than anything else. Charles, when do you start your work in the laboratory?'

'Too soon. The last of the stuff will be in within a couple of days.'

'Is it important—the work you will be doing?'

'Everyone seems to think so. Yes, I suppose it is.'

There was silence for a while. Charles patted the flat stones on which he was lying.

'Come on down,' he said. 'It's more comfortable than sitting up there.'

Lydia eased herself down on to the stones. She lay on her stomach beside him, resting her head on her elbows. Their bodies were not far from touching. She bent her head towards his; he would have thought flirtatiously except that her face was entirely serious.

She said: 'I've wanted to tell you——'

She broke off, and they both looked up. The fountain, abruptly, had cut off. The silence that took the place of its whispering linked them at once with the rest of the pool, with the garden, and the house on which it rested. Charles got up.

'That's funny,' he said.

He climbed up to the fountain head, to see if it had been blocked by anything, but there was nothing there. As he was climbing down again, he heard a call from across the pool. Ledbetter was coming out of the lift that gave on to the roof-garden. He had swim-trunks over one arm; he waved cheerfully to them, and disappeared into a robing cubicle.

157

Charles said to Lydia: 'What was it you wanted to tell me—before George comes over?'

Her smile was enigmatic, regretful. 'Nothing much, really. That I may have to leave here, quite soon.'

He said with surprise: 'Leave? Why?'

'There's some talk of a recall of P & M members—I'm not UC, remember.'

Charles looked at her; she was sitting, very decoratively, on the edge of the island, her feet trailing in the clear blue-green water.

'I hope you won't.' He saw Ledbetter come out of the cubicle and fling himself, flat-bellied, into the water. Thinking of Ledbetter's little scheme of applied psychology, he smiled to himself. 'I don't think you will.'

Ledbetter came snorting up to the island and levered himself on to it with one quick movement.

He said: 'Mind if I join you? Detroit's off for this afternoon, apparently. They got through to tell me the shipping has been held up.' He smiled. 'The usual Telecom foul-up, I guess.'

Lydia sat staring into the water. Charles said: 'Room for a couple of dozen on this contraption. How do you like Lydia's plastisuit?'

Ledbetter looked at her with calculation. 'I wouldn't be surprised to find she had blown half a dozen fuses in the rober. Lydia, my love, you were being paged on the callscreens just before I came up. I don't suppose it was important.'

Lydia got up quickly. 'I'll go down and find out.'

Charles said: 'It would have had an Urgent prefix if it had been important in any way.'

She smiled at him. 'I suppose so. But I'm silly about telecalls; once I know there's one waiting, I worry about it. See you both later.'

She dived in and swam strongly for the side. The two men watched her.

Charles said: 'Funny thing. The fountain's stopped. I thought your gadgets here were more foolproof than that.'

'It's hard to make gadgets foolproof,' Ledbetter said. 'Could be they've stopped it to change oil in the main pumps. In that case it should be on again soon.'

The fine spray leapt out just as Lydia climbed out of the pool and began to walk towards the cubicle where she had left her clothes.

'There you are,' Ledbetter said easily.

That was the last Charles saw of Lydia. Ledbetter mentioned her going at breakfast next morning. He smeared his roll with the new Hydroponics Breakfast Special, and said:

'We've lost Lydia, more's the pity.'

Dinkuhl looked up from scratching a leg. 'In what way?'

'Recall. Don't ask me why—P & M do that kind of thing at intervals. We couldn't properly hold her, and for that matter she was only supposed to be here in case of post-astarate complications in one of you two.'

'Nice of you to include me,' Dinkuhl remarked.

Charles said: 'She mentioned something about the possibility of recall yesterday.'

Ledbetter nodded. 'It was in the wind.'

'I told her it wouldn't go through.' Ledbetter glanced at him in inquiry. 'I thought my—my comfort would be put first. It seems I was wrong.'

Ledbetter laughed. 'You saw through our little stunt? I guessed you had—and that it hadn't worked. That helped to make Lydia dispensable, too, though we were all sorry to see her go. It was just an idea—P & M asked if we wanted any physical type of nurse—it seems there's a new craze of matching the patient's psychological needs in nurses. I

159

thought of you, and then thought it would be amusing to put the other girls in to create the right setting. So help me, it was all innocent fun. And I didn't really expect it to work.'

Dinkuhl said: 'One thing strikes me as odd. You haven't let the girl go back to her managerial carrying all the details of this set-up? Not that I should think she was the blabbing type, but it seems silly after the other precautions you have taken.'

'Hypnotic dememorizing. We have taken one week out of her life. She's been paid well for it, of course.'

'She agreed.'

'You can only do it with volition. She signed the agreement and took the preliminary hypnosis before she came here. We should not have taken her otherwise.'

'I take back,' Dinkuhl said, 'my unwarrantable suspicion that UC could have slipped up on so elementary a point as that. What a wonderful device is science! How easy, how simple, to erase us all from that universe which is the consciousness of Lydia. Snip, snip, and we are not even ghosts. We are only strangers.'

The news made Charles mildly sorry; he had liked her and he supposed that with long acquaintance the liking might have been deeper and stronger. As it was . . . a possible source of temptation, he felt, had been removed. Though it was rather disconcerting, as Dinkuhl had suggested, to think of oneself being so obliterated from the memory of someone one had known.

He said irrelevantly: 'I suppose she won't realize that she has actually used a plastic rober—she said she had never used one before.'

'Nor how well it became her,' said Ledbetter. 'I have some good news for you both this morning, by the way.'

'Not more blondes?' Dinkuhl commented. 'One can have too much of a good thing—at one time, anyway.'

160

'You can use the garden and grounds. The barrier has been completed. You'll have twenty or thirty acres to roam in. Not quite liberty, but the best we can do.'

Dinkuhl said: 'We don't have to use them?'

'Naturally not.'

With relief, Dinkuhl said: 'I have plenty to occupy me right here, and I'm not precisely the garden type.'

'I'll be glad of the change, anyway,' Charles said. 'I might take a walk right after breakfast.'

'Go right ahead,' Ledbetter said cordially. 'I'd join you but that the Detroit trip's finally on again.'

'What it is,' Dinkuhl observed, 'to be the passenger on a jaunt like this.'

Charles walked on his own in the grounds that morning; and the next—Ledbetter did not say anything else about joining him. He was glad of the solitariness, and glad also to be away, for a time, from the centrally-heated Cottage and its sub-tropical roof-garden. The weather outside had turned sharply cold, and it was bracing to walk through the bare outdoor garden and into the scattered timber beyond. The deciduous trees were bare, of course, but there was a belt of evergreens to the north and east from which the house was completely hidden.

The main track from the house led through these evergreens to a massive gate in the barrier fence which, heavily wired and with the ground cleared for five yards on either side, stretched around the perimeter of the grounds. Charles stood for a while gazing curiously at the gate. It was a check-point; a guard in UC uniform nursed his Klaberg rifle inside a small sentry-box with a plastic bubble top. The small nozzle in the plastic, just above the box's waistline, would be the astarater: a touch from the guard's finger could blanket the area around in a few seconds.

Quite an adequate safeguard. Theoretically someone might shoot the guard through the plastic, but that would actuate an alarm system, touch off the astarate, and bring a gyro from the house almost as quickly. A situation that would be infuriating to someone anxious to escape; he was pleased that he was not in that frame of mind himself.

He watched the guard changed. The gyro side-slipped through the air from the roof of The Cottage, and dropped on to the track just inside the gate. The new guard got out and, after a word or two, the old guard took his place. The gyro climbed back to its eyrie through the damp wintry air. Informal but effective. Charles walked on, his footsteps deadened by pine needles.

On the third morning, as he reached the edge of a clearing among the pines, he heard a low whistle. He turned quickly. Dinkuhl was standing by the side of a tree, watching him. He beckoned Charles over.

Charles said: 'Playing Indians?'

Dinkuhl, instead of answering directly, glanced at the massive watch he wore on his wrist.

He said: 'Charlie boy, time is short. Come over here and sit down.'

There was a fallen tree. They made themselves comfortable and Dinkuhl brought out cigarettes. They lit up. The smoke rose in straight plumes; it was cold but there was no wind this morning.

Dinkuhl said: 'You happy here?'

'Tolerably.' Charles glanced at him. 'You seem to be.'

'What's the difference between being held here and being held by Interplanetary—ruling out Luna City for the moment.'

'That's a lot to rule out. Quite a difference.'

The important difference—that here he was with his own

162

managerial—was one it would have been embarrassing to put plainly to Dinkuhl.

Dinkuhl glanced at him, smiling a little. 'Such as being in the bosom of United Chemicals?'

'I wouldn't rule that out. It's what I'm used to.

'And what makes you confident this is a UC set-up? That they wear the right badges?'

Charles looked at him in complete astonishment. He saw what Dinkuhl might be driving at, but it was a conception so fantastic as to be hardly within the bounds of sane speculation.

He said reasonably: 'You forget something, Hiram. Ledbetter was my Manager at Detroit.'

Dinkuhl nodded. 'For your work in the lab here—you said you were going to ask Ledbetter for your old assistant from Saginaw. Did you ever do that?' Charles nodded. 'And——?'

'He wasn't available. Reasonable enough. Ledbetter told me they have a couple of good youngsters they're bringing over from Europe.'

'So, apart from Ledbetter, there aren't any UC people here you can recognize?'

'It isn't likely there would be. They're mostly Contact Section, after all.'

Dinkuhl wrinkled the top of his head. 'Let that go. Where would you say we were before Ledbetter and the boys launched their Men of the Mounties rescue stunt?'

Whatever harebrained notion Dinkuhl had got hold of, the sensible way of treating it, Charles recognized, was to meet his points logically and sensibly. He said:

'In one of Interplanetary's spaceships—freighter, type 7, by your reckoning—in the Toledo pits.'

Dinkuhl grinned. 'Quite some Contact Section, as Ledbetter said. Breaking and entering the Toledo pits at a time when Interplanetary had their most treasured possession

163

stowed away on a freighter there. But that wasn't what roused my suspicions. I told you when I first met you in that phoney messroom that we should keep quiet about everything that mattered. One of the things that mattered was that that freighter was wrong in small details. Minor things. They had pop-out tables, but they'd missed the pop-up ashtrays; I had to stub my cigarette on the TV control panel. And the corridors hadn't taken the battering all round that they get from use in free fall—the track was all worn on the floor. Something else, too. I'll come to that.

'Anyway, the thing to do was to string them along, whoever they might be, and wait for something else to happen. In due course, it did. United Chemicals to the rescue. Virtue triumphant.'

Charles said: 'It strikes me as crazy. I hope you don't mind my saying that. Why should UC—or whoever you think it is masquerading as UC—do something as complicated as that? And what about the offer Interplanetary made me? I might have accepted it—what then?'

'That puzzled me a little,' Dinkuhl admitted. 'I wondered how they would fake the take-off, and the space flight, and the lunar conditions. Not impossible, but very very tricky. But there was no real need for them to do so. Had you taken the offer, there was nothing to stop them changing their minds and keeping you on an Earth base; it's easy enough to think of adequate reasons. You were never meant to take the offer, of course: it was put simply to soften you up psychologically, to ensure you were properly grateful for being rescued. Even if you had taken the offer, the rescue might still have taken place, for much the same reason.

'As for the complications, the people who pulled this job are not inartistic. They have you summed up as loyal to your managerial, and unlikely to be genuinely at ease under terms of constraint to any other. At the same time, you had shown

164

signs of initiative and some rebelliousness, so if they put on the UC cloak at the beginning and clapped you in custody for your own good, you might very well be awkward about it. Their solution was good: have you captured by—as you thought—Interplanetary, and then rescued by—as it seemed —United Chemicals. Up goes loyalty and gratitude; down goes rebelliousness.'

Thinking he saw a flaw, Charles said:

'The fact that the spaceship was a fake may show that it wasn't Interplanetary who had us at first, but it doesn't mean it wasn't UC——'

He broke off. Dinkuhl said: 'It does, though, doesn't it? When I woke up and saw Ledbetter, I wondered. When I heard him talk about rescuing us from Interplanetary, I knew the play was still going on. If it had been a genuine business, he would have mentioned the name of the real villains.'

'But what if the whole scheme you've outlined was planned by UC—for the reasons you gave, which would apply almost as well in that case as in the other?'

'Yours,' Dinkuhl said, 'was a simple-minded managerial, as managerials go. But in any case, I happen to know we are not now being run by UC. Come back to that. You didn't feel quite easy in your own mind, when you first woke up in The Cottage, did you?'

Charles said: 'It didn't amount to much. As I recall, it was you that put me at ease again.'

'I'm rather pleased with the way I've handled this.' Dinkuhl smiled. 'I have my vanity, difficult as it may be to observe it. But luck has run my way, too. The fact that I made such a business of warning you, on the spaceship, that the walls had eyes and ears, told in my favour when I carefully didn't warn you after Ledbetter and the boys picked us up. I played everything for the audience when I was

165

talking to you. Even, especially, when I put you on to the little scheme with Lydia. The safest man is the man who thinks he can see through things—so I let them see I thought I could see through things: little things. Like that spaceship being a 7 freighter, and Lydia being the velvet jewel in a sparkling setting. They had me taped. I gave you a couple of days on your own wandering through the grounds, too. I slipped out today.'

Dinkuhl grinned. 'I'd made me a schedule with Myra. Mornings about this time we spend happily together. My guess was she would have seen to blanketing her apartment; she has her modesty. I got some pills from Lydia for insomnia two or three days back. Myra is dreaming sweet dreams right now. Everyone else thinks I'm sharing them.'

Charles said: 'Lydia——'

Dinkuhl nodded. 'She left in a hurry, didn't she? My guess was she wasn't safe to have around any longer—she maybe thought you were too nice a guy to be fooled that way. Ledbetter read her mind.'

Charles said: 'Those spying devices—just how good are they?'

'Good enough.'

Charles saw now. He told Dinkuhl the details of his last conversation with Lydia.

Dinkuhl said: 'Right enough. She thought the noise of the fountain would knock them out, I guess. So as soon as she started to talk, they cut the fountain just to show her. Then Ledbetter came up to make things tidy. He had probably been waiting down below—they maybe guessed she wasn't safe before that.'

'But—telling me she was going?'

'She knew she was going. That way she could at least be fairly sure of going with a whole skin.'

'She might not have done?'

166

'This,' Dinkuhl observed, 'is the major league. No fooling.'

Charles said slowly: 'It's hard to believe that.'

'If it were easy to believe it, they would have slipped up. And they don't slip up on atmospheres—they've had plenty of training in them.'

There was a moment's silence. Then Charles said:

'All right. They're not UC. Who are they?'

Dinkuhl flicked the stub of his cigarette up into the gloomy branches of the firs.

'Who,' he asked, 'would be likely to have a mock-up of a spaceship? That was the big question. If not Interplanetary —who?'

'Go on. It doesn't mean anything to me.'

'It did to me. Something else confirmed it—a certain kind of track, marking the surface both in the corridors and the messroom. I knew what caused that track. TV camera cables. It was a mock-up Telecom had built for shooting spaceship interiors for the space opera serials. I made my final check after we landed here. Remember I told Ledbetter I wanted to send a message through to my assistant on KF—technical advice? Ledbetter said yes without hesitating. He would have hesitated all right if he had been UC, because UC don't have anyone who knows enough about TV operational jargon to be sure I wasn't passing a message outside. Telecom do.'

'Telecom,' Charles said. 'Well, I'm damned.'

Dinkuhl grinned. 'We both are. You'll soon see. It would take Telecom to have the kind of spy equipment this house has, too, incidentally.'

Anger was beginning to replace confusion in Charles' mind. He said tightly to Dinkuhl:

'What are we going to do?'

Dinkuhl looked at him. 'You're the H-bomb. The way I see it, you can do one of three things. You can go back and

167

get on with the job for your new employers. I take it that's out?' Charles nodded. 'Or you can go back and refuse to get on with the job. I don't advise that. Ledbetter has plenty on the ball, and he's playing for big stakes, remember.'

The confusion returned. Charles said:

'Ledbetter *was* UC. How does he come to be working for Telecom. I just don't get it.'

'*Sancta simplicitas,*' Dinkuhl commented. 'You wouldn't get it. I know a little about Ledbetter. He had a tough start— a background that would have been damn bad even in previous centuries. Both parents drunkards and fighting. He was a bright kid. He fought his way up to the top. But the top goes right up to the sky for that kind of climber. And managerial loyalty is only skin-deep, if that. No, George isn't the kind of playmate I recommend for you.'

'The third thing. What was that?'

Dinkuhl eyed him steadily. 'Escape.'

Charles looked around. Through the trees the barrier fence was visible, rising to perhaps ten feet.

He said: 'Easy. Which way do we do it? I throw you over first, and then you throw me over?'

Dinkuhl smiled. He consulted his wrist-watch again.

'The time approacheth. Leave it to your Uncle Hiram?'

'I'd prefer to have some idea of what you propose.'

Dinkuhl took his arm. 'We're going to borrow a gyro. There isn't time to explain everything right now. Down to the sentry-box. We've got a friend in the camp, though he doesn't know it yet.' Dinkuhl had begun to walk down the wooded slope towards the gate, and Charles, automatically responding to the pressure on his arm, walked with him. 'I told you—I never forget a face.'

Charles could see the gate now, and the upright figure of the guard inside his plaspex bubble. Dinkuhl went on talking, in a slow drawl that might be concealing nervousness.

'I've had enough time thinking about this. It should go O.K. I thought maybe it would be rushing things to try it this morning, but my principle is that it's always safer to act at once, unless you can act sooner. If not now, we would have had to leave it till tomorrow afternoon. That's when our friend is on guard again.'

They were approaching the sentry-box. Charles could see the tall immobile figure through the plaspex; he looked a very ordinary character, in UC uniform, with the UC badges. His eyes were fixed coldly on them as they approached.

'That was another thing,' Dinkuhl said. 'When I saw him before, he was wearing a Telecom badge. Though since his activities on that occasion would properly be classed as subversive, that wasn't conclusive in any way.'

Dinkuhl tapped on the plaspex. The guard unseamed his sentry-box and came out towards them; he had his Klaberg at the ready and was wearing the nose filter against astarate —presumably the Klaberg was fitted with an astarate release.

He said, his voice mid-way between deference and challenge:

'Anything I can do for you?'

Dinkuhl looked at him for a moment. When he spoke it was with the full resonance of voice that he could muster up when he wanted to. He said:

'Brother, are you damned?'

The guard only looked surprised for a moment. When he spoke it was in a liturgical tone of voice matching Dinkuhl's own:

'Damned to Hell. Brethren, are ye damned?'

'Damned to Hell.' Dinkuhl jerked his head towards Charles. 'In this brother's mind, Lord Jahweh has planted power and a sword. He must be free to serve Lord Jahweh whose Finger lights the sky to destruction.'

169

The guard inclined his head. 'To the Damned all gates are open.'

Dinkuhl looked at the gate; a little wistfully, Charles thought. It was a temptation simply to get out and trust to luck after that. Dinkuhl said slowly:

'We need a gyro, brother. Your relief will be along inside five minutes. I wouldn't fit in your uniform, but this brother will. I want you to let him take it. We will tie you up. The Will of the Lord Jahweh, brother.'

The guard nodded. Without hesitation he stripped his equipment and his outer garments from him. In the sentry-box there was the usual plastic exudator. Dinkuhl adjusted the nozzle to quarter-inch orifice, and at a touch the plastic rope ribboned out. Carefully and deftly he tied it round the unresisting guard. Charles watched him while he was himself putting the uniform and accoutrements on.

Dinkuhl said: 'You get the sticky job, brother Charles. The Lord Jahweh didn't see fit to provide me with the figure for it. Club him with the Klaberg if he's wearing his nose filter. In fact, it will be safer to do that, anyway. There doesn't seem to be a spare filter here, and you would have an even stickier job carrying me if I passed out. Hit him hard, for God's sake. I'll be crouched in the box and I'll come a-running if you get into trouble, but it's always better to make sure at the start, if you can.'

Charles felt tense; it was not an altogether unpleasant feeling. The prospect of doing something violent soothed that part of his mind which had been most outraged by Dinkuhl's explanation of the double trickery that had been practised on him.

Dinkuhl completed the tying up, and propped the guard in one corner of his box. He pointed towards the distant house. A gyro was lifting from the roof.

170

'There's your quarry. I'm getting inside. Don't forget—hit him hard.'

'Don't worry,' Charles said.

He stood just outside the box, Klaberg held loosely, waiting for the gyro. It arrowed down through the wintry air, rotors flapping idly, and perched on the road perhaps ten yards away from him. The left-hand door slid open, and a figure dressed as he was dressed jumped down. It was a relief to observe that he was only of middle height.

He walked up to Charles. He said curiously:

'You're not Herriot.'

Charles made an attempt at disguising his voice. He had his hood close round his face and was not seriously worried about his features being recognized.

He said: 'Herriot went sick. Didn't they tell you?'

'Where you from?'

Charles ignored the question. He stooped down towards the base of the sentry-box, and poked at it with his Klaberg.

'You know the condition this was in? Somebody should have reported it before now.'

He straightened up himself as the new man bent down to see what he was talking about. Behind the ear, he thought to himself. He didn't aim well enough, and the butt of the Klaberg landed at the base of the man's neck. He rolled over and lay slack.

Dinkuhl emerged from the sentry-box.

'Charlie,' he remarked, 'you're a man of action. I could not have done any better myself.'

The man lay still. With a rising of nausea, Charles contemplated the possibility that he might have done the job too effectively.

He said: 'I hope I haven't finished him off.'

Dinkuhl knelt down. He said: 'Fetch me a hank of rope. No, he'll live to explain to George what a sucker he's been.

171

Should make it less tough for Brother in there. For suckers the only safety is in numbers.'

When he had been adequately roped, the guard was pushed into the box with his companion. Dinkuhl led the way to the gyro. He clambered up through the open door and Charles followed him. Dinkuhl took the controls.

'Time,' he observed, 'is on anyone's side but ours. This is where we move.'

The gyro climbed steeply, and headed north.

6

THE rolling countryside of Vermont was spread two thousand feet beneath them. The clouds were low and from time to time wisps of them obscured the view. It was very peaceful. They were still heading north.

Charles asked: 'Montpelier?'

'Thereabouts.'

But Montpelier came into view below and their course held. Dinkuhl was apparently in one of his moods of concentration; it was abundantly clear that he had his plans and did not want to discuss them. Charles assumed that he had changed the immediate objective to, possibly, Quebec, perhaps because their escape had gone so well so far. Quebec would give more scope for losing traces.

Montpelier was three or four miles behind them when the gyro started to come down. The country was bleak and empty here, and Charles' first thought was that the gyro might have developed a fault. But Dinkuhl was directing the descent. They landed in one of Agriculture's vast potato fields. At Dinkuhl's gesture, Charles jumped clear; his feet sank into the moist crumbling earth.

Dinkuhl came out on to the gyro's running-board, but did not immediately drop from it. He was apparently adjusting the controls. The gyro began to rise again, and Dinkuhl fell, landing on hands and feet. The gyro's door was still open as it disappeared on a continuation of its northerly line of flight.

Dinkuhl wiped his hands on the back of his trousers. He looked after the retreating gyro, and said happily:

'They gave us too much time. I don't mind confessing a certain relief.'

'We were clear, anyway, weren't we?'

'That was Telecom we left. They have resources some other managerials don't. Their gyros can all be tracked from their control points.' He laughed. 'They can follow that now. Maybe they'll bring it down before it reaches the Hudson. But they will. They'll intercept from Montreal and Quebec.' He looked around expansively. 'We're clear, Charlie boy. I never really thought we'd make it.'

Charles looked round himself. It was a field of a hundred acres or bigger. Beyond the distant wire fences there seemed to be other similar fields. The sky was low and trailing strands of dark cloud. It was the first time in his life he had been isolated in the country without a gyro or some similar form of transport, and the experience was a depressing one.

'Clear,' he echoed. 'Clear to do what?'

'To walk back to Montpelier.' Dinkuhl grinned. 'A healthy and invigorating exercise.'

'And after that?'

'Taxi to Albany. Stratoliner to Detroit. Then we'll see. Meanwhile, the invigorating walk.'

Taking a southerly line, they trudged painfully across the ploughed field. They were nearing the first fence when Dinkuhl pointed to the sky. Two gyros were flying north. They stood and watched them until they were out of sight again. Then they climbed through the fence; another fence, perhaps a quarter of a mile away, gave on to a road. They headed for it with renewed energy; it was an east-west road, but at least the going would be less arduous.

They went westwards, hoping to find a southerly intersection, but the road not only continued without a break but also complicated matters by twisting off the original line. Neither Charles nor Dinkuhl had any experience in keeping compass directions in mind, and it was soon clear to them that they had lost their orientation. The road was D class, roughly metalled by Agriculture and used almost exclusively by them for field work. Since these fields were not being worked at the moment, there seemed very small chance of their encountering any other travellers.

It was a matter of more than two miles before they finally arrived at an intersection, and it was a disappointment when they did. The crossroads lay between flat empty fields, without a signpost or anything else that might give them a clue to their position.

Dinkuhl said sourly: 'Eeny, meeny, miney, mo. Damned if I know which way is south. Apart from the sun, I only know that moss grows on the south side of trees. Or is it the north side? Anyway, no goddam sun and no goddam trees. Find an acorn. We'll plant it and sit and wait.'

Charles pointed down the left-hand fork.

'One of the natives.'

They waited while the man came along the road towards them. He walked with a springy step but as he got nearer they could see that he was at least sixty; he had a head of white hair *en brosse* above wrinkled rosy cheeks. He was wearing the standard overalls of the workers, but without the managerial insignia.

Dinkuhl called to him: 'We're aiming for Montpelier. Can you direct us?'

175

He stopped in front of them; his features were not precisely smiling, but had a look of friendly amusement.

'I guess there are worse places to aim for,' he said. 'But you're not going there. You're going somewhere else.'

'Which is?'

'Heaven.' He broke into a real smile now. 'Or hell.'

Dinkuhl looked at him closely. He inquired:

'Brother, are you damned?'

The stranger laughed. 'I hope not, but it's one thing I would never lay money on. My name's Kirby—Stuart Kirby. You want Montpelier—I just left that place. A couple of miles back along the road. You care for a bite to eat?—I got bread and cheese in my wallet.'

He had a small rucksack on his shoulders. He loosened the straps and slipped it off. Charles and Dinkuhl accepted the bread and cheese he offered them. They also drank from a flask of beer he had.

Dinkuhl said: 'My name's Hiram. You don't wear any badges, Stuart.'

'Come to look at you,' Kirby said, 'neither do you.'

'I'm the Great Auk,' Dinkuhl said. 'I thought I was the last of my line. If you're drawing a pension, doesn't that oblige you to wear the fixings?'

'I resigned my pension. I was in Steel.'

'How do you live?'

'The Spirit of God has travelled every road I'm likely to find. Folks are kinder than someone like you might think, Hiram. I get food and drink, and times I get a bed.' He lifted one foot to display the kind of heavy boots the workers in Mining were accustomed to wear. 'Got these last night. A man who works in the quarries gave them to me. Almost new, and they fit me just right.'

'You live on charity?'

'All God's creatures live on charity, Hiram. They like

176

me to talk to them, and I like the sound of my own voice.'

Dinkuhl returned to an earlier suspicion. 'You're not one of the Cometeers?'

Kirby laughed. 'The man who gave me these boots—he and his wife were Cometeers. By the grace of God, they are no longer. The comet may be a sign, but then, all the stars are signs.'

Dinkuhl said: 'Signs are for some people.'

'That's true, Hiram. Have you found your sign yet?'

'Not yet.'

'You will. It may be the comet, at that.' He fastened his rucksack. 'Just now you want Montpelier. Travel in peace, friends. I have to be on my way.'

'Where are you heading?' Charles asked curiously.

Kirby smiled. 'Heaven. I hope. But I'm aiming not to take any chances.'

He walked jauntily off along the empty road, and did not look back.

Before they reached Montpelier, Dinkuhl had had second thoughts about picking up the stratoliner at Albany. As he argued, they had lost more time than he had expected and the possibility of Telecom having picked up the empty gyro could not be ruled out. If they had, then they might have alerted all their North American stations to watch for the fugitives; it would be a big undertaking, and difficult to explain without at the same time informing rival Contact Sections, but they might think it worth it.

Instead they took a gyro-taxi all the way to Detroit. They paid it off in the central taxi-park, and then, from a call-booth, Dinkuhl got in touch with Awkright of Genetics Div. Over Dinkuhl's shoulder, Charles saw the interior of the office to which he had been taken by Dinkuhl as the first step in his private commitment. Awkright's broad freckled face came into focus as Dinkuhl adjusted the controls.

Awkright said: 'Hiram! So they let you loose?'

'Call me Houdini,' Dinkuhl said. 'Can you pick us up—4th and Eisenhower? We don't want to stay on public view any longer than we have to.'

'Be right round.' Awkright grinned. 'Someone's been looking for you. For Charlie, anyway.'

'He's a popular guy, no kidding. Come right over before some more of his friends turn up.'

Awkright appeared in Dinkuhl's ramshackle auto; the smell of petrol went ahead of it as well as behind. Dinkuhl and Charles climbed in.

Charles said: 'A good way of travelling incognito, this.'

Awkright laughed. 'I borrowed this while you were away, Hiram. Hope you didn't mind. You mean someone's still after you? I thought you were with UC.'

'The trouble with having good contacts,' Dinkuhl remarked, 'is that you get to relying on them. And then someone else starts shooting the old moola along the pipeline. That was Telecom we just got away from. Where are you heading—not my place? They're likely to be dropping in again with false beards and astarate phials.'

'My place,' Awkright said. 'I told you—Charlie already has a visitor.'

Charles said: 'Look, you mean there's someone out there waiting to see me? Anything but that.'

Dinkuhl said: 'I'm not inclined to look with great favour on the idea myself. The situation's liable to be difficult. They badly want what Charlie's got, and there's something of a tendency to grab instead of asking nicely. It might be easier to run along to Louie's place.'

Most dangerously Awkright threw back his head and

178

roared with laughter; the auto swayed perilously close to the pavement. Dinkuhl said acidly:

'I noted the left front fender was dented. I'm not surprised. Keep your sense of humour till you stop driving.'

'I'm just a naturally happy guy,' Awkright said. He laughed again. 'I can't help it.'

The auto drew up before a big apartment block fronting the lake. It looked ridiculous beside the rows of battery saloons in the parking space. The three of them went inside and took a lift to the top floor. Awkright whistled sharply at the door. He grinned at Charles.

'I warned the visitor we were coming.'

The door opened and they went through into the lobby. The floor was plaspex bricks over a tank of tropical fish; presumably Awkright's hobby since it was too expensive an affair to be an incidental fitting in this kind of suite.

Awkright said: 'You go ahead, Charlie. Straight through to the lounge. I want to show Hiram something.'

There was no doubt that something was waiting for him. He pushed the door open and walked into the lounge—a big bright airy room with a lake view. Someone was standing by the main window, looking out over the waters. She turned as she heard him come in. It was Sarah.

Charles went right over to her. She smiled, hesitantly and then with warmth. He took her by the elbows, eager to feel the realness, the solidity, of her body. It might have been some trick of projection cameras.

But it wasn't. She was real, flesh and bone, and her breath caught as he touched her. He wanted to bring her closer, to take her altogether into his arms, to turn the knowledge of her return to him into the conviction of embrace. He was fairly sure she would not refuse him this time, either. But

179

something prevented him. Instead he took one of her hands between his own, caressing it.

'Sarah,' he said. 'How did you get away? Who was it took you?'

He waited for the pleasure of hearing her voice again, and was not denied it.

She said: 'Get away? There wasn't any difficulty. Why should there be?'

'But you were captured in the first place—by someone? It was made to look like suicide.'

'Captured, but very politely.' She shivered. 'That was the unpleasant part. A pre-set lock was put on the gyro controls. After about five minutes I found the controls just didn't respond. I had to sit there while the gyro took me.'

'Took you? Where?'

'Sacramento. In the first place.'

'Sacramento. Atomics!'

'Of course. Didn't I mention that? But I didn't know until the gyro came down right alongside one of their pylons. I just didn't know what was happening. Things weren't much clearer when I had landed, for that matter. I was taken into the Atomics HQ building. They were very nice about everything, and most apologetic. They had had to pick me up, they said, for questioning on a matter of what they called managerial importance. I was to have a bed there for the night, and leave for Philadelphia the next morning. There was nothing I could do about it. I was relieved enough that my worst fears had not been realized.'

'You couldn't get any message out, of course?'

'Well, no. I was fed up about that. But it was understandable. They gave me a direct undertaking that I would be a free agent again in three days, and I had to be content with it.' Her face clouded. 'During that time, Daddy—you know. But even that wasn't their fault. They asked me whether my disappearing for three days would be likely to have any serious effect on him; they were willing to pick him up as they had done me, if I preferred it. It was my error of judgment. I didn't want him to have the shock of being captured; I guess I underestimated the shock to him of having that happen to me.'

Charles said: 'I didn't think he was dead, either. I thought it had been arranged to look like that, as with Hans and yourself.'

She shook her head. 'Only too true, I'm afraid. But I suppose there was more to it than my disappearance. Hans before that, and his feeling that his own life was empty now. Teaching history to two students; not much of a life for a man who had hoped to rule Israel.'

'I'm sorry.'

She smiled wryly. 'Nothing we can do now. I was upset at first, and angry—but it was nobody's fault. Just bad luck. They had to act when they did; it was a matter of forestalling others—Telecom particularly. You will know about that.'

He nodded. 'Yes. I know about that. What happened— when you got to Philadelphia?'

'I saw Raven.'

Charles whistled. Raven was Chief Director of Atomics, Chairman of the Council of Managerials.

'And . . . ?'

'I liked him. In fact I think he's the first person I've met over here that I've genuinely respected.' She smiled, dimpling. 'In a daughterly way, that is.'

Charles said: 'He sounds a regular guy. Not the kind who would be trying to get you to complete Hans' work for the benefit of his own managerial at all.'

Sarah released her hand. 'Come and sit down.' She led the way over to a wallseat; it slid out as she buttoned it. She sat down, and Charles sat beside her.

'Naturally you would have that reaction,' she went on. 'I did myself at the beginning. Remember, I was never sold on the values of managerialism to start with. Anyway, I'm not going to argue with you about this. I want you to see Raven yourself.'

'He did want something, though. Can you tell me what it was he wanted?'

Sarah fixed her eyes on him. 'He wanted me to transfer from UC to Atomics. Officially, and above board. I can tell you that he would like you to do the same.'

Charles stared back at her—in amazement. He said:

'You don't mean—you consented? That you applied for transfer?'

From a pocket she took the Atomics flame badge, and pinned it on her tunic. 'Yes. I didn't wear this at the beginning because I wanted to explain things to you.' Her face softened. 'Charles, I should have liked to talk it over with you first, but then they had to tell me that you had been captured by Telecom. They were trying to get you released, but meanwhile what was there to do?'

'Go back to UC. Why not?'

'UC,' Sarah said, 'is so ineffective as to be impossible. The only Managers they've got that are any good are those who, like Ledbetter, are careerists. When Hans disappeared, the Atomics Contact Section were on to it. They tried to get co-operation from UC—from the top, from Graz—but they didn't even know what had been happening in their own laboratories, and didn't care either.'

'They didn't know,' Charles said, 'because Ledbetter had been routing the important stuff through to Telecom.'

'That's what I mean,' she said. 'Ineffective. They still didn't act when I disappeared, or even when Ledbetter had you picked up. And meanwhile they had allowed the lab to be raided and anything that was of any value picked up.'

182

Charles remembered Isaacssohn's reports arriving at The Cottage; of course, Telecom would have got them.

'Yes,' he said. 'I know about that.'

'You see,' she said. She showed him her wrist, and the small radio banded to it. 'With this, I can call help from Atomics at any time. If I had gone back to UC it would merely have been a matter of presenting myself as a sitting duck to whichever managerial felt like taking aim.'

Reluctantly, he began to see her point of view. He himself had been shocked enough by having the familiar world split and quake beneath his feet, and he had not been an exile, in a strange land, a strange world almost.

'It wasn't as though I had any ties to UC, was it? They took us in when we came over from Israel, but any managerial would have done. We were skilled technicians— Hans and myself, that is. They didn't do anything for Daddy.'

'I suppose not. And you're working for them?'

She said frankly: 'Not very well. I suppose I'm the collaborative type—I don't work terribly well on my own.'

'But how does it happen that you're here—in Awkright's suite? He's not working for Atomics, too?'

'I was flown over here. Three or four hours ago, Telecom alerted their whole organization for triple security checking. Atomics guessed what it meant—that you and Dinkuhl had got clear somehow. The Telecom line seemed to be directed towards Canada, but the Atomic guess was that you would be heading this way. They knew something of Dinkuhl's circle—more than Dinkuhl would like to think, I fancy— and assumed he would get in touch with Awkright as soon as possible. As he did, of course.' Her hand moved, to touch his own. 'You didn't mind my coming over to meet you?'

He smiled, grasping her fingers. 'No.'

183

'Not even when I come as an emissary of a strange managerial, trying to seduce you from your duty?'

'It's always nice to have someone try to seduce you, even when you have no intention of giving way.' He grinned. 'Isn't it?'

She looked at him appraisingly for a moment, and then coloured. 'I suppose so.'

He thought for a moment. 'You do recognize that my duty should be towards UC—my own managerial?'

She shook her head definitely. 'No. I was looking at it from the point of view I was afraid you might adopt. But I'm not going to argue about that. Will you come over and see Raven? I can promise you that you can do what you like afterwards. There will be no question of holding you against your will.'

He said: 'Of course I'll come. It will be quite an experience seeing Raven, in any case.'

With relief, she said: 'I'm glad.'

He warned her: 'That doesn't mean I'm transferring.'

She shrugged, very prettily. 'As long as you're coming.'

Something that had been teasing Charles' mind returned to bother him now.

He said: 'Your watch . . .'

She lifted her finger, looking at him curiously. It was the same watch, or a duplicate.

'You got it back, then,' he said.

'Got it back? Oh, I see what you mean. I didn't know you knew about that. I put it in to Allied Electrical for recharging during that week-end. Daddy said he would pick it up for me on the Sunday afternoon—he had to go fairly near the automat delivery—but he forgot. His memory was not very good the last few years. He was going to have it sent on to me, but of course . . . I had it sent on to Philadelphia eventually.'

Charles said: 'Well, I'm damned! As simple an explanation as that. It was that watch that convinced me you really were alive.'

She smiled. 'Well, I am.'

'Yes, but the evidence was unsound.'

'Does the evidence matter?'

The grave air of formality, to some extent characteristic of all Atomics posts, was paramount at the Philadelphia HQ. They deviated from the norm also in having the Chief Director's office on the roof; brass, in other managerials, took the first floor. There was a private lift giving directly on to the Chief Director's suite, but the more usual route, and the one by which Sarah took him, was through the roof-garden. A bowery walk, dripping with honeysuckle, gave on to a small courtyard, with three fountains, surrounded on three sides by walls plasticized to the effect of cool white-washed simplicity. The Chief Director's private office was directly facing the walk; it was a long room, with one window on the courtyard and the other on Philadelphia, spread out thirty floors beneath. The desk the Chief Director was using was the one by the courtyard window. The uniformed precise flunkeys ushered them in, and Raven stood up. He bowed slightly, and smiled.

'I had the pleasure of seeing you approach, from my window. Miss Cohn, I am very glad you were successful in your mission. And you, too, Mr Grayner—it was very good of you to be willing to put some of your time at my disposal.'

Atomics for some reason retained the archaic forms of address in polite conversation. Charles was not certain whether it was etiquette to extend the usage to Raven himself, though. In any case, there was no reason why he should fall in with Atomics customs.

He said: 'Naturally, Chief Director, it's an honour to be invited to meet you.'

Raven directed his attention to Sarah. 'Do take a seat, Miss Cohn. And you, Mr Grayner.'

Sarah remained standing. She said: 'I think it would be better, sir, if I left the room for the present.' She glanced sideways at Charles. 'Mr Grayner knows of my transfer, and knows something of my views on it. I don't think it would help at all for me to stay.'

'As you feel best,' Raven said. He nodded to the two flunkeys by the door, and they opened it again to let Sarah out. 'You will be within call?'

She nodded. 'In the garden.' She smiled at Charles, and left.

Raven said: 'I think an entirely private conversation would be most satisfactory, don't you, Mr Grayner? Rogers, Barczywski—wait outside, please.'

The doors closed, and they were alone in the long and carefully ordered room. It had been built, and furnished, a long time ago; this was one of the first major edifices of the managerial world. Charles noticed that the old-fashioned projection TV was installed; there was the small slit in the ceiling which would release the hanging screen.

'You will have a chair, anyway, Mr Grayner,' Raven said. 'Cigar, cigarette?'

Charles took the chair indicated, and a cigarette from the box. 'Thank you, Chief Director.'

Raven went through the motions preparatory to lighting a cigar. He chuckled; it was a restrained but friendly expression.

'If you were to decide to come over to us—I say *if*, Mr Grayner—it would be incumbent on you to address me as "sir." We have our little ways which must be preserved, *ruat coeli*. Am I right in taking it that you would not find an insuperable objection in that small point?'

186

The flame moved over to him, and he lit up. He smiled. 'No. No objection, sir.'

'Well,' Raven said easily. 'That's something. I always prefer to start off with a measure of agreement, however tiny it may be.'

He paused, drawing on his cigar, and Charles waited. While he waited, he studied the man.

He was a little under average height, and slimly built. He wore London clothes—a dark rust suit with a lime shirt and cravat—and wore, as a button-hole ornament, a white carnation. His features were somewhat sharp in outline but entirely relaxed in expression; it was impossible to imagine him getting excited over anything. He was probably in his early sixties; his hair had already turned white, and to good effect.

All his appearance combined to be impressive, but the impressiveness, it seemed to Charles, was much more than the sum of the individual features. The man radiated confidence, and integrity. Charles thought of Ledbetter—Ledbetter friendly, frank and assured, but with so much else battened down behind that front, battened down and fighting to be free. He could feel sorry for Ledbetter's vaulting ambition, which yet had to meet this reality, at the top.

Raven said: 'Well, that seems to be going. Now, we can get to the business. I hope you will let me indulge my age, Mr Grayner, in running over a number of things with which you must be familiar—in some cases, only too familiar. But I want to put things in their perspective. You are, I am sure, a shrewd and eminently sensible young man, but with the experiences you have so recently had, it would be surprising if your judgment had not been knocked a little out of true. And then, for some time now you have had the advantage of the company of Mr Dinkuhl, a man of acute and perspicacious intelligence but of rather fixed ideas.' He glanced at

187

Charles. 'Could you, I wonder, give me some idea of your present views?'

'On what?'

'On fundamentals. On society.' He glanced down into the viewer on his desk. 'Your record is a good one. It shows genuine stability when loyalty traits persist so strongly in someone who, quite frankly, has had less than a square deal from society. For an integral part of our society is the right of the able man to use his ability.'

He paused. Charles said warily:

'That's something I have found confusing—the implications of what you have just said, sir.'

Raven looked at his cigar. 'I believe I am safe in claiming that no previous society can show as good a record as ours in encouraging intelligence, in whatever circumstances it shows itself. The odd mistake, as in your case, merely sets off the record.'

'No. It wasn't quite that I was referring to. I simply meant . . . It's rather hard to explain.' Raven looked at him benevolently, encouragingly. 'Until the recent events you mentioned, I took things for granted. I think that what has probably surprised and shocked me more than anything else has been the realization of the mistrust and hostility that exists between managerials. The world seems to have broken up, and it isn't easy to put the pieces together again. Dinkuhl's group of malcontents—you seem to know about them—and the Cometeers—and you probably know about them, too—and then finding that Telecom had access to all my records—through Ledbetter, I suppose. Now you have my records as well. The whole set-up seems to be riddled with double-crossing.'

Raven nodded. 'Not a very pretty picture, is it? The managerial society, with all its running sores on show. And even if none of those sores existed, there still remains a constitutional weakness which a healthy mind might easily turn from in horror. The spectacle of a society chasing its tail, right hand fighting left hand, for the possession of the skills of three people—two of whom are not even its own children —is one to strike fear. I suppose Mr Dinkuhl would describe such a situation as the ultimate throes of decadence.'

Charles smiled slightly. 'He does.'

'And I,' said Raven, 'must take a large measure of the blame, I suppose. I have been Chief Director of this managerial for fifteen years, and Chairman of the Council for twelve.' He leaned forward slightly. 'Ten years ago, to the month, I reminded the Council of the urgency of re-organizing the research and technical development sides of managerial life. It was not a new proposition—several of my predecessors had drawn attention to the same need. The matter was ventilated—and dropped. Nothing got done.'

Raven gently tapped cigar ash into his disposal cup.

'As you know, the Council does not come to many decisions; the sovereignty of the individual managerial is too much cherished for that. Perhaps I can excuse myself on that ground. But can I excuse myself for my failure to apply reforms of the kind I was envisaging even here—in Atomics? I'm not sure. Shall I tell you what I did?

'I launched in this managerial a propaganda drive in favour of science and technology. We spent quite a lot of money on it. It was directed principally at the class which was then in process of graduating. I did everything I could to persuade those young people to opt for the research side. Do you know what the results were? A bare handful of 120+ IQ candidates volunteered—and every single one proved to have disabling personality characteristics!'

'In UC,' Charles said, 'there was no question of opting.'

Raven smiled. 'Nor, in any other year, was there in this managerial. I thought of enforcing the reversal of policy,

189

and even made tentative plans, but it did not prove possible to carry the idea through. I met local opposition. There are limits, my dear Mr Grayner, even to the powers of a Chief Director.'

Charles said: 'Then Dinkuhl was right. This society is too far gone to save itself.'

'Sometimes,' Raven said, 'I have thought that. But, you know, there never has been a historical situation which was final. Rome fell, but Byzantium, as closely pressed, gathered its defences and survived for another eight hundred years. It is the law of averages that destroys empires, and that is a law that doesn't help you at all in assessing the particular.

'No, in any historical situation, the best one can do is to assess probabilities—and after you have assessed probabilities you have still got to decide about taking sides. For you will appreciate that there must always be times when it is better to fight for one chance in a hundred than for the remaining ninety-nine—for instance, when the one chance in a hundred entails your living, and the other ninety-nine your dying.

'It is here that Mr Dinkuhl and I part company. It is a relatively simple matter, I think. Mr Dinkuhl—and you will be best able to judge whether I am doing him an injustice in this—Mr Dinkuhl is eager for destruction. He wants the world to crash. No doubt he has his reasons, and no doubt they are very strong ones, but I do not appreciate them, nor share his views. If society is sick and looks like dying, my instinct is to do what little it may be possible for me to do, to save it. The death of any society is a terrible thing, as Mr Dinkuhl—as a student of history—must know. It may be that people today are not as happy as the TV screens portray them as being. They cannot be, if so many of them have resort to these peculiar rites of damnation associated with the comet that happens to be visiting us. But I regard the

190

kind of unhappiness they may now have as different in kind from the utter misery and wretchedness that would attend a breakdown in civilized life. We are entitled to count our small blessings, I think. And to reject the destructive solution to our problems is not the same as rejecting all solutions. It may be a long pull—it may be an entirely vain pull—to get society back on its feet, but I see no harm in trying it.'

Ceasing to speak, Raven kept an inquiring look directed on Charles' face. It was impossible not to be impressed by the man's realism and confidence; nor to fail to compare it favourably with Dinkuhl's realism and despair. Charles argued, but already he was arguing automatically, without conviction:

'Whichever way you look at the situation, it's black enough. And it isn't as though there's been any attempt to make people understand it.'

Raven bowed slightly. '*Mea culpa,* again. Or partly so. But it is well-nigh impossible to preach the sobering message to which you are referring. The public will put up with many oppressions—taxation, invasion of privacy, loss of liberties —but it will never bear nor forgive Cassandra. In any case, one of the minor disadvantages of the present state is the disproportionate part Telecom play in the forming of opinion, and the direction of Telecom has been in mildly paranoiac hands for some little time now.

'As for the situation being very black—yes, of course it is. A crisis is ahead of us. But you must remember that a crisis is precisely what it says it is: a moment of decision. For a decadent society, it is the periods of non-crisis that are dangerous; the crisis presents the challenge and a response must be made to it. Cassandra gets a hearing in a crisis, and sometimes speaks to good effect.'

Charles said: 'How is it going to help Cassandra—my working on the diamond-solar power source for Atomics?'

191

Raven hesitated slightly. 'You force me into the embarrassment of asking you to make an estimate of me, personally. From what you have recently encountered yourself, and from what you have gleaned from Mr Dinkuhl, would you regard me as typical of the Directors of managerials?'

Charles said promptly: 'No. Of course not. The reverse.'

Raven laid small, neatly manicured hands in front of him on the desk. Charles expected him to contemplate them, but he did not; his eyes were on Charles.

'This is the picture I give you, Mr Grayner. Either you help to destroy managerialism, or help to save it. You will be saving, as I have explained, something very imperfect, but destruction is a terrible thing. Should you choose what seems to me the more human course, then you must decide in what direction your help will be of the greatest value. Were other things equal, I should counsel you to work on behalf of your own managerial, for a number of reasons which I will not go into now. But I don't think other things are equal, and I do not think you yourself think so. I ask you to throw in your lot with us, because it is my own belief that we are most capable of helping you and of using your work wisely.' He paused. 'You might like time to think matters over?'

Charles said: 'You already have Sarah. If I should ask for transfer as well—aren't UC going to object to this wholesale suborning of their research workers?'

Raven nodded. 'It is very likely. But one of the few intermanagerial regulations the Council did agree on was that entailing the full and free right of transfer, with the consent of the person seeking transfer and the new managerial. The consent of the original managerial is specifically not required.' He smiled. 'Although it was much before my time, I believe I am right in saying that United Chemicals, along

192

with Steel, Allied Electrical and a few others, formed the group that urged the regulation, and that this managerial opposed it in the first place—it was used in a campaign against us. Things make the round. Anyway, you may leave UC's objections to me. It's my job to deal with them.'

'One question, sir. You haven't got Isaacssohn?'

'No.'

'And you don't know where he is?'

'We have had some lines to work on. Frankly, we know very little yet. He may even be genuinely dead.'

'You know that he is the real brain behind the diamond power source—that the original work was all his?'

'We know that. Let me ask you a question, Mr Grayner. What stage would you say the work has reached?'

'Development stage. When I first examined it, I wanted to pass it on for routine development—the essential creative work had been completed. Sarah persuaded me to carry on for a time. Of course, I did not know then that there was no one in fact capable of doing the development work.'

'And how long, in your view, should the development work take?'

Charles shrugged. 'It's practically impossible to give an answer—snags always crop up, but you can't estimate the size of the snags nor their number in advance. Not less than three months, I should say. And probably not more than a year.' He glanced at Raven. 'Once again, it's worth remembering that even if you hold two out of three, it's the third that's the heavy-weight.'

'I'm not so sure. Einstein did the early mass-energy conversion research, but his work on applied nuclear fission was confined to a recommendation of its feasibility. Isaacssohn may or may not be able to work faster than you and Sarah, whoever he is working for. I doubt if he will be able to work much faster?'

G   193

'Probably not. The snags stage tends to level things out.'

'And our chief concern is to prevent whoever is using Isaacssohn from having the monopoly on the completed invention. For that purpose any fairly close finish will do.'

Charles said: 'Yes. I see that.' He looked around, at the dignified solidity of his surroundings. Suddenly he didn't want to leave them. Raven would let him go if he wanted to—but where should he go? And how would he remain free from Ledbetter and the others? And was he prepared to lose Sarah, so recently found again?

He said: 'I'll transfer. I'll work for you, sir.'

'I'm glad,' Raven said. 'I'm very glad, Mr Grayner. But you can still have time to think it over, if you have any reservations at all.'

'No. No reservations. You don't mind my continuing to see Dinkuhl?'

'See whom you like.' Raven smiled. 'You will be seeing a lot of Miss Cohn, since you are to work together. I did not wish to influence you by stressing that aspect of things, but I imagine it has its interest for you.'

'I noticed it—that you weren't stressing that.'

'Well, perhaps you would care to go along and tell Miss Cohn the news now; she said she would be in the garden, did she not? Eventually—there's no hurry—I should like you to go and see Mr Tehchen, and fix up this transfer application. Mr Tehchen looks after that side of things for us. Tenth floor—room B97. But you will be directed by one of the pages.'

Charles got up. 'Thank you, sir.'

'Thank you, Mr Grayner. I shall be dropping in on you at the lab, so it won't be long before we meet again.'

Mr Tehchen—Manager Tehchen—was a man of expedition, and the transfer was filed with the Secretariat of the

Council that afternoon. The following morning, Charles was given the option of starting work, and he was glad enough to take it. He had residual guilt feelings about UC; he had expected to have them, and the pangs were not as bad as he had guessed they might be. Nevertheless they existed, and work seemed the most obvious way of eliminating them— work in Sarah's company.

He found it difficult to make up his mind about Sarah. It had been inevitable, as he saw, that the course of his acquaintance with her—knowing her for so short a time and then separated suddenly and left to brood about her under very abnormal circumstances—should have produced an uncertainty when he found her again; but the uncertainty seemed to be more than was natural. She was different, was his first reaction. He found a softness in her which was disconcertingly unfamiliar.

The explanation dawned on him unexpectedly. He had left out half of the equation; accounting for the effect of shock on his own attitude he had not remembered that Sarah's shock had been a worse one. It would naturally produce changes in her—perhaps far-reaching ones. Adrift from all her moorings, both the links with that world of her childhood snapped, it was only reasonable that she should look for someone who might give her reassurance. He could count it as his good fortune that it happened to be him.

Having come to this view, he was prepared to make excuses. On their first morning together in the lab, she seemed unsure and, in a way, apathetic. She had already, it appeared, been two or three days in the lab, but nothing substantial was there to show for it. He suggested that she should sketch out again her scheme for the rectifier, and she retired into her small office—they had one each—to get on with this. He himself was checking the installation of the

195

scaifes, when the wall screen glowed with a call from the roof lobby.

The flunkey radiated politeness, but they all did here. He began to speak: 'A visitor for you, Mr Grayner——' He stopped in surprise and well-bred annoyance as someone appeared behind him on the screen; the visitor had clearly made his way round the barrier to join in the call himself. Charles smiled. It was Dinkuhl.

Dinkuhl said: 'Charlie boy, so they tied you down already. Any chance of your taking a break for coffee?'

Charles asked him: 'You mean that you've got KF back into running order as quickly as this?'

The flunkey began again: 'Excuse me——'

Dinkuhl patted him solemnly on the shoulder. 'That's O.K., son. Run right along.' To Charles, he said: 'The assistant—still no cap A—managed better than I had expected during my enforced absence. He picked the lock of the vaults and found the encapsuled telecasts of the last seventy years. If any of our clients are much over seventy they may be won over to a cyclical philosophy. What about this coffee?'

'I have it on the job. Should be up soon. Why not come down and have it here?'

Dinkuhl said: 'A real live laboratory, where scientists work. Get the wistful tone? Am I allowed?' He put a hand back on the flunkey's shoulder. 'How about it, junior?'

The flunkey said: 'I'm not sure——'

Charles said crisply: 'All right. I'll vouch for Manager Dinkuhl. Have him brought down, will you?'

Dinkuhl looked around him with interest when he was brought in. He shook his head, wonderingly.

'Not that I know anything about anything, but how does this stack up against the set-up Ledbetter arranged? As good?'

196

'A good deal better. We operate smoothly in Atomics—smoothly and fast.'

Dinkuhl grinned. 'Ah, the new fledged patriot! You moved fast, all right. I always had my doubts about making a pessimist of you. There was one argument you kept at the back of your mind. Where is the argument, by the way?'

'The argument?'

'Sarah. I've been painting a sign for you. "Here is good horse to hire. Here you may see Charlie the married man." '

'Not quite as bad as that yet. Or as good. Here she is.'

Sarah came out of her office. She had the sketch in her hand. She stopped when she saw Dinkuhl.

Charles said: 'This is Hiram, Sarah.'

Dinkuhl said: 'I've seen your picture, lady. But you look nicer.'

She smiled. 'Thank you. Charles has told me about you.'

'About our death-defying escape from an impregnable fortress dripping with milk and honey and Circassians? Sometimes I think my brain is beginning to soften. I've spent damn near fifty years looking for an establishment like that, and what do I do when I find it?—bolt myself, and drag Charlie here kicking and screaming at my heels. It doesn't make sense any way you look at it.'

Sarah laughed. 'No, I suppose not. I'm glad to know you, Hiram.'

Dinkuhl looked at her searchingly. 'You are?'

Charles said: 'You've got that sketch? Run it through the projector, will you?'

Dinkuhl looked at the screen with interest. 'Doesn't mean a damn thing. Is that the super-diamond-bomb or a section of the New York subway?'

'Neither.' Charles flicked a circle round a salient point on the pilot screen and its blown-up counterpart glowed on the

197

wall screen. 'Only a rectifier. But a rather unusual one, and most elegant. Sarah's work.'

Dinkuhl said: 'Tell your Uncle Hiram how it works, honey.'

Sarah gestured towards Charles. 'Charles makes the explanations. I'm just the help.'

'Wouldn't help to tell you, Hiram,' Charles said. 'No chance of your ignorance becoming vincible.'

'I guess not.' Dinkuhl turned to Sarah again. 'You both look happy. What's it like being in Atomics? You got the secret of ultimate bliss? Think I should maybe join up, too?'

'Why not?'

'Yes, why not?' Dinkuhl echoed. 'It makes a nice bolt-hole. Comes the big bang, bolt-holes are going to be handy. They give you at least five minutes extra, before someone comes along and pumps gas in from the top.'

Grinning, Charles switched the screen off.

'You're an anarchist, Hiram, and anarchists always under-estimate the reorganizational powers of society.'

'Five minutes,' Dinkuhl insisted. 'Five minutes, and then a gentle hissing sound.' He shot a glance at Sarah. 'What do you think, honey?'

She said: 'You may be right, I suppose. But we might as well try to do what we can while we have the chance.'

'Pollyanna in her moated grange,' Dinkuhl remarked, 'believing where she cannot prove.'

Sarah smiled. 'I suppose so.'

Charles said: 'Philosophy—even so wise and bitter a philosophy as yours, Hiram—must attend on more practical matters. Sarah, I'd like you to tell me what you think of installing the polishing bench in the little room. You coming along, Hiram? Do you know anything about diamond polishing benches?'

'As much as I do about rectifiers. I'll stick here and steal

198

the odd secret to flog to Ledbetter. Maybe there's a chance I can put KF back in the black.'

When they returned to the main room, perhaps five minutes later, Dinkuhl was sitting on one of the stools watching the TV screen. He switched off as they came in.

'In the act,' Charles said. 'Cosy Bright?'

'The practised ascetic knows where to draw a line. Red League's good enough for me. Whenever the springs of optimism begin to well up in my unlikely breast, I only have to watch the old Red League for a couple of minutes. Realism infallibly sets in again.'

'Preserve your perspective,' Charles said. 'At least, Red League's no worse than it would have been in the later Roman Empire, if they had had TV then.'

Dinkuhl shook his head. 'Inferior by omission. We haven't got any Christians, and all the lions have been emasculated. I won't keep you two from the great work any longer. Nice to see the place, though. I'll drop in again.'

'You were going to have coffee with us. It'll be up any minute now.'

'Drink a toast,' Dinkuhl said, 'to absent friends. I've remembered there's someone I want to look up while I'm here, and I've got to be back in Detroit for the afternoon.' He bowed solemnly to Sarah. 'I am glad to have known you, too, lady. I hope I shall see more of you in the future.'

'We'll always be glad to see you here, Hiram. Both of us.'

Dinkuhl nodded. 'I'm touched.'

Raven came through on the screen soon after. He was half smiling, half stern.

'I've had a complaint about you, Mr Grayner. Already.'

'Yes, sir.'

'The duty page tells me you have had a visitor?'

'Mr Dinkuhl.'

199

Raven smiled openly, approving, Charles guessed, his use of Atomics idiom. 'So I guessed. The point is that the page has had instructions that your lab is top secret. He was ruffled, I fancy, by the somewhat cavalier approach of Mr Dinkuhl, and by your support of it. You had him brought down?'

'Yes. There could be no question of Mr Dinkuhl being any kind of danger to security. For three reasons: he's a trustworthy friend, he wouldn't recognize a technical secret if he saw one, and there isn't anything lying about, anyway. I had Miss Cohn demonstrate an improved rectifier layout in his presence. Even if it meant anything to him, it wouldn't help anyone else.'

Raven said: 'My dear Mr Grayner! There was no question of security having been endangered or damaged. That which was damaged was something even less palpable, though not necessarily less important—the duty page's self-esteem. What I should like you to do is to have passes prepared for admission to your laboratory. Ask Mr McGuire of Contact Section to arrange them for you. You may present Mr Dinkuhl with the first, and I should be happy to have the second. I hope to come along and see you soon.'

Charles said: 'Yes, sir. I'll do that.'

He broke contact, with his mind in a not unpleasant confusion. He was impressed again by the warmth and urbanity of Raven. Dinkuhl was all right. He owed a great deal to Dinkuhl. But there was no denying his clownish aspect.

They worked late that night and started early the next morning. The first hitch occurred soon after lunch; the plasbestos they were using for heat insulation turned out to be badly flawed. Charles got through to Conway, who was handling the supplies for them. He was a man of melancholy appearance, but of surprising charm and forcefulness whenever the need arose. He listened to Charles' explanation carefully.

He said: 'UC material. Not really surprising. But we asked for grade A plus and we paid grade A plus prices for it. Leave it to me. I'll send a man down right away to collect a sample of the dud stuff.'

'And replacement?' Charles asked. 'How long will that take?'

Conway smiled. 'UC replacement schedules are twenty-four-hour jobs. Normally they take two to three days. I'll have the stuff with you in six hours.'

As the glow died from the screen, Sarah said:

'Six hours. We could take a break.'

Charles nodded. There were a number of minor jobs which they could get on with, but he didn't have much enthusiasm for them.

'What do you suggest?'

'It's a long time since I went airsphering. There's a good wind. It ought to be fun.'

The airsphere hangar was reached through the roof-garden. Above and beyond the summer through which they walked, the sky was grey and angry, and tossed with scudding clouds. Airsphering afficionados had always held, with near fanatical dogmatism, that the sport should not be described as airsphering at all with winds at less than force 5, but, as in most sports, they were outnumbered by the casuals. The hangar was full. Atomics HQ apparently did not boast many really keen airspherers.

'Singles?' Charles asked.

The singles were the small one-man spheres; there were also doubles, and multiples capable of taking parties of six.

'I'd rather a double.'

Her look was of uncertainty and trust; very feminine and very flattering.

201

He said: 'My preference, too. All right if we take a blue?'

The blues were spheres whose plaspex was delicately tinged with azure, and whose Sokije valves had hair-trigger sensitivity. It made them fast in response, but correspondingly risky in inexpert hands. Charles had not done a great deal of airsphering, but he knew himself to be competent at it. Just at present, he recognized with inner amusement, he was playing up to the situation caused by Sarah's choice of a double: the masterful male.

They pulled the sphere clear of the hangar, and climbed in. There were two seats, each with controls but the controls had automatic cut-offs which prevented both being used together. The seats were adjustable from ninety degrees to a hundred and eighty. Charles took the right-hand seat and controls. He decompressed and there was the slight hiss of air being driven out and helium taking its place. The sphere rose gently through the quiet air trapped in the roof-garden. Then it emerged, above the conditioning range, above the plane of sunlets, and the wind struck it like a giant's bat, lifting and swinging it away into the outfield. The blustering sky was suddenly all round them; the shock of the transition was a thrill in itself.

'Cut off,' Sarah said. 'Quite cut off from everything.'

They had jumped to a thousand feet in a few seconds, and were still rising. The Atomics building had fallen away behind them; with the plaspex giving them vision all round—above and below and to all the corners of the horizon—they could see with sharp clarity just how isolated they were.

Philadelphia was drifting away, too. There were a few gyros battling through the wind and a stratoliner was coming in to land at the field by the city's northern limits. They were in a private world, more isolated with each passing moment.

'See the sun?' Charles asked. 'The real sun?'

'Love to.'

They were in cloud, a sea of mist pressing about them, now lighter, now darker. Like a bubble bursting through depths of water, the sphere burst free. The sunlight was radiant everywhere, and reflected from the dazzling white surface of the world through which they had just emerged. That world was one of continual movement—a plain where crevasses sprang out and were swallowed up again, where tentacles, reaching slimly from the ground, became squat towers until the towers themselves collapsed back into the ground from which they had risen. And all white, all feathery snow.

Sarah gasped. 'It's wonderful.'

'Perhaps we should stay here.'

She smiled. 'And live on?' She poked in the side locker and produced three bars of candy. 'On these?'

'On angel's food,' Charles said. 'On light.'

The air was less turbulent here; the sphere continued to rise, but only slowly. The enchanted landscape merged more and more into a great glistening plain stretching in every direction. Charles compressed slightly, and the sphere began to drop. The landscape opened up again, in shifting whorl and contour. They grazed the woolly surface and he manœuvred the controls with fine delicacy so that they bounced along, as though sledging on living snow. At times a dazzling upflung cliff would appear in front of them, and the sphere would plough through its pearl-grey interior, to re-emerge into sunshine. And again the cloud beneath them would open up into some vast ravine, through which, once or twice, there were brief glimpses of the other world two thousand feet below—the world that held them on an elastic rope, the managerial world.

Sarah said: 'Up, Charles, up now.'

'To the sun?'

'Or higher.'

203

As he decompressed to the full, the sphere shot up, and cliffs and ravines dwindled again and were lost in the all-extending, all-embracing white of the plain. Soon it was bereft of all individual features. It was a carpet of dazzling snow that stretched in every direction to the downward curving horizon. It was difficult to believe in the real existence of the world beneath the cloud belt.

Charles adjusted the controls for height stabilization. The altimeter needle bobbed gently just above the 3,000 figure. He did not know what horizontal orientation they might have; the airspheres were equipped with position-fixing equipment based on the triangulation of Telecom's beacon transmitters, but there was no hurry to find out how far they might have drifted from Philadelphia. However far it might be, it was always possible to find a return current at some altitude. It was enough at present to relax in a warm sea of golden light, under an azure sky.

Sarah slipped her tunic-coat off. Beneath it she was wearing a short one-piece dress; it was a shade of blue that went well with her dark colouring. She pushed her chair back to horizontal, and lay back. She looked up at Charles, shading her eyes against the sunlight.

'Aren't you hot?'

He slipped his own coat off, and tossed it to the back of the airsphere; it lay beside Sarah's discarded garment. There was a significance about that, which he was not sure if he wanted to think about. He was wearing the sleeveless shirt and shorts he normally wore when off duty in conditioned atmospheres. The sun was very pleasantly warm on his arms and legs.

He looked down at Sarah. Her eyes half closed, she was looking at him quizzically. She showed to her best advantage: the bronze of her skin against the deep crimson of the

204

airfoam, and the faintly blued white of the far-away background.

He said: 'I think I might relax, too.'

She smiled, but made no reply. He pushed his own chair back, and turned to face her. The smile still lingered.

'I wondered . . .'

Her lips barely parted. 'Yes?'

'A scientific question.'

'If I can help you . . .'

'The well-known Israeli inhibitions—I wondered if they functioned with the same precision at all altitudes.'

The smile deepened. 'I should think, a very interesting question. What would be the scientific approach to it?'

'Experimental.'

He moved towards her. Her willingness was certain even before she opened her arms to him.

Dinkuhl had explained that he was only stopping off at Philadelphia in the course of a trip to New York. He had had the idea of making the detour simply in order to have a meal with Charles, on the way. On his expense account, he further explained. He was at Oak Ridge, which was the Atomics men-only club, so Charles had to make his excuses and leave Sarah.

Dinkuhl had tall glasses of hot rum and ginger waiting when Charles arrived.

He said: 'Drink it up, Charlie boy. How's life. You look like a cat that's been living on alcoholic cream.'

Charles eased himself into a chair, and took the glass from the adjoining table. 'Very fair. No complaints. How about you? No trouble from Ledbetter?'

It had been Charles' idea that Dinkuhl should be given an Atomics bodyguard in view of his having been concerned with Charles both in imprisonment and escape. Atomics had been willing, but Dinkuhl had laughed at the idea. In his view, Telecom would be anxious to keep the defeat of their plans as private as possible. Taking it out on him would merely be an exercise in vindictiveness; it would give them no material advantage and might well provoke the reverse, should Charles urge Atomics into retaliatory action.

'Trouble?' Dinkuhl laughed. 'You know, the first morning back, Gillray called me up? Asked me if I'd been taking a holiday. If that character were any smoother, his face would slide off the screen.'

They had lunch together. While they talked, Charles was aware that there was something worrying Dinkuhl; he talked and joked but the talk and the jokes were perfunctory. He made no attempt to find out what it was; Dinkuhl was not the kind of person who encouraged solicitous probing into his troubles. But Dinkuhl brought things out into the open himself, over coffee.

'I've got a problem, Charlie boy,' he said.

Charles nodded. 'Unusual. So unusual that I'll offer my help. If I can help.'

'I'd appreciate your advice. It's not personal. That is, it's not my worry actually. It's Burt's.'

'Awkright's?'

'Yes. You know your new outfit used him to get in touch with us—with Sarah. They spun him a yarn about the wonders of Atomics Contact Section that enabled them to know he was one of my little gang of rebels—by God, if the PRO's don't get the fattest salary in the Contact Sections they ought to, the line of guff they hand out. He was happy enough thinking it was just Atomics that were exceptionally clever—still is.'

Someone at the next table flicked a shaker through a pool of aromac, and a cloud of delicately tinged bubbles danced up through the air, filling the room with their fragrance.

Charles did not himself care for perfume with his meals, or even after his meals, but it was too accepted a custom for any protest to be possible. He thought of holding his breath until the first impact had evaporated but decided, as he had done before, that it was more sensible to inhale deeply and de-sensitize his olfactory perceptions.

Breathing deeply, he said: 'And?'

Dinkuhl glanced at the adjoining table. He commented in a loud clear voice: 'The world's turning into a garden of goddam pansies. Roll on the gardener in white.' He permitted his voice to resume its normal level. 'I wasn't as happy as he was. I started looking around. I found that Atomics were not the only people in the know—very far from it. I had known that Telecom knew, of course—they had to know to pick you up through me. But it was more than two, even—Mining, Steel . . . Genetics Division——'

'Genetics?'

'Yes. Burt's own managerial. The boys took some precautions, but not that many. We thought we weren't interesting. We weren't, but I guess it kept the Contact brigades in practice. We are all neatly docketed and ticketed.'

'For action?'

'For information. The boys are all useful workers, and they find that useful workers mostly have aberrations nowadays; they put up with them providing there's nothing dangerous there.'

Charles said absently: 'Then I don't see what's worrying you.'

'Burt,' Dinkuhl said, 'is a more complex person than you might guess. I've known him for some time, and I know what he would do if he found out his seditious associations with me and the boys were known to the Genetics brass. He'd transfer—anywhere so long as it was outside Genetics and away from Detroit. He can't stand to be pitied or laughed at.'

207

'Most folk don't enjoy it.'

'They get by; Burt wouldn't. You get it, though? Do I tell him the truth or not? He's not likely to find out unless I do tell him. If I tell him, he'll leave and he'll be unhappy. If I don't tell him . . . where I want your advice is there : a guy's living in a fool's paradise—which is best, to leave him lie or to give him the jolt?'

Charles' thoughts were partly on Sarah, partly on the problem of the miniaturization of a thermoelectric conversion system. He gave Dinkuhl's question lukewarm attention, until he realized it was a question of principle on which advice was being sought. He brought his mind to focus.

'I should tell him. People are always entitled to be told the truth. No one has the right to decide in advance that it's bad for someone else to know the truth about his own affairs. Whatever it is, and whatever he may do as a result.'

Dinkuhl pursed his lips. 'I guess you're right. Maybe I was thinking of myself; I'll be sorry as hell if Burt does light out for somewhere else.'

'Tell you what,' Charles said. 'Affiliate KF to Atomics and bring the works over to Philly. Raven would fork out, if only to make Telecom sore.'

Dinkuhl smiled. 'I'll think of that. I'll let you know—I'll be dropping in on you again soon.'

Things ran smoothly meanwhile. Raven himself dropped in at the laboratory now and then; he showed a good deal of friendliness and an intelligent interest. Charles found him standing beside him one day while he was completing the polishing of a stone. He heard Raven's voice above the nervous grinding whine of the scaife.

'I'm interested to see you grind your own stones, Mr Grayner. Though, I must say, not surprised.' Charles straightened up. 'That one will be almost completed?'

Charles picked up the stone, set in its metal-plastic mount. He flicked the switch, and the scaife spun gradually to a halt.

'That one is finished, sir.'

'Mind if I have a look?'

Charles handed him the mount. Raven picked up a loupe from the bench and gave the diamond quite a professional going-over. Putting it down at last, he said:

'Brilliant cut. Brown-brilliant?'

Charles nodded; he was surprised but cautious. 'I didn't know you had worked in this line, sir.'

'Not worked.' Raven smiled. 'I've got what used to be known in earlier ages as a butterfly mind—or perhaps a jackdaw mind would be the more appropriate expression. Minor studies fascinate me—obscure crafts. Tell me, Mr Grayner, why is it that later excellent diamond cuts, like the brilliant, disappeared, although the earlier cuts, like the rose, managed to survive?'

'I wish I knew. I've often wondered.'

'It was simple enough. Luckert's synthetic—borbide. It was one of the last technological developments before the interregnum. In the war and post-war period diamonds jumped in value, as always, for economic security holding. Luckert's borbide fooled enough people to put a premium on diamonds cut in the old styles; they presumed those at least would be genuine.'

Charles said: 'But there's no great difficulty in telling borbide from diamond—it discolours, and there's the piezo-electric test.'

'It discolours—within a year or two—but that didn't help the purchaser at the time, did it? As for the piezo-electricity check, you have to remember that diamonds were sold by small shops. The special equipment required wasn't available in any case during the breakdown period. It was simpler to concentrate on primitive cut stones.'

209

'I should think the borbide people would have got on to that.'

'They did. But the brilliant cut didn't come back. That, Mr Grayner, is how aspects of craft, and even crafts in their entirety, pass out of the world's cognizance.' Raven walked about the small room which held the diamond polishing bench, picking things up, looking at them, and putting them down again. 'Mr Grayner, are you finding it pleasant working here?'

'Very pleasant, sir.'

Raven looked about with an air of deprecation. 'Not magnificent. Not at all magnificent. You would have fared better with Telecom; from the material point of view, at least. Still, we must try to do what we can for you. Any complaints, for instance? Are there any complaints, Mr Grayner?'

Charles hesitated very briefly; the hesitation was involuntary, and he spoke quickly to cover it up.

'No complaints, sir. I have everything I want.'

'You and Miss Cohn are getting on all right together?'

He said, with no hesitation this time: 'Very well.'

'That's good. I hope you won't hesitate to come to me if there should be anything. Don't hesitate to waste my time. It is yours that is the more valuable.'

Raven went, with his jaunty old man's step, and Charles had to master an impulse to go after him, or to call him back. He mastered it as he had covered up the earlier hesitation, and for the same reason. It was not that he doubted Raven's willingness, nor even his ability, to help him. It was that it was impossible to frame any of his doubts or his worries without criticizing, if only by implication, Sarah.

Outside the laboratory, their life together proceeded very harmoniously. They did most things and went to most places

210

together. Charles did not let his doubts carry over to spoil this part of their association. All of love was a new experience for him, and he was determined it should not be spoiled in any way.

They spent a lot of time airsphering—mostly together, but occasionally each in a single bubble. Then there would be the delight of chasing each other over the invisible hills and valleys of the air. Along the rivers of the wind they would chase each other, and they were rivers capable of turning, without warning, into precipitous waterfalls that plunged the spheres hundreds of feet, either up or down, in an instance. Close on her heels, Charles might suddenly find himself looking down on her far below, or gazing up, blinded by sun, to where her sphere drifted high and remote.

The Alleghenies provided them with a pleasure ground. There they could ride the updraughts, close against the rocky mountain sides, and glide dangerously alongside the knife-edged spurs that could so easily rip the plaspex skin, spilling the sphere's occupant down great cliffs of fall to distant midget valleys.

And, of course, there was the delight of bringing the spheres in to some sun-splashed ledge of rock, on the world's roof, of tethering them to the mountain face with impact suckers, of eating and drinking in that warm silent isolation, of sitting and talking or simply sun-bathing. Of making love.

Charles had sent Sarah to check personally some supplies that had been queried by Conway when Dinkuhl paid his next visit.

He said: 'Hi, Charlie.'

Charles said with facetious sternness: 'Where's your pass, Mister?'

Dinkuhl managed a wry smile, but he clearly wasn't amused. Charles said: 'Burt asked for transfer?'

211

Dinkuhl nodded. 'He left last night. That advice you gave me. Tell the truth and let the chips fly what way they will. You still think it's good?'

'The best. But I'm sorry you've lost Burt. Where's he gone to?'

'Lignin. Somewhere north of Finland. Lignin should be pleased all right. They're shorter of good men than most managerials. And they're all short, with the notable and glorious exception of Atomics. Sarah?'

'Checking supplies. She'll be back soon.'

Dinkuhl leaned back against one of the benches; he had a restless look and his voice had taken on the slightly affected drawl that indicated some inner excitement.

'That the set-up now?' he asked. 'You do the work and she checks supplies in? I thought her middle name was Einstein.'

Charles said angrily: 'What the hell do you mean by that, Hiram?'

'Brother,' Dinkuhl said softly, 'you're worried. You're plenty worried. Tell Uncle Hiram.'

Charles stared at him. 'For God's sake! Have you gone crazy? Who's worried?'

'What is it, Charlie?' Dinkuhl asked. 'She isn't as bright any longer? She doesn't grasp things that should be simple going? You wonder even if maybe she had a knock on the head during that fortnight you were apart?'

Charles restrained his voice to quietness. 'I don't know what's got into you. Burt transferring, maybe. Anyway, I want you to keep it for somewhere else, Hiram.' He turned away. 'You'll be welcome in a different mood.'

'I'll carry the invitation in my heart. Here the lady is now. Hi, Sarah. Been copying any good sketches lately?'

Charles had no idea what Dinkuhl was talking about, but the tone was unmistakably offensive. He expected Sarah

212

to flare up or to treat him with icy contempt. She did neither. She said placatingly:

'Glad you managed to get along, Hiram.'

Dinkuhl watched her for a moment. Then he smiled.

'What we all need,' he remarked, 'is a drink. You both have a drink?'

Charles hesitated. Sarah said: 'Be glad to.'

Dinkuhl brought a flask out of his back pocket. It had two small plastobeakers attached. He filled them, and looked about him inquiringly.

'A glass for Uncle Hiram? You find me one, Sarah?'

While Sarah was getting it, Dinkuhl picked up the two already filled. He gave one to Charles; the other he held in his hand, holding it with his palm cupped above it. When Sarah came back, he gave it to her, and took the glass she brought and poured out a tot for himself.

'To all honest men,' he said. He bowed to Sarah. 'And honest women.'

She coughed a little as she drank. 'What is it?'

'All right? Liqueur grappa. I have a source.'

She smiled. 'A good one, I should say.'

'All my sources are.' Dinkuhl considered her speculatively. 'You know something? Charles here has been telling me he's disappointed in you. He thinks you're lying down on the job. He——'

Charles stepped across to stand in front of Dinkuhl. He said tightly:

'I don't know what's got into you, Hiram. But, for the last time, lay off. Lay off!'

Dinkuhl said: 'You know, I never met Sarah. But I know enough about her to know she wouldn't have needed your help in a slanging match, Charlie.' To Sarah, he said: 'Well, honey?'

She said uncertainly: 'I feel dizzy.'

213

Dinkuhl took her gently round the shoulders. 'Come and lie down, honey. You need rest. Easy now. Couch over here.'

He got her on to the couch, and made her comfortable. She shook her head, as though trying to shake off cobwebs.

Dinkuhl said: 'You're going to sleep, honey.'

His voice was significant, and as though in response she jerked up. 'You mean . . . ? The drink!'

Charles demanded: 'Just what have you been doing?'

Dinkuhl said gently: 'What's your name, honey? Before you go to sleep, what's your name?'

Her speech was becoming slurred; unable to sustain the effort she had made, she sank back again. 'Sarah Cohn. You know——'

Dinkuhl shook his head. 'No. Not that. Your real name.'

She tried to speak again, but it was beyond her. For a brief moment she looked at them in agony and fear, and then her eyes closed, and she was unconscious. Charles had rushed over to her, and he sat beside her now, holding her limp hand. He turned to look up at Dinkuhl.

'Something good, Hiram. It had better be something good.'

Dinkuhl said: 'Don't think I'm happy. I wasn't happy when I told Burt, either. That was why I put the question to you the last time I was over. I could see you were happy with the girl, and it made it hard. It was a relief that you should make it so clear things were worrying you, when I came this time. They were, weren't they?'

Charles felt that anger, and every other positive emotion, had been drained from him. He looked at Sarah's quietly breathing body. Sarah's? A Sarah surprisingly unhelpful in the work, a Sarah he could almost think of as trying to cover up her own ignorance. The doubts that he had dammed up were now flooding round him; his thoughts bobbed like chips on the tide.

Dinkuhl said: 'You see, I had had access to those UC

214

Contact Section reports—they included Sarah's psychoplan. A wench of spirit. But even if that line hadn't been so strongly marked, it was still reasonable that a girl who showed herself so clearly to be interested in you should have had a different reaction to me. The first time I came over here, I clowned, I made snide remarks. She took them, like a little woolly lamb. It wasn't right, Charlie. It wasn't right for a normal girl, and it was very wrong for one with a psychoplan like Sarah's.'

Charles looked at him, and back to the girl's figure.

'You mean, they've done something to her? What? And why, in God's name?'

'That isn't Sarah, Charlie. It never was Sarah.'

Charles shook his head. 'I know her. It's Sarah. Her voice alone——'

Dinkuhl bent over the girl. He pulled the neck of her tunic down a fraction, and pointed. There was a line on the skin, barely visible, perhaps an inch long.

'Gannery's operation. Re-formation of the vocal cords. You can get precision with it and I guess this job was a precision job.'

'How did you know that would be there?'

'It had to be. I knew she was a phoney. You remember the time she'd been showing that blueprint-thing on the wall screen? You took her off to show her the diamond polishing bench. I had a look in her little room while you were away. She had been copying that sketch from a photostat of the original that Sarah did. Why should she need to copy, unless it was because she wasn't Sarah at all? They had primed her well, but you can't prime a person with years of scientific experience.'

Charles stared at the motionless girl. 'I can't believe it. That little scar . . . it could be something else.'

Dinkuhl stood beside him. 'You remember being Charlie

215

Macintosh, Charlie? Macintosh was a real guy—works at an obscure GD station in South Africa. Would have been a laugh if you'd met up with him. Burt went to some trouble to pick him: he had to be someone who matched you closely, but with extra flesh at all points. You can build up; you can't whittle down. He had full cheeks, while you have thin ones.'

He paused, gazing at the face of the girl who had been Sarah. 'An interesting face. Good looking, but not precisely beautiful. The temples bulging a little just above the brow line. Unusual, that.'

From his pocket, Dinkuhl took a small knife; he flipped the catch and the sapphire blade leapt out, gleaming dully. Charles watched in fascination as he bent down towards the unconscious face. He heard himself saying: 'Stop ...!' With a deft motion, Dinkuhl sliced the girl's flesh at the base of the forehead.

He held up a strip of flesh that he had cut away. There was no bleeding from the incision. The cut had laid bare not flesh but plastic. Now, beyond any doubt, Charles knew he had been loving a mask. Dinkuhl tossed the strip into a disposer; he walked away from the girl, and leaned against a bench on the opposite side of the room. He looked at Charles.

'Well, Charlie boy? What's it going to be?'

Charles said dully: 'You tell me. How do you expect I should know?'

' "People are always entitled to be told the truth." No, I'm not riding you, Charlie. I'm not the strictly monogamous type, but I can guess how bad it is. This way, though, it's quick. You would have had to find out sooner or later. They still operate on the assumption that scientists are dumb. Hell, you were finding out already. It was better this way.'

216

Charles shook himself. He saw the truth of Dinkuhl's statements, but that still didn't make it easy to act on them. To find that he had been deceived in this way was somehow worse than when he had thought Sarah killed. He looked up at Dinkuhl, almost in inquiry.

'Raven——?'

'Just a fine old Southern gentleman. Ledbetter was no more than peanuts. Raven's good. All these tricky arrangements made on the assumption that they were going to get you away from Telecom. We only made it easier for him by arranging the break ourselves. Raven's the kingpin, all right. You've reached the managerial top, Charlie. You can't go higher. This is where they put gloves on before they reach for their knives.'

Charles looked at Dinkuhl helplessly. 'What's the best thing to do? I should like to see Raven. Is that silly?'

'No. Not at all silly. Inevitable, I should say.' He glanced around the lab. 'I should hazard a guess that the usual precautions are in operation. Even if they aren't, I can think of easier things than just walking out of a place like this. The air of casualness has, to my mind, a somewhat studied look.'

'I guess so. That kind of crook doesn't take chances.'

'Don't be bitter, Charlie—not about individuals. It doesn't pay any percentage.' Dinkuhl raised his head slightly. There was the sound of a door sliding open in the lobby. 'A visitor. Red-handed. In this same country, and besides, the wench is not dead.'

It was Raven himself. He stopped just inside the door. His bright amused eyes took in the tableau—Dinkuhl leaning against the bench, Charles still sitting on the couch beside the girl's recumbent body.

Raven said: 'Good morning, Mr Grayner. And Mr

217

Dinkuhl.' He peered towards the girl. 'The lady would appear to be indisposed.'

Automatically, Charles said: 'Good morning, sir.'

Dinkuhl leaned back a little further. He drawled:

'I guess the lady drank something that disagreed with her. Would there be any objection to your introducing her to us, Director, so we shall know whom to apologize to?'

Dinkuhl watched with bland unconcern as Raven walked across to the couch, and bent down to examine the girl. Raven straightened up again a moment later, and looked at them both.

'Would you gentlemen object if I were to arrange for Miss Levine to be taken away and put properly to bed? I doubt if she is likely to recover her faculties for some hours yet.'

Charles did not say anything. Dinkuhl nodded.

'Go right ahead. It's your home territory. We should appreciate it to have Miss Levine attended to.'

Raven went across to the callscreen. They heard him asking for two stretcher-men. Then he switched off and turned his attention back to them. He said:

'This has been rather unfortunate. I had hoped it would be delayed for some time—a few more weeks, at any rate. But we must put up with events as they fall out.'

'Life,' Dinkuhl said gravely, 'is like that. I hope you will arrange to convey our regrets to Miss Levine when she wakes up. She will understand it was nothing personal.'

Raven said: 'And you, Mr Grayner? Your regrets as well?'

The implication was obvious, and Charles resented it. But he was prevented from saying anything immediately by the arrival of the stretcher-men. They put the girl gently on to the stretcher. Raven said: 'To her rooms, please, and then get a nurse for her.'

Charles felt Raven watching him while the little procession

left the room. He said, as the door slid closed behind them:

'A lot of regrets, Director. But they are all concerned with being made a fool of. No regrets about finding the truth out. Assistant Levine was doing her duty, I guess. No one's fault if it came out this way.'

'If we must use these titles,' Raven said softly, 'we should use the right ones. Manager Levine. An exceptionally brilliant and talented young lady, and we are very proud of her.'

'With the views I now hold of Atomics,' Charles said bitterly, 'that fails to surprise me.'

'Your views are understandable. They would be understandable even if you had not had the benefit of Mr Dinkuhl's tutelage. But I hope they will not be permanent. You are an intelligent man, Mr Grayner—that is not flattery, but a statement germane to the situation. Mr Dinkuhl is also of high intelligence, but his intellect is hampered by his emotions; particularly by that over-riding urge to destruction, which is so marked a feature of his attitude towards society. I have discussed this point with you before.'

Dinkuhl said lazily: 'That's me. Samson, with each arm around a pillar.'

Charles said: 'You convinced me that Hiram had taken an unreasonably pessimistic view. But part of the conviction at least was from believing that you, and Atomics, represented something higher than the others.'

'To my great regret,' Raven said, 'I felt obliged to give you that somewhat exaggerated impression of my personal integrity. It was made necessary by the experiences you had already undergone. I should like you to believe that I would have preferred to be frank with you or, since I could not be frank, dishonest in the normal human fashion.'

'You can tell the truth?'

219

'From this time on, Mr Grayner, I shall use nothing else with you. There would be no point.'

Charles said: 'Where is Sarah Cohn? Who has her?'

'I do not know. We have looked very hard and we have not found her—neither her nor Isaacssohn. You can imagine that we have spared no efforts to find both of them. They may be dead. It is a conclusion to which the absence of any information is tending to force us. You see that I am being frank now, Mr Grayner.'

'Are you?' Dinkuhl asked. 'Or could you be trying to persuade Charlie that he might as well make do with a near-miss? Another dab of plastic, and Miss Levine's as good as new.'

'No, Mr Dinkuhl,' Raven said. 'You misjudged me. I was being frank. You are putting things in their worst aspect though I will admit to hoping that Mr Grayner may overcome his present resentment against Miss Levine. But that was not in my mind at that time.' He glanced at Charles. 'Miss Levine took this duty on with great reluctance. She accepted the task only on my personal plea, and because she was the one person available who could be made to resemble Miss Cohn physically, and at the same time be capable of deceiving you for a time on points of personality and technical skill. Her failure—for I'm afraid it was failure—in this latter is a pointer to its difficulty. No one else could have done it anywhere near as well.'

'She made one big error,' Charles commented. 'And one easy enough to avoid. Sarah is essentially chaste. Didn't her psychoplan show that?'

Raven nodded. 'So,' he said, 'is Miss Levine.'

'Then the orders she was given were at fault.'

'There were no orders. I think I take your meaning, Mr Grayner. Whatever may have happened between you was not a part of the attempt to deceive you. You will give

220

me credit, I hope, for not committing so egregious a blunder.'

'Then?'

'Miss Levine was surprised—and not pleased, Mr Grayner —to find her duty in some respects more attractive than she had anticipated. She quickly became fond of you.'

'She told you that?'

Raven ran a neatly manicured hand through his white and well-groomed hair.

'She had to, Mr Grayner. It was necessary, to explain her request to be relieved of her duty.'

'She asked that?'

'Three times. The latest occasion was yesterday evening. I was forced to refuse her requests. I told her I hoped that within a week or two you would have settled well enough in this managerial to have the truth explained to you. I did not reckon with Mr Dinkuhl, who appears to have a talent for unveiling indiscreet secrets.'

Incredulously, Charles asked: 'You think, under those circumstances, I would have stayed?'

Raven said: 'Mr Dinkuhl, that is a flask I see in your pocket? Might we not all have a drink—unadulterated this time?'

Dinkuhl grinned. He poured into the two plastobeakers and the glass. He retained the beaker the girl had had for himself, and handed round the others.

'I'll take the residual Micky. Your health, Director.'

Raven took the drink, sniffed it, drank, and smacked his lips lightly. 'A good liquor, Mr Dinkuhl.'

'I always find the best is good enough.'

'A good motto. Now, Mr Grayner—would you have stayed? I hope you would. I hope you still will.'

It was clearly the beginning of a long disquisition. Charles broke in.

'Before you go any further, Director, I should like to express my views on something—on the ties that can exist, that should exist between the man and the managerial. I can see two, and only two: natural loyalty, and trust. I still retained some loyalty to UC after I had seen it as inefficient and corrupt, because the loyalty went back a long way. It isn't possible for me to have that kind of loyalty to Atomics. That's where the necessity for trust comes in. And it's a vulnerable growth. It won't stand up to the kind of treatment you have given it—with whatever good intentions. I can assure you that it is dead. Dead and stinking.'

There was a short silence, as though Raven were waiting to be certain that Charlie had finished what he was going to say. Then he said:

'Loyalty to a managerial—trust in a managerial—those are sentiments apt for the lower levels of society. You have left that stage, Mr Grayner, as Mr Dinkuhl had done before you. Nor can you get back to it. Could you go back to UC from this managerial? Could you even contemplate such a return? You have joined the emancipated, and perhaps that is your misfortune. But one thing is certain: it doesn't make life easier, and it most certainly does not make the course of your future acts obvious or assured.

'Your disillusion is nothing new to me, Mr Grayner. I became acquainted with it many years ago. The Chief Director of a managerial is the last person who could possibly be a starry-eyed managerialist. He sees a number of distasteful things, and he is forced to take part in some of them. But he must continue to work through his managerial on behalf of the higher loyalty he holds.'

'Which is?' Dinkuhl asked.

'Loyalty to the human race. It is a far-reaching loyalty and not always easy to grasp—it is not *possible* to grasp it until

222

the earlier loyalties have been superseded. But it is, of course, the fundamental loyalty of man.'

'And the fundamental loyalty,' Dinkuhl suggested, 'demands that Charlie goes on working for Atomics—though you don't need to call it Atomics? What shall we call it? United Preservers of Mankind—how's that?'

Raven was not ruffled. He smiled dismissingly at Dinkuhl.

'Not one of the things I said at our first meeting is invalidated by your discovery that I have been deceiving you in the matter of Sarah Cohn. As I have said, it was certain that the deception could not be maintained for very long in any case. I risked the disappointment and resentment that you were bound to feel then because of my confidence in your fundamental level-headedness. And in your ability to rise above your own needs and desires.

'I am asking you to do that now, Mr Grayner—to forget your personal problems for a moment and to study things in a more general and detached light. The human race is facing one of its moments of decision, and you personally can be of great importance in the way that decision goes. Even without Isaacssohn's discovery, the situation would have been critical, but it now becomes urgently so. I put it to you with all seriousness that the world may be facing devastation.'

Dinkuhl said: 'Not for the first time. They sacked Cnossos five thousand years ago. And shall Atomics live?'

Raven walked across to Dinkuhl. He stood before him, his hands folded together.

'Have you thought of what the sack of Cnossos must have been like, Mr Dinkuhl? Is it not possible that the lethargy, the flabbiness of spirit, that you so rightly chide in the world about us may have blinded you to the sleeping furies? For they are no more than sleeping—the Cometeers show us that. It is this social fabric you despise that prevents them from waking. Destroy it, and you will see them rub their eyes.'

223

Dinkuhl looked at him and smiled. 'They are rubbing their eyes already, Director. What is more, their bellies are rumbling.'

'Do you think, then, that man was made for murder—for torture and rape and brutality?'

For a moment Dinkuhl was silent. He said: 'I don't know what he was made for. Maybe he was made to sit in front of a TV screen. If he was, I'll take the torture, rape and brutality; it has a healthy ring to it.'

Raven swung around, an easy unhurried movement, to look at Charles.

'This is the point, Mr Grayner: do you share your friend's view of cataclysms? Do you feel with him that Red League and Cosy Bright cry out for cannibalism as a counterweight? I do not ask you to place any trust in me, nor in this managerial, but I ask you—forgetting your own needs, forgetting Sarah Cohn—to answer a question truthfully. The question is this: do you know of any capacity in which you can serve your fellow-men better than—no, as well as!—you can here? Never mind whether they have deserved destruction and damnation. That is the sort of question we can leave to the Cometeers. But from the simple point of view of avoiding pain and suffering, where else can you do as much?'

'One small item,' Dinkuhl cut in. 'A necessary item on that premise. Charlie produces the power source and the weapon: then he has to trust you for the using of it.'

Raven said, with absolute confidence: 'I will leave that point to Mr Grayner. He knows that I have deceived him, but he knows also that I did this with a larger end in view. I apologize for deceiving him, but I do not regret putting the world's needs first. It is precisely because I have already done that, in fact, that I can appeal to him to rely on my integrity in the future.'

Dinkuhl said: 'Charlie, my view is we've heard enough

from Chief Director Raven. We know just what kind of a noble and altruistic lover of mankind he is. I think that at this point we can prepare to move on.'

Raven said to Charles: 'Well, Mr Grayner? Destruction or salvage? A corrupt and decadent world—do you destroy it or do you try to mend it?'

Charles stood in silence; he felt that his irresolution must be written all over him. Raven and Dinkuhl were both looking at him—Raven with calm confidence, Dinkuhl with the trace of a mocking grin.

He said: 'I don't know——'

Dinkuhl said: 'I suppose a key point is whether even now you have all the facts in the situation. All the relevant facts. Has he had all the relevant facts presented, do you think, Director?'

Raven nodded. 'As far as I am concerned—yes.'

Charles glanced quickly at Dinkuhl; he knew him well enough by now to know that something was due to follow.

'You wouldn't consider it a relevant fact,' Dinkuhl asked, 'that you have been personally losing ground both on the Atomics Board of Directors and the World Council of Managerials for some years past—that your touching desire to save the world from itself is bound up with an anxiety to restore your own prestige?'

'It would be relevant if it were true. But it is not true.'

'The advantage I have over you, Director, is that Charlie has not yet caught me out lying to him. There is a motion down for the next Board meeting of this managerial, expressing no confidence in you as Chief Director and calling for your resignation. It is subscribed by Ramaseshan of New Delhi and Burlitz of Munich.' He paused. 'You can now remove my advantage by calling your secretary from this room and asking her to put on the screen the draft of agenda for the meeting in question. In case your memory needs refreshing, the meeting will be held on February 23rd, at New Delhi.'

There was a brief silence. On Raven's face there still remained the faint smile he had called up at Dinkuhl's first charge of his personal interest in having Charles in Atomics. He made the gesture Charles had expected him to make on their first meeting; he lifted his hands and examined his nails. The control was admirable.

'I could defend myself, Mr Dinkuhl,' Raven said at last, 'but for the second time I have been caught in deception—and this time it was most certainly an error of judgment. Twice is too many.'

He shrugged delicately. Dinkuhl was observing him closely.

'So now,' Dinkuhl commented, 'for our own good, for the good of suffering mankind, and last and least for the good of the prestige of Chief Director Raven, you must—regrettably, regretfully—adopt the methods of such inferiors as Ledbetter. You must use force.'

The shrug was repeated, more delicately still. 'With very great regret, I assure you, Mr Dinkuhl. I am not under any illusion that the work will progress as swiftly in such conditions. But there is no alternative.'

'Should your colleagues, Ramaseshan and Burlitz, become aware of your having had such a prize and of your having jeopardized it through what they might think of as a desire for personal aggrandisement, I feel your position would become less secure rather than more, Director.'

Raven smiled. 'I am inclined to agree, Mr Dinkuhl. Fortunately they are not likely to become aware of it. I have better security control here at Philadelphia than possibly you might imagine.'

'I've got a good imagination. I hope you have, too, Director. Just about now, Ramaseshan is receiving a radio

226

report. It explains to him how, for the good of Atomics—we omit mankind for the moment—you took steps to obtain the services of Official Grayner, late of United Chemicals, who is—to your knowledge—the sole person capable of carrying through a project that will bring final power to that managerial which obtains it exclusively. Unfortunately Grayner has been got at by some outside group and either abducted or persuaded to desert. You have reason to think the destination is Asia, and probably India. Ramaseshan's aid in recovering the fugitive will be appreciated. The report is signed Raven.'

Raven looked at Dinkuhl. He said slowly: 'Your destructive potential is very high, Mr Dinkuhl.'

'Don't bother to make any formal good-byes. At my guess, Ramaseshan will be on the screen to you without much delay. Oh.' Dinkuhl fished in a pocket. 'A copy of your report. You'll need it.'

Raven said: 'Sometimes I see your point of view, Mr Dinkuhl, and am even minded to share it. You two have now ceased to be an asset, and become instead a nuisance. Have you any good reason why I should not eliminate a nuisance?'

'The best. We're persuasive talkers. I doubt if you have an executioner you could be sure of, since we should naturally claim access to Ramaseshan. Besides, you really are very busy, Director. I should get back to your desk, if I were you.'

Raven smiled. 'The points are not overwhelming, but you have me. I lack the essential vindictiveness of a Chief Director; it accounts for my present awkwardness. Ramaseshan, for instance . . . Ah well. I take it you will not reconsider simply for the sake of helping me save my skin, Mr Grayner? I thought not. What do you plan to do now, by the way?'

'Leave us to our worries,' Dinkuhl said. 'You have your own.'

227

'Very true. Good-bye, Mr Grayner. I wish I could say I believed you to be in good hands. Good-bye, Mr Dinkuhl.' Walking jauntily but without haste, Raven went out.

There was no hurry this time. They went along to Oak Ridge for drinks and a meal.

'An enviable position, Charlie,' Dinkuhl said. 'You can even use that wrist transmitter to call up the Atomics bravos if anyone else shows awkward. For a few days you can describe yourself as in Atomics but not of it. No longer than that, I think. The Chief Director is versatile if not vindictive. He may still make a deal with Ramaseshan. Or even, for that matter, eliminate him. I told you the stakes were high.'

Charles contemplated his gin and vermouth.

'Hiram,' he said, 'the last few weeks I have spent chasing my tail. I don't entirely blame you for this, though I do have the impression that you've provided a twist once or twice when I showed signs of slowing down, but I would have you know I'm tiring rapidly.'

'Telecom came and took you. You put yourself into Atomics. I only got you out of those two havens.'

'Right. For what purpose?'

'Purpose?' Dinkuhl grinned. 'I'm not Raven. What do you want yourself?'

'To find Sarah. If she's alive.'

'O.K. Any clues?'

'None. As you know.'

'As I know. Well, we've tried the overworld. I never thought we'd get anything there. Now we try the underworld.'

'The underworld?'

Dinkuhl's face changed, hardened. His voice dropped an octave. 'Brother,' he demanded, 'are you damned?' He resumed his normal expression. 'After a lifetime preaching culture, I guess I can preach damnation.'

'What do you expect to get from the Cometeers?'

'I don't know. Nothing. Anything. At least, it's where Contact Sections are least likely to look for us. With a couple of natural beards, we'll be impenetrable. Put not your trust in plastics when nature can lend a hand. I'll do the preaching, Charlie. You can go round with the hat.'

Charles said doubtfully: 'You think you can get by?'

'I've made a study of it. I'll have the rest of the preachers tearing their beards out by the roots.'

'It seems crazy.'

'When sanity calcifies, madness is the only solution. Any better ideas?'

Charles shook his head.

7

THE night was very cold and dark with clouds. Inside in the square box-like room, even the heat generated by the massed ranks of the Cometeers failed to raise the temperatures perceptibly. Charles wrapped his cloak more tightly about him. Dinkuhl, above him on the rostrum, had thrown his cloak wide, presumably warmed by his own eloquence. While waiting for their beards to grow sufficiently they had taken on artificial ones—tapering in Charles' case, square-cut in Dinkuhl's. There was some discomfort in the wearing of them, but coupled with the preacher's long cloak they provided an impressive spectacle. In Dinkuhl's case particularly.

Dinkuhl was cooing now, like any nesting dove.

'Are there some who shall say that Love walks in the world? Are there some who shall say that out of Evil will come Goodness? Is there then Love in Flesh? Is there Goodness in Evil? My friends, is there Life in Death? Does Purity spring from Corruption? Let them see, who have eyes. Let them hear, who have ears.'

He paused. 'My friends.' His voice was low but carried, Charles knew, to the very last row. 'Are you Saved?' His voice rose in volume, with the diapason of an organ. 'Or are you Damned?'

'Damned!' they chorused back, raggedly at first but

developing unison as they went along. 'Damned to Hell, and in Hell. Damned! Damned! Damned!'

'And if you are damned,' asked Dinkuhl, 'shall any be saved?'

'None shall be saved! None shall be saved!'

Charles had an oak staff. He leaned on it now, unmoving and silent in the midst of the rising clamour. That had been a touch of Dinkuhl's—that he should stand and watch. He himself had no clues at all as to the reactions these people might possibly have; no feelings about them, in fact, except repulsion and amazement. But Dinkuhl handled them like an orchestra. He let the echoes of their affirmation of despair die away, before he continued, and in an almost conversational tone.

'My friends,' he said, 'let us babble of green fields. To minds racked by sin and by remorse—for the damned cannot know repentance—let us call a vision of the childhood meadows of innocence. Let us dream a moment of spring and early roses, of sunlight bright beyond bearing and yet more sweet than life itself, of the dew that sparkled gem-like in the hedgerows. Let us think, if we can, of that long-lost time when pleasure could exist without sin, when laughter was gentle, and god-fearing hearts were gay. In the mind at least, let us retrace our stumbling footsteps while they yet walked the narrow path, carpeted with flowers, that led to the high blue mountain. Let us think of what we were, my friends.'

He let it sink in. Covertly Charles observed the effect. Several were crying openly.

Dinkuhl's voice changed again; not very much but simply by the taking on of an edge.

'Are your hearts sad, my friends? Do they know the bitterness of grief? Does the knife twist deep when the mind recalls the world that it has lost? For it is lost, my friends. You will never know that spring again. You will never see those meadows, those roses, that beaded dew. Your doomed

231

faces will never be warmed by that sunlight. And the path you walk now does not lead to the high blue mountain. It leads to the pit. To the pit!'

The shuddering moan, by now familiar, as though the rows of hunched figures were not several, but one. One flesh. Leviathan grieving. Charles let his eyes flick over them. He could see the badges of those in the first two or three rows. Steel . . . United Chemicals . . . Interplanetary . . . Genetics Division . . . Agriculture . . . Mining . . . It was a roll-call, representative if not complete. Somewhere, he thought, Ledbetter, Raven are going about their ordinary affairs—plotting, manœuvring, struggling with God only knew what mixed motives for the control of the safe and imperturbable daylight world. Why did they not bend a little of that energy to the world below? Surely they realized that it might crack their towering edifices even before they could erect them?

'You will never see those enchanted places. You will never know that halcyon time again. But you will remember them, my friends. For the damned keep three things. Their flesh. Their sins. Their memories. Their flesh for their torment. Their sins for their damnation. And their memories for that last agony of the mind which is the awareness of loss. You will remember them in flames, in the burning dust, in ice, in the desolate frozen wastes. You will remember them, and you will curse the bitter memory.'

From somewhere at the back, a man's voice cried out, in a deep monotone:

'Damned! Damned! Damned! Damned! Damned!'

The same inarticulate groan responded to it. With horror, Charles guessed, and wondered if he could have guessed right: that Ledbetter, even Raven, might have other reasons for doing nothing than unawareness or indifference. That it might be fear that held them back, fear of unleashing the storm.

232

'Damned,' Dinkuhl said, heavily but without emphasis. He let the words drop like stones into oil. 'Damned.'

From different parts of the room the echoes came back. 'Damned.' 'Damned.' 'Damned.' A woman began sobbing— dry rasping sobs that sounded as though they might go on forever. They were still continuing, as Dinkuhl lifted his right hand.

'Tonight the Lord Jahweh hides from you even the sight of his Finger of Wrath. Nevertheless we will go out and make our plea. That which you wish to give for the bread of the Preacher and the Preacher's Friend you must cast down by the door as you go out. No more than a dollar from anyone. Let us go out.'

Some of the men among the Cometeers took the rostrum out and set it up in the open. It was bitterly cold, and very dark. Charles helped Dinkuhl to find his way up on to the rostrum. He stood beneath it himself, shivering. There was no point in attempting impassivity; he could see no more than a vague blur of white which was presumably the faces of the damned. They would not be able to see him at all, even if there was any likelihood of their looking at him.

'The Lord Jahweh hides from our eyes his Finger of Wrath, but it is there, approaching in space and time. The Finger that points to a world of doom! The Finger that will strike a people given over to iniquities! The Finger that brands the cattle for the slaughter! The Voice of the Lord Jahweh will be a thunder from the mountains, a quake from the depths of the earth! None shall escape the words of judgment—none shall escape!'

The wind clung close, prying and biting. Dinkuhl, however, made the pause that the ritual demanded. His voice leapt out suddenly, shouting, savage:

'Down! Kneel! You dogs, you bitches! Down, down, down! Down to your damnation! Down on your knees, and cry, cry to Jahweh the Eternal: "Lord Jahweh, we are damned! Send us your whips, your scorpions, your fires to sear our tenderest flesh!" '

'Lord Jahweh, we are damned! Send us your whips, your scorpions, your fires to sear our tenderest flesh!'

'Unleash your demons!'

'Unleash your demons!'

'One mercy only, Lord Jahweh. One mercy only!'

'One mercy only, Lord Jahweh. One mercy only!'

'After a million years of torment, grant us oblivion!'

'After a million years of torment, grant us oblivion!'

Their responses had been growing, both in volume and unison. Now Dinkuhl pulled another trick out for them. It was effective; Charles' own flesh crept slightly. Out of silence Dinkuhl's voice, like a whisper but a whisper that outroared the wind, was the very intonation of despair.

'We, your damned, kneel before you, Lord Jahweh.'

And raggedly, shaken, the final response:

'We, your damned, kneel before you, Lord Jahweh.'

It was over. Dinkuhl climbed down from his dais, and Charles and he stood together by the door of the shed while some of the people made their personal good-byes. The atmosphere now was entirely different: friendly and casual. It was now that they picked up information—the Cometeers to get in touch with at the next port-of-call—news of other preachers in the district. Their other questions did not seem unusual in the general asking and answering.

'Brother,' Dinkuhl said, 'we are looking for two instruments of Jahweh. They hold power in their hands. A young woman whose name is Sarah Cohn, a man whose name is Hans Isaacssohn. Wherever they are, they are being kept secret. They may be captive. Have you heard anything of these two? The Will of Jahweh, brother.'

A short barrel-figured man with an Atomics badge: 'I don't know of anyone under those names, Preacher.'

234

'They are scientists.'

'No. I don't know any scientists.'

The same question, substituting only Sister for Brother, addressed to a dark intense Hydroponics woman.

'I don't see anything of that kind of business, Preacher. Tell me, Preacher—my Manager . . . now and again he has a look of the damned. You think I ought to put it to him—ask him along to one of the meetings?'

'Sister, every man is entitled to understand that he is damned. Invite him along.'

A cynical-looking middle-aged man in Steel said:

'I know enough dirt about my managerial to prosecute them before the Throne, Preacher, but I don't know of them keeping anybody secret or captive. Not right now, anyway.'

The last scatter of the faithful departed to their gyros, leaving Charles and Dinkuhl together.

Dinkuhl said: 'Let's get inside and collect the offerings, brother. It'll be something to get in out of this goddam wind. too.'

They picked the money up from the floor and Dinkuhl, who carried the Preacher's purse, put it away.

'I find it possible,' he said, 'to regret that the custom has hardened of setting a dollar limit. I've thought of forgetting that line, but I guess the customers would remember, anyway. There must be a useful angle to this racket, but I haven't found it yet.'

'Good performance tonight,' Charles said judiciously.

'Yes. I was quite proud of myself. Halcyon and roses and the high blue mountain. It's better than KF. I can ham away to my vulgar heart's content.'

'The bass at the back helped.'

'I should hire him.' He glanced speculatively at Charles. 'Or station you out back to do the job.'

'My voice isn't good enough.'

'I could fit you up with a bass amplifier.'

They laughed. Charles said: 'I'm glad you're enjoying things, Hiram. It doesn't look as though we're getting anywhere much.'

'Brother, we're only starting.' Dinkuhl rummaged in an inside pocket of his cloak and brought out a square flask. 'To help us on our way. The successful spy is the guy who manages to enjoy life on the side. Where's the next call? Kentucky?'

'Kentucky's right.'

Charles had a drink, and passed the flask back to Dinkuhl. He gulped, and smacked his lips.

'We ought to count our blessings, Charlie boy. As that there's no ban on gyros for Preachers—not even on gyros with airfoam mattresses. Though, come to think, I don't see how the Preachers manage to fit themselves out with gyros on a take of a dollar a head. I knew there was an angle to the racket. And once you know there's an angle, you're half way to finding it.'

Charles shook his head. 'The local community chests provide them. One of the brothers was telling me they provided a gyro for one of their young hopefuls who felt the call to be a Preacher only a couple of months ago. They reckon it pays off in a faster circulation of the Word.'

'And the Word is circulating fast, brother. I suppose there's some kind of objection to a Preacher handling the community chest? There would be, I guess.'

'I guess.'

'Well, count our blessings, anyway. I could use some sleep right now.'

They moved in leaps of a hundred or a hundred and fifty miles, and at random. There was no control of the movements of the Preachers—it was their duty to travel as the

236

spirit moved them, and they were welcome everywhere. Charles and Dinkuhl moved in a vast circular swath: east to Ohio, south to Kentucky and North Carolina, north again along the Atlantic seaboard. At Norfolk, they arrived the day after another Preacher, but the congregation was still numerous and enthusiastic.

Dinkuhl commented: 'What happens if we coincide with one of these guys?'

'No flattery, Hiram,' Charles said, '—you'll take the kudos. Brother Lucas was telling me yesterday that he'd listened to upwards of fifty Preachers, and none of them came within acres of you.'

'The point that I was brooding on was who takes the dollars? Well, we can worry about that when it happens. I've had another idea, Charlie. I think it would help for you to carry a skull—hold it in your hand while I talk. I'll have to look one out for you.'

'Staff in one hand, skull in the other. That still leaves my feet free; maybe I could play a treadle organ with one of those.'

Dinkuhl chuckled. 'Another six months with me and you'll have a sense of humour. Take things lightly: it's the only thing to do if you don't want them to bury you.'

'That means eliminating regrets. How are you for regrets, Hiram?'

'None. Precisely none. Occasionally the vagrant thought takes me that my proper place is back in Detroit, presiding over the funeral rites of culture's last outpost. And what response does that evoke? The simplest: the hell with it.'

'Better than playing the fool, though?'

'Brother, the world is sweeping over the lip of an interplanetary Niagara into an interstellar cauldron. No guy's got a future unless he can learn to live backwards. At times like these, there's nothing better than playing the fool.'

*　　*　　*

It was at Boston that they finally coincided with another Preacher. They had been told to get in touch with a man called Brogden, of Psycho & Medicine. He was the Manager at the crematorium.

He turned out to be a top-heavy-looking individual—big head and shoulders and chest, and then tapering down—with a sullen appearance punctuated by flashes of nervous merriment. His white overall, which he wore very long, had the look of a shroud, but an oddly incongruous shroud: it was punctuated by a great scarlet buttonhole.

He said: 'I got word you were coming, Preacher. It's the way it is. We haven't had a Preacher for three weeks, and now we get two on one night.'

'Maybe we should go on to our next preaching place, brother,' Dinkuhl said.

Brogden shook his head. 'No call for that. We've heard about you, Preacher—that you're a fine preacher of the Wrath. Preacher Robinson and you will preach together. We've got a big hall, and the Word's strong in Boston. The Word's as strong in Boston as anywhere in New England.'

'And the Word's strong in New England,' Dinkuhl agreed.

Brogden looked at him. 'Outside New England, Preacher, I guess folks don't know what it is to be damned.'

He burst into a bellowing laugh, in which Charles found himself joining. Dinkuhl permitted himself a wintry smile. His laugh completed, Brogden said solemnly:

'You'll have a bite with me before we go down, Preacher? You too, brother?'

They nodded their agreement, and Brogden led them through the long corridors of the crematorium to the suite of rooms he had at the back. He paused once, and reversed the polarization in one of the side-panels with the flick of a switch. They looked through transparency to a room studded with raised platforms, each bearing its corpse awaiting cremation.

238

'An impressive sight, Preacher, I always think,' said Brogden. 'The bodies for the flames, and the souls already in the flames.'

Charles expected him to laugh again, but he didn't. He shook his head soberly, flicked the switch back, and led them on once more.

Apart from one evening on Mining property, Dinkuhl had preached previously in sheds, outside the towns, belonging to Agriculture. Brogden led them, by gyro, down to the waterfront, to a stretch that was apparently unused now though still nominally under the control of Telecom. It was a very decayed sector altogether, crammed with broken-down warehouses that seemed ready to slip off the water-front into the unhealthy-looking water. The gyros already parked showed that Brogden had been right in his promise of a good attendance.

They met Preacher Robinson inside, and made their salutations. Preacher Robinson was a gaunt man and there was something odd about his speech.

'I've heard you're a fine teller of the Wrath, Preacher,' he said. 'Would you like to lead off?'

Dinkuhl replied: 'Better if you lead off, Preacher. You've been preaching longer than I have.'

Preacher Robinson inclined his head. 'As you like.'

He preached well, with a cold bitter fervour. But Dinkuhl, following him, was in tremendous form. The audience that had listened in silence, betraying only by an occasional shuffling of feet that some charge of iniquity had sunk deeply home, was roused to a pitch of sobbing and shouting by Dinkuhl's playing on their emotions. Dinkuhl passed them back to Robinson for the liturgy that took place in the open but, under his influence still, it was the crowd rather than the Preacher that dominated the responses.

When it was over, Charles and Dinkuhl stood beside

239

Preacher Robinson and made their informal good-byes to the faithful. They had decided that in the presence of Robinson they would not put their usual questions about Sarah and Isaacssohn. Charles stood in silence while the two Preachers listened to the small talk and small problems of the departing congregation. The comet was plainly visible at the top of the black chasm between two warehouses. A few yards away there was the slow lap of water against rotting piles.

Brogden said: 'Will you all come back with me for the night? There's plenty of room in my suite for the three of you.'

It was Preacher Robinson who answered first. He said:

'The Preacher and I will have some things to talk over in private. We may come up to your place afterwards, brother, but you should go along now.'

Brogden said: 'I'm in no hurry, Preacher.' He laughed, but his laughter had a hollow sound in the night air. 'Nothing waiting for me but Hell.'

'Go along,' Preacher Robinson said. 'The Will of Jahweh.'

'The Will of Jahweh.'

There was enough light for Charles to see Dinkuhl stiffen slightly. He was surprised and made wary himself. It might be the usual thing for Preachers to compare notes when they happened to meet in their travels, though it was something they had not heard of before. But even if there were no more to it than that, it foreshadowed a situation that would require careful handling. And if there were something else . . . Charles comforted himself with the thought that they were two to one.

But there was still a handful of the congregation left when Preacher Robinson started to talk. He said to Dinkuhl:

'How long have you been telling the Wrath, Preacher?'

'Not long, Preacher. The call only came to me a few weeks ago.'

'You tell it well.'

'An instrument of Jahweh, Preacher.'

Dinkuhl's voice, Charles noted, had relapsed into the drawl that signified alertness. The remaining handful of the damned had moved in closer; they were surrounded by them. There could be very little doubt that they were followers of Preacher Robinson. It was not two to one; it was two to half a dozen.

'Tell me, Preacher,' Robinson said, 'these other two you have been asking questions about—a woman called Cohn, a man called Isaacssohn—are they instruments of Jahweh, too?'

It might still be no more than a routine check-up; the fact that they knew of the questions they had been asking did not necessarily signify anything more than that the Cometeers were a tighter-knit organization than had seemed likely on the surface.

Dinkuhl said: 'Every man and every woman is an instrument of Jahweh.'

Preacher Robinson laughed, and his laughter was the dropping of a cloak. It was the laughter of cynicism. They had reached an inner circle; that was clear enough. And it was an inner circle dedicated to something other than the fanaticism of the Cometeers. But to what? The general inference was clear enough. Some managerial. But which? Which managerial was capable of controlling an organization like this—an organization of which Ledbetter and even Raven were unmistakably afraid?

'You put that well, Manager Dinkuhl,' said Preacher Robinson. 'We're still curious, all the same. What do you want Cohn and Isaacssohn for?'

'Would you believe it,' Dinkuhl drawled, 'if I told you it was for no other reason than the pangs of aching love?'

'For both of them?'

I

'Well, one each. Charlie for Cohn and me for Isaacssohn. It's just that I'm built that way.'

Robinson laughed again. 'You know,' he said, 'I think we'd take you in for that sense of humour, if for no other reason.'

'Take us in—where?' asked Dinkuhl. 'And are we expected to come willingly?'

'You'll find out where. Willingly if you like. Otherwise not. We've come prepared.'

Dinkuhl groaned. 'Not astarate again.'

'No,' Robinson said, 'not astarate.' He drew something out from beneath his Preacher's cloak. 'We're the more primitive type.'

His followers were making similar dispositions. Charles recognized what it was they carried from having seen something of the sort on a Red League historical soap opera. They were old-fashioned blackjacks.

Dinkuhl said: 'Mind if I have a word with Charlie—on our own?'

'A word. Don't make it longer than half a minute.'

Dinkuhl drew Charles to one side. 'Can you swim?' Charles nodded. 'The blunt instruments are all they've got; they would have produced something else if they had it. Probably don't carry anything metal in case someone puts the detectors on them. Anyway, it's worth trying a rush. There's only a couple between us and the water. Right over them and in. Swim left. There's a main artery within a hundred yards, and they can't get at us before then because of the warehouses. They won't try anything under lights.'

Charles said: 'O.K. When do we go?'

'We'll walk back to them and I'll take out a cigarette pack and a lighter. When I toss the lighter in the Preacher's face, we move.'

The watchers appeared to relax as Charles and Dinkuhl

242

walked back together to where Robinson stood. Dinkuhl drew his pack of cigarettes out, slowly. He felt in his pockets for the lighter.

Robinson said: 'Are you prepared to be reasonable? We play ball if you do.'

Dinkuhl brought out his lighter, and pressed the flame button. The small blue glow shot up to its full height of three inches.

'A lot depends,' Dinkuhl observed, 'on the brand of ball you play. For instance——'

He roared: 'Now!' as he flicked the lighter in Robinson's face, and Charles leapt for the man immediately between himself and the waterfront. The man went down, but he brought Charles down with him. Charles rolled clear, but by the time he had got to his feet another of them had him by the arm and yet another was between him and the water. Dinkuhl had got clear. He stood by the water's edge, and looked back. They were making no attempt to go after him. Me again, Charles thought.

He called: 'Beat it, Hiram!'

As he tore his arm free and dived for the man in his path, Charles saw Dinkuhl bull-rushing back to his assistance. He did not see anything else. Something hit him on the back of the head.

He came back to consciousness once to the sound of a high-pitched buzzing roar, recognizable as the noise of a stratoliner's engines. He sat up, and had time to see that he was in the hold of a cargo-plane, and tied up. Dinkuhl, also tied up, lay a little way off.

A voice said: 'No trouble. We don't want trouble.'

Another blackjack blow smashed him back into oblivion.

8

THE next time Charles came to, he was free of his bonds. He sat up carefully, and then stood up. His head ached, but no more than it had done after astarate; probably the bludgeoning effect of a blackjack was no worse than that of a drug.

He was in a small neat cell of a room, but there was no question of this being a cabin in a real or fake spaceship. There was an armorplex window in one wall, and outside light came through it. His first attention was to Dinkuhl, though. Dinkuhl was lying on the floor; he had a nasty blue and black bruise on his left temple. Charles tried to rouse him, but without success. There was no water in the room, and slapping his cheeks brought no result. At least, he was alive.

Leaving him for the moment, Charles went to the window and looked out. The building they were in was on a height, and looked across a city that pricked his memory without quite yielding to it. A mixture of styles, but predominantly very old, and with more than a hint of the oriental. A museum city. That narrowed the possibilities quite a bit—there were few cities that had escaped both the War's destructions and the subsequent pattern of standardization in civic reconstruction that had marked the beginning of managerialism. He tried to think which this could be, but without being able to persuade himself of one likelihood over another. The sky was busy with gyros; that didn't help either.

It wasn't until the door of the room opened, and he saw the man who stood in the threshold that he guessed where he was. A number of things fell into place then, not least the trace of unfamiliar accent in Preacher Robinson's speech. He had never seen this man in the flesh, but he had seen a deep-view of him, and in the same dress.

It was Hans Isaacssohn, and the dress was the Israeli military uniform.

'You're awake,' Isaacssohn said. 'But not Dinkuhl?'

'He's been roughed up badly.' Charles felt his own head. 'Your men seem to get some pleasure in the use of blunt instruments.'

Isaacssohn smiled. He had a slow smile that warmed his normally severe features. 'The need for secrecy precluded the use of more advanced methods of repression. I won't say that some of them may not have been a little heavy handed. Enthusiasm is a good fault in the military. But they know where to hit without doing permanent damage. And that was in their instructions—to avoid any permanent damage.'

'Very thoughtful. Do you think something could be done about making Dinkuhl comfortable, now you've got us here?'

Isaacssohn nodded. He pressed a wall button. 'You have not been here long. They dropped you here, and then informed me. I came almost at once. You must have been coming round when they left you.'

'Anyway, we're here.' Charles gestured towards the window. 'In——'

'The capital of the world.' Isaacssohn smiled again. 'Jerusalem. The Einstein Institute. Seventh floor. Room 93.

245

I take it you recognize me? You will have seen my records. How are things in California?'

'Yes, I recognized you. California—it's a few weeks since I was there.'

Two orderlies, also in uniform, brought a stretcher in.

Isaacssohn said: 'He should have been taken to sick-bay. See that he's looked after.'

As they left the room, Charles said urgently: 'Sarah—she's all right?' Isaacssohn nodded. 'And her father?'

The remark amused Isaacssohn. 'Yes. Professor Cohn is in good health and spirits. Very good spirits. He wants to see you.'

'And Sarah?'

'That's a matter for Professor Cohn. We'll go along now, if you're ready.'

Charles held his hands up. The rope had cut deeply, and it had been oily. 'A wash would be useful.'

'Yes, of course. Our sanitary arrangements are not quite managerial, but I have a lavatory attached to my office here. Come on down.'

Isaacssohn's office was two floors below; they went down and Isaacssohn showed him to the lavatory.

'You'll find me back in the office when you're ready,' he told him. 'Soap, towels—got everything?'

Charles tidied himself up as well as he could, and went out to rejoin Isaacssohn. He got up from his desk, and then sat down again.

'Something you may be interested in, before we go along to Government House. Have a cigarette? Take a chair.'

The cigarette was very welcome, and Charles was not reluctant to sit down. He glanced round the office. Nothing unusual, except that it was rather untidy. There was a TV screen inset in the wall.

Isaacssohn spoke into some kind of tube: that was new.

He said: 'Get me Gathenya—Neues-Werke.' He glanced up at Charles. 'We use wire more than you do for communications. A result of being closely knit and centralized. There's a saving on power, and we have had to learn ways of economy.'

The screen lit up to show a man sitting at a desk. He apparently recognized Isaacssohn, and saluted him.

Isaacssohn spoke to him in German, and he nodded. '*Ja, General.*' The screen blanked, and opened up again to show a factory interior. It was a mass-production layout, but not automated: there seemed to be far too many workers. Isaacssohn said something else in German, and the cameras switched to a close view of the end of the line. The products were being picked off the line and carefully stacked for transfer somewhere else. They were small, metal, egg-shaped.

'Recognize them?'

Charles shook his head. 'Should I?'

Isaacssohn gave another instruction in German. This time the scene cut to a courtyard, enclosed but open to the sky. It was filled with a swarm of monstrous bees. Men flying.

These, too, wore Israeli military uniform. Each was encased in a skeletal framework of metal. The framework had a footrest, a seat, and a waistband with certain controls. From the waistband the metal rose in a hoop above the flyer's head. At the top of the hoop were the vanes; horizontal for take-off and inclinable in various directions for routine flying and manœuvre. As the scene became more clearly visualized in Charles' mind, he understood that quite a complicated aerial parade was taking place. One flyer, hovering motionless at one end of the courtyard, was an instructor; the rest were obeying his commands.

'A very neat design,' he commented at last. 'Powered by . . . ?'

247

'As you will have guessed, by the diamond-solar battery. Those were the batteries you have just seen coming off the assembly line.'

'Congratulations. But I don't know how you did it, in the time. I saw at least six months' work in the development stage, quite apart from the time required for production—tooling up, and so on.'

Isaacssohn smiled. 'Of course. That's why I can't accept the congratulations. We have had people working here on it right from the beginning. My job at San Diego was a stalling one for the last year. Not as easy as you might think.'

Charles looked at him sceptically. 'Two questions. How could you have people working on this here in Israel, when you and the Cohns were refugees? And if you did have them, why give any information at all to United Chemicals? You gave enough to interest more than one managerial.'

'So I understand. The answer to the first question is that this is a capitalist country, not a managerial one. Disorganized, ramshackle, inefficient. So inefficient that it was not at all difficult to carry out research work unknown to the government of the time. Professor Cohn was Director of this Institute before our misfortune. The President was badly misinformed; the man he appointed in succession was one of our group. It was quite easy to camouflage the work.

'As for your second question, the idea was in a very embryonic stage indeed when we left Israel. I needed a laboratory and funds very urgently. I had to wave some kind of carrot under the noses of those donkeys at Graz. And I had to continue to give them enough to persuade them to maintain the project—though I understand a good deal of what I did send was being intercepted by Ledbetter for another managerial?'

Charles nodded. Isaacssohn went on: 'And I was fairly confident that there wasn't one of them with the training and

248

brains to make anything of the information, anyway. From what Sarah told me about you, I discovered that I had made a mistake there. Our men tried to locate you, but various other groups got on to you first. I should be interested to learn why they didn't manage to keep you. Anyway, you dropped very neatly into our hands.'

'Into your hands?'

'The Cometeers.'

'The Cometeers are an Israeli organization?'

'Let's say, we provided the first spark for the powder trail. Its success has rather overwhelmed us. Our psychological advisers plotted it out, but I think even they have been surprised by the results. The present membership figures are astonishing, and there's a steep upward curve for the rate of increase.'

'The instruments used by Israel are not such that they commend Israel to me,' Charles said.

Isaacssohn shrugged. 'A pity. Unfortunately, the Cometeers are necessary to our plans. We aren't fond of them ourselves, but at the same time they could never have succeeded unless the society in which they flourished was corrupt. And there's another point. We expect them to be the means of saving thousands, perhaps hundreds of thousands of lives. The majority of them not Israeli.'

'In what way?'

'You will be told, I fancy. We should be getting along. There's one other thing you might be interested in first.'

Isaacssohn spoke into the tube again, and again the TV picture changed. A larger courtyard. More of the flyers. They watched them drop down towards a row of black canisters laid out at about three-yard intervals on the ground. The frameworks supporting these flyers carried on each side a small barrel-like affair, terminating in a nozzle. Suddenly, and presumably at a word of command because the effects

249

were nearly simultaneous, there was a lambent flickering around each of the nozzles, and on the ground the canisters —or all but two of them—burst into flame.

'The heat ray,' said Isaacssohn. 'Beloved by managerial TV serial writers. The other diamond application. Unfortunately limited to use in conditions of sunlight, but, granted those conditions, most effective. Variable focus, but only between certain limits, of course, and the range is not very great. The heat, at point of impact, is. I won't give you a figure, because I don't think you would believe me. A surprise, you think?'

'Only in its actual appearance,' Charles said grimly. 'A few people have grasped the idea.'

'Then they will be surprised, to see their idea marching on the wings of the wind.'

Isaacssohn switched off the screen, and got up to go.

Charles said: 'One thing. How much of all this did Sarah know—when she was with you at San Miguel?'

'Our conventions are perhaps peculiar. There are some things we don't regard as suitable for women—they include counter-revolution and military strategy. Sarah didn't know anything.'

Isaacssohn said: 'May I present you? Charles Grayner—Professor Cohn, President of Israel.'

The gyro had brought them to the grounds of a modest little house on the outskirts of Jerusalem, and the room in which they now were was as unassuming. Professor Cohn got up to greet them from a scratched and shabby desk; there was no large TV screen in the room, but a portable callscreen beside the desk. Professor Cohn smiled, and Charles remembered and recognized the humorous slyness he had seen on the morning of Sarah's disappearance.

Professor Cohn said: 'Our apologies, Charles. You've

been somewhat roughly handled, too? That wasn't intended. We've been inculcating aggressiveness into our soldiers, and it's difficult to prevent them from overdoing it at times.'

'President?' Charles asked. 'Since when? I haven't been seeing the newsreels very lately.'

'Would your newsreels regard it as worth the recording? I suppose they might. But this has been a very secret palace revolution. We thought it best not to let the news leak out just yet. The *coup d'état* coincided with Hans' return here. It was well planned and went without a hitch. I was called back when it was all over.'

'Sarah——'

'I felt it was necessary to bring Sarah with me. There were a number of good reasons for that, not the least being her value as a hostage if left behind. She expressed unwillingness when I told her.' Professor Cohn looked at Charles keenly. 'She wanted to tell you, but of course that was impossible. I was afraid she might have left some clue, though I took all precautions.'

Charles remembered the incident of the finger-watch; with the false-Sarah's explanation out of the way, it assumed its earlier importance. He smiled slightly.

'I gather she did,' Professor Cohn said. 'Well, never mind that now. The point of all the preparations was to throw United Chemicals, and any other managerial that happened to be interested, off the scent. We seem to have been helped by the local rivalry; even when the genuineness of the deaths was suspected, they were too eager to lay the blame at each other's doors.'

Charles nodded. Only now was he beginning to grasp the scope of the plan underlying the work of Isaacssohn, the disappearances, his own abduction. Keeping his voice even, he said:

'The idea, I suppose, is of some sort of aggression by Israel against the rest of the world—a foray for fresh territory.' Professor Cohn was smiling at him benignly. 'How long has that been in preparation?'

'A very long time. On an old Japanese analogy, Hans and I were members of the war party. There was a peace party; our temporary eviction was the result of a temporary defeat in an earlier skirmish. The position has now been rectified.'

'You want war. Why?'

Professor Cohn raised his hands. 'Wanting doesn't enter into it. The world outside is breaking up. There will be chaos there, anyway, within a couple of decades, and, as the only state with any vitality at all, we should have to go out then and reclaim the chaos. It would be a long job and a painful one—unnecessarily so. It is simpler, and a lot more efficient, to precipitate matters. Has Hans mentioned the Cometeers to you? We've found confirmation for our views there, and it is of great help in the softening-up.'

Charles said: 'Let me see if I can understand what you are talking about. You mean—Israel taking the whole planet over?'

'Exactly.'

'With a handful of aerial soldiers and a heat ray that only works at close quarters, and when the sun happens to be shining?'

'I should put it somewhat higher than that,' Professor Cohn said judiciously. 'Let me explain something of the art of warfare to you, Charles. That art, throughout the centuries, has seen a continual alternation in the status of the individual warrior, through the alternation in the kind of weapons at man's disposal. To render the situation down, you may say that artillery dwarfs the individual soldier, while small-arms magnifies him. Of course, you can pick your own variations on the theme, from the conflict between the giant sling and the javelin in Roman times, to the conflict between the big guns and the musket in the eighteenth century.

'During the twentieth century, the balance swung—irretrievably as it seemed—away from the soldier. Massed artillery barrages, pattern bombing, and finally the atomic and hydrogen bombs seemed to tilt the scales finally towards the mass-weapon. And weapons, of course, affect society. The musket was typical of capitalism, just as the H-bomb is typical of managerialism, even though it was the last stage of world capitalism that produced it.'

'The managerial world,' Charles observed, 'still has a stock of H-bombs.'

'Which are quite useless. The mass-weapon has grown too big to use. Yes, I know it was used in the last war, but the results bear me out, don't they? Do you think your friends will use H-bombs? On what targets? We shall have Africa within a week, Europe within ten days. Do you know what the situation resembles? It resembles a small iron-walled room, full of big men holding Klaberg pistols. And a child comes in with a water-pistol and drenches them. They can't hit back because they haven't got any water-pistols, and wouldn't know how to use them if they had. And if they fire their pistols, the charges will ricochet off the walls; they are as likely as not to kill themselves, and they know it.'

'As far as I can see, a longbow would out-shoot your new weapon, Professor Cohn.'

Professor Cohn smiled. 'And which managerial has a stock of longbows? I take your point, though. The heat ray is not the weapon that restores the initiative to the soldier. The flying apparatus is. We've had the essential design for some time, but it's heavy on power—as you might expect. The sun, fortunately, is an inexhaustible power-house. That makes the weapon worth having. Wings on every soldier. A flying army. Even without the added advantages of surprise and an enemy that has, in the main, lost interest in everything but its hypothetical damnation, this new factor would be sufficient to do the trick. In all probability. We have taken the elementary precaution of mapping out the key points. There isn't one that can't be taken by half a dozen of our flying soldiers. And we have more than that to spare.'

They could do it, too. Charles could visualize the situation very clearly. The Cometeers running hog-wild ... he had already learned that a Cometeer did not pause to consider managerial loyalty when a call came in the name of Jahweh ... and then the trained, disciplined and efficient Israeli troops dropping through the air. . . It was a cast-iron scheme. Understanding this, it occurred to him to wonder why it had all been explained to him. His skill wasn't wanted now. The only advantage he represented to Israel was the negative one—assurance that he would not be doing anything for the managerials.

He said: 'One thing interests me.' Professor Cohn raised his head slightly. 'Why you have told me all this.'

'A reasonable question. Because I am going to ask you to give me your parole.' Charles looked baffled. 'An old expression—your promise of honour that you will not try to escape or communicate with anyone outside Israel. That given, you will have a good deal of liberty. And if you are to give it, I think you must be told enough of your situation to make its implications clear to you. This is the world's new capital. We want you to understand that.'

'How long before you attack?'

'Not long.'

That startled him. 'Now—in winter? It will take the edge off your weapon, won't it?'

'Unfortunately. Though not as much as you might think.

254

The cloud is generally low at this time of year, and it will not be difficult to rise above cloud height for recharging.'

Charles, with a twinge midway between guilt and regret, thought of airsphering with the false-Sarah, and the world of blue and gold and stillness.

'But in any case,' Professor Cohn went on, 'timing is now a matter of some urgency. It isn't that we have any fears of the managerials duplicating the battery or the weapon within six months—for that matter, within six decades—but they might get round to suspecting the true state of affairs, given six months' grace. We can't bank on their mutual mistrust holding out. And surprise is going to be very important. So we shall go ahead in the very near future.'

'In which case,' Charles said, 'surely it would be simpler to keep me under lock and key?'

Professor Cohn smiled benevolently. 'There are personal considerations.'

Sarah. It was a warming thought. As though he had been tunnelling towards her for months, through miles of rock and had become aware of a tapping, answering him and directly ahead. At the same time——

He said: 'I'd like to have the opportunity of talking things over with Dinkuhl.'

Professor Cohn nodded. 'Naturally. Hans will take you back.'

Dinkuhl was sitting up in bed, in a small but not unattractive room. There was a table beside his bed, with a large bowl full of fruit on it. Dinkuhl grinned wryly.

'Come to devour the grapes?'

Isaacssohn said: 'I'll leave you here, Charles. I'm afraid we have to post a guard outside, for the time being. He will take you to me whenever you want that.'

'Adios,' Dinkuhl said. 'Back to the detector screen? Why not just crawl under the bed?'

Isaacssohn looked puzzled for a moment. 'Oh, I get it. No, you're private in here. Our privacy regulations forbid the installation of detector equipment.'

He smiled and went out. Dinkuhl looked after him.

'You know,' he said, 'I believe he's telling the truth.'

'Probably. How are you feeling?'

Dinkuhl rubbed his head gingerly. 'Regretful. Death was more welcome. But it will pass. The number who takes my pulse will help it to pass, I feel.'

Charles said: 'It will need to. You will need all your faculties to think up a scheme for geting us out of this.'

Dinkuhl's look was quizzical. 'Maybe you'd better let me have anything you know.'

He listened in silence while Charles told him what he had been told by Isaacssohn and Professor Cohn. He said at last:

'I can think of one thing that's likely to prevent them from doing it.'

Charles said eagerly: 'Yes?'

'The sun blowing up.' Dinkuhl looked at him. 'Relax. Relax, Charlie boy. You want my advice? Give your parole. And then enjoy yourself.'

The flippancy was the same, but it didn't seem to be the same Dinkuhl. In the past the flippancy had been only the cover for a mind driving hard on its course. He examined Dinkuhl's features more closely; he thought he could detect something he had never seen there before: indifference that somehow was more harsh than despair.

Dinkuhl took an orange and began to peel it. 'Help yourself, Charlie.'

Charles said: 'I don't know about getting out of Israel. The odds are against us. In fact, they're so much against us

256

that a more limited objective might be a good deal easier than it seems on the surface.'

Dinkuhl dropped a curl of peel on the floor. 'A limited objective?'

'I don't believe there is a detector on this room. It's part of the business of one guard outside the door, of being taken around by Isaacssohn, in person and alone. They are so confident that we couldn't get out of the country that they take hardly any precautions on the spot. Listen, Hiram. This building is served for TV by a single transmitter-receiver room. I know where it is because Isaacssohn took me past it and the door was open. There is only one duty operator—I suppose they can manage with one because so much is covered by landlines.'

Dinkuhl sectioned his orange. 'I am ahead of you by a neck. We are in the TV room. We have laid out the solitary operator. Pick it up from there.'

'To my mind there's only one man who might be able to do anything worth while with the information we could give him.'

'Raven?'

'Yes. Do you agree?'

Dinkuhl nodded. 'I agree.'

Charles said: 'Right. I suggest we call the guard in, and I'll stand behind the door and hit him as he comes in. It may be elementary, but I think it will work.'

Dinkuhl shook his head. 'Charlie boy, it's you should be in bed. Wait till I recover a little more, and you can have it. I'll go get the nurse for you. Don't thank me. It will be a pleasure.'

'What's wrong with the idea?'

'Look,' Dinkuhl said. 'You wanted the girl. You're within ten minutes of her. You only have to go and tell Isaacssohn you are retiring from the cloak and dagger business. You never were cut out for it, anyway.'

257

'You won't come in on this?'

'The nail goes to the woodwork in. I won't.'

'You'll be content to see the Israelis running the world?'

'That nurse can run me any day. The hell with the world.'

'I'm serious.'

'That's your bad luck. I lost my girlish laughter too long ago to be serious at my time of life. Lookit, Charlie, you've got what you wanted.'

Charles paused. He said slowly: 'What about you, Hiram? What was it you wanted?'

There was another silence. Dinkuhl said: 'O.K. What did I want? Your girl for you? I wish I could rate myself as high for altruism. I told you once, Charlie—you were the H-bomb. You were what was going to blow the top off. You were the Destruction, and I served the Destruction. You aren't now, are you? Go in peace, brother, if go you must.'

'You've found a bigger bomb?'

'Just that. Now I wait. I don't know what I wait for, but I wait. I don't kid myself the Israelis have got much more than the managerials, except in the military line, but it looks like being an interesting year. Go and get the word through to Raven, if your loyalties are still stronger than your common sense. I don't say it won't affect the issue. But it will still be an interesting year, whatever you do.'

Charles looked towards the door.

'I'm a neutral,' Dinkuhl said. 'I won't call for nurse. That's a big sacrifice I'm making, the way I feel right now.'

Charles called the guard. His own voice seemed unnatural to him. He posted himself behind the door, grasping, by its projecting handle, the heavy wooden fruit bowl; he had emptied the fruits on to Dinkuhl's bed. Dinkuhl was watching with every sign of interest.

The door opened and the guard came in. He wasn't very tall; it was an easy matter to crash the bowl down on the

258

back of his head. He pitched forward in a falling arc and hit the floor with a cracking thud. Dinkuhl leaned down to look at him.

'Pretty. I see now what they mean about the spectator seeing the wood for the trees. You have at least quarter of an hour, Charlie boy. I should take the bowl with you.'

The corridor was deserted and it was no more than ten yards to the service lift. He called it down, and got in with relief—leaving the scene of the crime. The TV room was ground floor. He made his movements in closing the lift gate studied and deliberate. There were two or three people in this corridor, between him and his quarry. He walked along, swinging the fruit bowl casually. A girl looked at him curiously as he passed her, but no more.

The door of the TV room was closed now. That was bad luck. Fortunately whistle locks did not seem to be in use in Israel. The door had a handle; he was going to turn it when he found it gave under the pressure of his hand. He pushed it open, gently.

The operator was sitting at the main control panel with his back to the door. He had not yet become aware of the open door, but he might at any moment. Charles ran towards him, raising the fruit bowl above his head as he did so. The operator turned round, in time to take the blow on his forehead, instead of on the base of his skull. It was as effective. His breath exhaled in a dull groan and he slumped forward on to his desk.

Charles went back and closed the door. It had a lock on this side—an old-fashioned key lock—and he secured it. Then he went back and examined the operator; he was out, all right. On the panel in front of the desk a spotlight lit up a figure. 21. Someone wanting attention. How long could he count on before someone came to see why there was no

259

response? Perhaps as long as it would take the guard to come round in Dinkuhl's room. The point was, with a meagre knowledge of TV communications, to get on to the outside circuits and get Raven in that time.

It would have been easy with Dinkuhl, of course.

It took him five minutes to master the controls to the extent of getting through to Athens, the nearest managerial booster station. He had rolled the operator on to the floor, out of sight of the screen.

The sight of the neat chrome-and-plastic Telecom desk stirred strange feelings; after recent events and the time spent earlier with the Cometeers, he had almost forgotten what it would look like. The operator was a girl; above the neat uniform her face had the typical dreamy remoteness of a mesc-taker. She registered no surprise at his bearded and dishevelled appearance; after all she would take him for an Israeli, and would hardly be surprised at anything.

He said: 'Jerusalem for Atomics HQ, Philadelphia.'

Even that did not surprise her, although it was a safe bet that that particular link was not made once in a decade. She said sleepily:

'Jerusalem for Philadelphia. Stand by, Jerusalem.'

He said: 'It's urgent.'

She smiled and barely nodded. 'Yuh.'

He thought, while he watched her making the call to the space station that would provide the junction between the world's continents, of what Raven would do when he gave him the news. He would put it on record, of course, to carry weight at the Council meeting he would have to call. The managerials, under such a threat, would be forced into unity. They would have to unite, if they were to defend themselves.

And then? The Israelis would go through with it—they had gone too far to draw back now. A bitter war, a long war. They would be unlikely to save Africa; Europe might go, too. But the Americas were defensible, especially if Raven took the obvious precaution of rounding up the leaders of the Cometeers.

For Raven, it would be a good war: the natural, the automatic leader. His thoughts were wrily humorous. Let Raven have it. All he wanted himself was peace of mind: the feeling that, dragged from obscurity into temporary greatness, he had kept his faith with the society that had bred him—whether shot through with evil, whether condemned to die despite everything, he had kept faith. For that he was willing to let the rest go—his personal liberty, his life if they required it . . . and Sarah.

The girl was talking again, though not to him.

'Station Q5? Athens has a call for Philadelphia.'

Was there a discrepancy between his action now, and his refusal to stay with Raven and work for Atomics in the past? Perhaps, perhaps not. Raven had seen catastrophe coming, but Raven's word had been suspect. And it had been a different catastrophe even so. Civil war is something you never believe in until it breaks out. So is the collapse of a state from within. It was the outside shock that stimulated half-forgotten patriotism.

It was hard to think of losing Sarah when he had come so very close to finding her again. So hard, that he mistrusted his ability to keep his purpose steeled if he did think of that. The picture was plaguing him now; he thrust it back, finding crazy jingles of thought to keep it at bay. 'Raven the Raven, Raven's ravin'——'

'Raven's ravin——'

It became a real thought, with the clear sharpness of ice. What would Raven do? Call the Council—round up the leaders of the Cometeers? He saw suddenly that he would do nothing so half-hearted as that; he had been underestimating Raven. Professor Cohn had been contemptuous

261

of the H-bomb because by the time the managerials had awakened to the fact of invasion, the airborne Israeli armies would be all over Africa and Europe. In those conditions it would be impossible to use the H-bomb. But Charles was creating different conditions—the Israelis still locked within their relatively small territory were a target impossible to miss. Raven would not miss it.

Well, he thought—my life, if they require it. He had lost Sarah, anyway.

The girl said: 'Philadelphia coming in, Jerusalem. They will be transferred as soon as focused.'

It hit him so hard that for a moment there seemed to be blackness before his eyes.

. . . Sarah was in the target.

The girl said: 'In focus. Will you accept, Jerusalem?'

He stared at the screen, wondering what it was he had been going to do. He heard her voice again, mesc-tolerant and weary:

'Philadelphia is in focus, Jerusalem. Are you ready to accept the call?'

To the right of the desk there was the building's code of numbers. Isaacssohn was 71.

'Philadelphia . . .' the voice began again.

He didn't look up. He said: 'Cancel it.'

She said: 'O.K. Cancelled.'

The picture faded. He connected to 71. He said, when Isaacssohn answered:

'This is Grayner. I'm in the TV room. You can come and collect me.'

Looking at her, he wondered how he could ever have been taken in by the false-Sarah. The thing about her was not the lines of her face, her body, but the sparkle, the altogether inimitable glint of personality. And, although she was smiling, she was watching him warily; how could he have forgotten that wariness which was more a part of Sarah than the tiny bulges just above her eyebrows? He remembered the flesh, peeled off by Dinkuhl's knife . . . it should not have needed that.

He said humbly: 'I've been getting into trouble, Sarah, since I lost you.'

She laughed. 'If being just on the point of calling down H-bombs on us is to be labelled as getting into trouble . . . anyway, you didn't.'

'There was more to it than that . . . I meant, back in North America. I didn't think of H-bombs. That call I tried to make'—he looked directly at her—'I was prepared to not see you again, Sarah. I didn't want it to happen —the take-over—with any consent of mine. You understand?'

'Within limits.' She patted the plastifoam couch. 'Come and sit down.' She was wearing the very full skirt which was the common dress of Israeli women, and she drew it away to let him sit by her. 'This other trouble. Details?'

He told her about the false-Sarah; it was a relief to make confession. Sarah said thoughtfully:

'You went airsphering with her?'

He nodded. 'Yes.' He wondered if he looked as uneasy as he felt; he supposed so.

'It's a very romantic occupation. A cousin of mine did a thesis on the aphrodisiacal effects of airsphering. He had to go outside Israel for the practical work, of course . . . our young ladies don't go airsphering except with their fiancés. He went to Greece.'

Charles looked at her unhappily. 'Yes?'

'The correlation was positive.' Sarah paused. 'Tell me. What was I like?'

'It was a very good disguise. Just like you, physically—of

263

course, they had had access to your records. But I shouldn't have been deceived by it. It wasn't you, Sarah.'

'Not even in the airsphere, high above the clouds?'

He grinned shamefacedly. 'Least of all, then. I was surprised.'

'But pleased, I guess.' She got up from the couch and stood facing him; the trace of a smile made her face expressionless. She leaned forward slightly and slapped him, stingingly hard, on either cheek. He put his hand up and rubbed first one side and then the other. She stood looking at him.

'What was that for?'

The smile deepened, but he still could not read the inward expression. She said:

'The first was on behalf of the other Sarah. She should have done it, so I'm doing it for her. The second was on my own account—for your still having thought it was me, afterwards.'

He nodded, in gloom. 'I'm sorry.'

'Sorry! What about doing something to show you really are sorry?'

He looked up. 'I'll do anything, Sarah.'

He thought her composure was going to desert her for a moment; there was the beginning of embarrassment, but she controlled it. She said brusquely:

'This afternoon then . . . you can take me airsphering.'

He grasped her hand, and she let him pull her down beside him on the couch again. She averted her face from his kisses, but she was smiling happily now. He hesitated in the attempt as a thought struck him.

'But you said . . . no airsphering except with——'

'——Fiancés. Idiot! Don't you realize you are being proposed to?'

He drew her to him, and now she took his kisses, and

kissed him back. When, after some minutes, he released her, he offered her his cheek.

She looked at him thoughtfully. 'Well?'

'Since you are going to marry me, I'd prefer to get all my punishment over in advance. I went airsphering more than once.'

Sarah raised her eyebrows. 'How many times?'

'About half a dozen.'

She looked at his offered face, and at her hand.

'No. Not just yet. A good wife always keeps something in reserve.'

The Director's garden on the roof of the Einstein Institute was almost exclusively made up of evergreens and roses; the roses were made to bloom all the year round so the seasons did not touch it. From the garden, on this morning, it was a small party that looked out, away from the centre of Jerusalem, towards the military camp on the outskirts. The party was made up of Professor Cohn and Isaacssohn, Sarah and Charles, and Dinkuhl. The sky was a sparkling blue, and the great sun itself dimmed, by comparison, the sunlets that were strung above their heads.

Professor Cohn said: 'Hans has been telling me about your idea, Charles. We'd considered the idea of utilizing the space stations as solar power collectors, of course, but the distribution is impossible. They can collect all right, but the only power they use is for TV boosting. We can't run cables up to them.

'This idea of yours—of maintaining a collector on airspheres; it might work. We could run cables there, for reasonably low cloud levels at any rate. There's one thing—wouldn't they drift?'

'They couldn't if they were cabled, could they? At least, not far. The airspheres take care of the buoyancy, and the cables take care of the drift. You could have an operator up there, as well.'

Professor Cohn nodded his head. 'Cheap power all the year round. Make a big difference in the cloudy territories—the British Isles, and so on. What do you think, Hans?'

'Very nice. I can foresee some lively problems. I suggest this presents a good first job for the Hebron lab.'

Sarah protested: 'Let's get over the honeymoon first. We haven't officially accepted Hebron yet.'

Isaacssohn said: 'I speak with my full military authority.' He grinned. 'Any recalcitrance and I'll split you—Charles to Cairo and you to Constantinople. I can make that opposing hemispheres once the take-over is accomplished.'

'Managerialist!' Sarah said. 'We wouldn't go.'

Professor Cohn said: 'It's a pity we can't do anything about utilizing power in space. Such a waste. But short of developing a power transmitter, it can't be done.'

Charles said: 'There's one way of utilizing it.'

'And that is . . . ?'

'Atomic-powered spaceships are clumsy and hellishly expensive. Diamond-solar power would make them a different proposition altogether.'

Professor Cohn nodded slowly. Isaacssohn said:

'Get thee to Hebron. *Malesh* the honeymoon.'

'*Malesh* the spaceships,' Sarah said. 'First things come first.'

Charles said: 'What about you, Hiram? Decided on anything yet?'

The indifference that Charles had first noticed behind Dinkuhl's ordinary flippancy, when he tried to persuade him to join him in warning Raven, now, for the most part, had taken its place. He did not talk very much, and then laconically.

He said: 'I'm not sure.'

266

Isaacssohn said: 'I've offered him the job of running the Telecom units, as we take them over. It's still open.'

Charles asked: 'What about it, Hiram?'

Dinkuhl appeared to rouse himself. 'Very kind of everybody. I guess I'm not an organizer, though.'

Charles said: 'When we first met in this business—in Detroit—you said you had thought of trying to get KF transferred to Israel. Well, here you are. Why not?'

'A misconception,' Dinkuhl said. 'KF was a legacy from capitalism—Israel was capitalist. I missed the nuances. KF stemmed from philanthropic capitalism, from capitalism in decay. Israel is a different kind of capitalism. Military capitalism, maybe. Nearer to the roots, anyway. And the root of capitalism is giving people what they want—what they want, not what they ought to want. They never wanted KF, except the cranks, and a sane and healthy society doesn't cater for the cranks.'

Charles said: 'Isn't there anything you want?'

'There is one thing——'

Isaacssohn looked at his finger-watch. 'I think . . . now!'

They looked. From the camp the leather-jacketed swarm was rising, like locusts, into the sharp blue sky. At this moment, throughout the Israeli territory, similar swarms were setting out. Like locusts they would fasten on the neighbouring lands, stripping them of their nerves and moving relentlessly on. Locusts with intelligence, locusts with a purpose. The kaleidoscope of civilization was being shaken; one could only guess into what new pattern it might settle, or whether there would be a pattern.

'Mankind is on the move again,' said Professor Cohn.

'They'll get by,' Dinkuhl said. 'Mankind is like Charlie; mankind is adaptable. You'll be happy at Hebron, Charlie. A wife and a line of research—two lines of research. What more could you want? I hope you're glad I didn't come in

267

with you on the last break. There was no one I wanted to save from the H-bomb.'

'You had thought of that? Why didn't you, then? You wanted destruction.'

The swarm had already become a cloud on the horizon, a fading cloud. Dinkuhl gestured towards it.

'I prefer it spread well out.'

Isaacssohn said: 'I interrupted you just now. You were going to say there was something you wanted. If we can provide it, it's yours.'

Dinkuhl nodded. 'Very kind of you. It isn't much. I'd like the use of a camel.'

Coda

I⊤ was a part of the country from which even the aggressive Israeli agriculture had fallen back in dismay—rocky barren ground useless for everything except grazing sheep. He had passed several flocks, tended by young boys who would presumably grow into the leather jackets that awaited them, the sun-powered wings. But this section was deserted. Dinkuhl was alone, with the camel and his thoughts. He had grown used by now to the uneasy rocking motion of his passage, and to the camel's grunts, the flapping pad of its feet and what he suspected was the creaking of its joints.

It was night. Stars, but no moon. The stars themselves were big and brilliant in a cloudless sky. Weather, he reflected, was still on the side of Israel. He wondered where the locusts had reached by now—Cape Town, Gibraltar, London, Moscow, Delhi?

The comet looked very big, too, and almost overhead. Great for the Cometeers. He tried to rouse disgust, or even the more detached feeling of ironical contempt, but indifference possessed him and would not be set aside. Indifference was a good armour, but a poor companion. A close one, though, and a determined one.

Indifference had come with the death of hope, and hope had died with the news Charlie had brought him, in the

269

little room at the Einstein Institute. He had not known it then, because he had not known that hope had been with him at all, but he had understood it later. 'Destroy!' his mind had said. 'Destroy!' He had not heard its quieter whisper: 'That good may come from the casting down of evil.'

And suddenly he had seen Destruction in the wings, ready to move on stage, and he saw it for what it was—an ordinary player, supplanting, but essentially no different from the other players. And hope had died, unrecognized.

The Israelis, the Managerialists, the Cometeers. . . . There was nothing to despair of losing, and so there could be nothing to hope for. What was he doing, riding a swaying camel through the clear winter's night? Nothing. Progressing in time and space from nowhere to nowhere, with the only consolation that of knowing what he was doing—that he was doing nothing.

He was tantalized by a thought . . . someone else with no aim in view . . . a different road——

Kirby. The white-haired wanderer on the Vermont roads. But Kirby had been happy, he protested to himself—you could see that guy was happy.

That made it a joke. Happiness. Happiness in a world of Israelis and Managerialists and Cometeers, a world of Ellecotts and Ledbetters and Ravens, of Cohns and Isaacssohns, for that matter of Charles's and Sarahs—of Dinkuhls. You needed to be a fool to stay happy in that world.

The only thing was: Kirby had not struck him as a fool.

For the first time since it had come, indifference left him, retreating a little way before the upspringing of that which had been dead. Hope without despair? Hope for hope's sake? His mind cried irrationally: 'Stay with me! Stay with me, anyway!'

Hope came with innocence, and went with knowledge. And can a man unlearn what he has learned?

270

'Stay with me!' his mind cried again. 'Let me be a child, but stay with me. I was willing to give up everything to despair, except my knowledge. Take that, too, if I can have hope.'

He rode his swaying camel under the frost-bright stars. Ahead he could see the lights of a village, a small village but lit as though for carnival. He could hear voices singing; it was puzzling, because the village was still too far away for the songs to be from there. The voices were nearer, and at last he saw the singers, coming towards him along the stony path. They were young Israeli lads, shepherds.

They were rejoicing, and he was happy in their happiness. He tried to catch the words of their song, but he had very little understanding of the dialect. As they came abreast of him, he called out to them in German:

'What is the name of this village?'

Several of them answered him, but he knew what name it would be before they said it. He pricked the camel with the goad, urging it to greater speed.

He said aloud, crying to the black sky, to the stars, to the plunging comet:

'I was ready to give up knowledge for hope. And now hope and knowledge are the same.'

From the rag-bag of memory he found words—words that it surprised him to remember.

'Nunc dimittis . . .'

———————● ★ ●———————

Lightning Source UK Ltd.
Milton Keynes UK
27 January 2010
149183UK00001B/167/A